MW00911426

Intimate Terrorist

Susan Grace Napier

Intimate Terrorist is a work of fiction based on the author's research and contact with domestic violence victims. Names, characters, places, and incidents are a product of the author's imagination or are used fictitiously. Any resemblance to actual events, locales, or persons, living or dead, is entirely coincidental.

PLEASE NOTE:

The author has used a few **cuss words** in this book in order for readers to feel the intense power of these words slamming into victims from their abusers. If these words make you cringe or are offensive to you, just imagine how devastating they would be if someone yelled them at you over and over. Ms. Napier's desire is to bring the reality of a taboo subject out of darkness into the light to increase awareness about domestic violence and its impact victims. Resources are readily available in the appendices for reader(s) who realize they are ready to make changes in their lives and for people who want to make a difference for victims who are living in domestic violence situations.

Cover designed by Erin Carter

Library of Congress Cataloging-in-Publication Data is available.

ISBN ISBN-13: 978-1470101787

DEDICATION

This book is dedicated to one of my surrogate mothers

Grace Laverne Napier Thompson

in loving memory

and

To all victims of 9/11 and domestic violence.

ACKNOWLEDGMENTS

To my Heavenly Father who has opened the right doors in my life in a perfectly timed procession as this book has progressed from inception to publication.

To my children and grandchildren who continue to love me in spite of my poor choices and mistakes in the past.

To my friends in the Kansas City Monday Night Writers Group whose invaluable feedback and critiques have been essential in making this book what it is today – Tim Anderson, James Barton, Rachel Ellyn, Greg Gildersleeve, Kara Hoffman, Kenneth Hursh, Ben & Kate Kort, and Denny Young.

To my friend and presentation coach, Evelyn Anderson.

Table of Contents

Intimate Terrorist

Susan Grace Napier

Prologue

"Why the hell'd you wake me up?" a voice screams at me.

In my nightmare, I'm in New York City, standing across the street from the World Trade Center. With thousands of other Americans, I watch the North Tower collapse so orderly, floor-by-floor, that it appears to be a controlled demolition. I cannot get my feet to walk or run.

"Damn it, Sara. Wake up!" yells a familiar voice.

"Huh . . ." I say, sitting upright in bed, "Why are you shaking me?" I ask, still half asleep.

"'Cause you're kicking me! I have to go to work in two hours!"

"Sorry," I say, timidly.

"I've had it with your damn nightmares," Ronnie screams, flopping back on his side of the bed.

I lay down easy, turning my back to the man I've been married to for 11 years. Ronnie curses under his breath as he goes back to sleep and flip-flops back and forth like a fish out of water. The undulating waves feel as if they are going to roll me right off the waterbed onto the floor. But this night his noisy movement is welcome. It keeps me awake, staving off the nightmares. As his breathing evens out and the snoring begins, I know it is safe for me to move to the sofa.

Moving carefully, I slide from between the sheets and go down the seven steps to the dining room, carefully stepping to the side of the creak in the fifth step. Resting on the sofa is better than being in the same bed with that monster. Plagued by a fluttering stomach, clamminess from the cold sweat, and vivid but disconnected images from the nightmare realm, I toss and turn. As I wonder how many weeks a person can function sleeping an average of four hours per night, my eyelids touch together. I'm out.

Ronnie's alarm clock jerks me awake. I hear the step creak as he comes down the stairs going to the kitchen for coffee and his first cigarette. I drift into light sleep.

"Wake up, bitch," jars my senses. Ronnie taps my dangling hand with his foot. "I said, WAKE UP!"

"What?" I look at my watch. "It's only 4:15, not time for me to get up yet."

"You messed with my sleep. Now you're going to stay awake till I go to work."

"That's ridiculous," I say, closing my eyes. *Lord, I'm so tired. Make him go away.*

I smell his morning breath in my face. "Get your lazy ass upstairs right now," he growls. "Or I'll be screwing with more than your sleep!"

Reluctantly, I stand and go upstairs with him guiding me by tapping on my back. "Get in there and sit while I shave."

Sitting on the stool lid, I know there will be hell to pay if he catches me closing my eyes or leaning against the wall. With him between me and the door in the four-by-four-foot bathroom, my claustrophobia builds. To distract myself, I open the bottom door of the wall cabinet in front of me and shuffle things around.

Finished shaving, Ronnie turns and yanks the upper cabinet door open. It swings within one-half inch of my head.

I frown up at him.

His lips start to curl into a smile but stop. "Okay, bitch, back in the bedroom."

I sit on the edge of the bed, trembling with anger and exhaustion.

He pulls his work clothes out of the dresser drawers and closet, slamming them shut. "When are you going to quit having those damn nightmares?"

"I don't know. I don't know what's causing them," I answer, determined he's not going to see me cry.

"That's because you're such a stupid piece of shit that doesn't know anything about anything." He admires himself in the full-length mirror on the closet door. "Gotta get going," he says. He puffs his chest out, turns and leans down, giving me a peck on the cheek. "See ya tonight."

As soon as his foot touches the first step, I run to the bathroom, scrubbing my face. I don't want any of him on me. Exhausted, I collapse into bed. *Only one hour till my alarm goes off.*

Chapter 1 – The Early Years

"Our dream of having a split-level house has finally come true," Ronnie says. The empty living room echoes his excitement. He sweeps me off my feet, spinning me around like I'm on a carnival ride. The revolving room slows as he puts me down and holds me close. I lean back and look up at his face.

"The only thing we need to make our lives perfect is to have a boy and then a girl," I say.

"Maybe that will happen by the time we fill this house with furniture."

"Hopefully, since we just got approved by the adoption agency.

I wiggle out of his arms. "I think the first thing we need to do is go buy a bed." I tell him over my shoulder, "One night of you pushing me off that air mattress onto the cold floor is enough!"

"You pushed me!" he says, chasing after me as I run for the car.

* * *

I thumb through home decorating magazines, .purposely avoiding the ones with happy children and mothers in them as I wait to see my gynecologist. Dr. Slocum's nurse leads me directly to his office instead of a treatment room. I check out my doctor's medical degrees hanging on the wall and a family photo on his desk. After what seems like forever, he enters, grinning from ear to ear.

"Hello, Sara. How are you feeling?"

"Okay, Doctor. Why am I in your office? We usually talk about my tests on the phone."

"Please sit down. I have a couple of questions first; then we'll talk about your tests." He lays my file on the corner of his desk and crosses his arms in front of him. "Have you been sick at your stomach lately?"

"Yes, off and on. There's been a bug going around the office."

"Have you started your period yet?"

"No . . . but you know how irregular I am."

Instead of going around his desk, he sits in the chair next to me. He takes my hand. "One of your blood tests came back with unexpected results." He pauses. "Sara, you're pregnant!"

I feel queasy. "*What*? Are you sure? But the tests have shown for years that I'd never get pregnant."

"I know. I know. For that very reason, I had the lab redo the test. It's still positive. And you exhibit classic symptoms of pregnancy."

I jump up so fast the chair rocks back and forth. I pace with excitement.

Dr. Slocum scribbles on a prescription pad, chuckling. "You will need prenatal vitamins."

"I can't believe we're having this conversation." I stare down at my stomach as if I would be showing already.

His smile has been continuous since coming through the door. "God pleasantly surprises me occasionally."

"It is a miracle, isn't it?" I am trying to wrap my mind around it . . . pregnant! "When is my due date?" I ask.

"May 12th."

"Now I'll be like other women, always talking about *my* baby." I giggle.

"Because of the chronic yeast infections you've had, we're going to do checkups every three weeks instead of the usual four. For the first trimester take things a little easy. Eat a well balanced diet, exercise at a moderate rate, and take naps when you feel the urge. You can schedule your first appointment on your way out."

"Okay, I'll do that. Thanks, Dr. Slocum."

"You're welcome. If you have any questions, don't hesitate to call."

When I walk out the front door of the medical building, I look both directions. No one is in sight. I cup my hands around my mouth like a megaphone and yell, "I AM PREGNANT!" A voice from the nearby parking garage says, "Congratulations."

***

I park in front of the Royal Grocers warehouse where Ronnie works. Still trying to believe the news, I practice how to tell "Daddy" about it. I move to the passenger side of the car and wait. After several long minutes, Ronnie and two other drivers come out the front door and stop. I try to be patient as they talk and talk. I honk the horn. Ronnie waves at me and keeps talking. I honk again.

Aggravation shows on his face as he walks toward the car and opens the driver's door. "What's the hur—" He stops mid-sentence when he sees my face. "What's going on here? I've never seen you look so excited." As he sits down in the seat, he asks, "Has the agency found us a baby?" He leans back, smiling. "Do we have a baby?"

"Sort of."

"How can we sort of have a baby?" He turns sideways, looking at me. "Either we do or we don't. Which is it?"

"I went back to Dr. Slocum's office this afternoon."

"Why? You were just there last week."

"I know, but he wanted to discuss the results of one of my blood tests."

A smile starts at the corners of his mouth. "You can't be pregnant! *Are you?*"

"Yes, yes, I am! We're pregnant!"

He hops out of the car, jumping in the air, raising his fist in victory. "Hey guys, we're pregnant!" he yells at the cars leaving the parking lot.

Back in the car, his gaze caresses my face, making me feel like the most beautiful woman in the world. "Sara, this is the best news ever."

"I'll call the adoption agency Monday to tell them we're making our own baby," I tell him.

"Hot damn! That bitch social worker won't be nosing into our business anymore."

* * *

On April 10, 1994, at 6:33 a.m., Logan Michael Farley comes into this world three weeks early. He is a lightweight at 5 lbs. 2 oz. As I hold him, Logan wraps his small hand around my little finger while Ronnie strokes our son's cheek. Everything is perfect in our world.

* * *

At the sound of a car pulling into the driveway, 2½-year old Logan runs to the front door welcoming Daddy home. Ronnie comes into the kitchen carrying him.

"Sorry I'm late, but I got some overtime."

"That's great."

Ronnie puts Logan down and comes over to kiss my 7½-month pregnant stomach. When he rises up to give me a kiss, his smile disappears. He bends down to Logan's level. "Hey, buddy, how about practicing your Sesame Street game? I'll play with you after dinner."

"Okay, Daddy," and he is gone to his bedroom.

"Are you and the baby okay?" Ronnie asks, looking concerned.

"Dr. Slocum said I've started dilating."

"So, the baby's coming soon?" he asks, excitedly.

"I hope not. Dr. Slocum wants me to stay in bed until my delivery date." Tears slide down my cheeks.

Ronnie takes me in his arms and kisses away the tears. "Calm down Sara. Why are you so upset?"

"Staying off my feet for six weeks is bad enough, but there's no way I can take care of Logan from the bed and sofa."

"That is a problem, but we'll find a way to handle it. Why aren't you off your feet?" He puts his arm around my waist and guides me to the sofa in the living room. "You're going to rest while I finish dinner and figure out a plan."

"Thanks," I say, settling in on the sofa for a nap.

Some time later, I am roused by a sweet kiss on the end of my nose. When I open my eyes, there's Logan, three inches away. "Daddy bring dinner."

Ronnie sets a TV tray with a bowl of soup on it down by the sofa as I sit up. "Let's eat, and then we'll talk about your vacation." He winks at me.

He joins Logan at his low plastic table on the floor. Logan gets into his little chair, immediately grabbing crackers to crumble into his soup. *What a Kodak moment! Wish I had a camera.*

After enjoying several spoonfuls, I ask, "What did you do to the soup? It tastes different."

"Do you like it?"

"Maybe." I wink at him.

"Um, um, good," Logan says.

"Okay, okay, I really like it."

"Did you hear Mommy say something?" Ronnie ignores me, chit-chatting with Logan. Teasing me is his way of distracting me from our after-dinner conversation.

Logan bobs his head, imitating his bobble-head Ernie. "She likes it," he answers.

With a finger to Logan's lips, Ronnie says, "We won't tell her I put Mexican cheese in it, will we?" Logan turns his bobble-head from side to side.

When our bowls are empty, Ronnie stands up, comes over to me, and puckers up for a kiss. "Stay off your feet while I get the little guy ready for bed." He leans down and kisses me. "Then you can read him a story while I clean up the kitchen."

"But – " He points his finger at my stomach, shaking his head no.

A short time later, I lay beside Logan on his bed and read the same Ernie book, again. As Ernie goes to sleep in the book, Logan's eyelids flutter shut. I kiss him and move back to the sofa.

It isn't long before Ronnie comes in, sits down on the sofa, and lifts my feet onto his lap. "While I was in the kitchen, I made a few phone calls to see who's available to help us out." He starts our nightly routine of massaging my feet to minimize the swelling. "Mom said she'll come over to see if she can keep up with Logan."

"I appreciate her giving it a try." I lean forward and reposition the pillows behind my back. "Annie is the only one on my side of the family who isn't working, but I'm sure Gary won't let her come."

"Probably not," Ronnie answers. "We both know what a bastard he can be if she doesn't have dinner ready when he gets home." His strong fingers knead soreness out of my foot. "I also talked to Earlene. She's going to freeze food in single-size servings and bring it to us on the weekends."

"That's great! My brother has a great wife." I reach my hand out to him and he takes it, pressing a kiss to my palm. "Honey, you're absolutely wonderful."

"I know," he says. I kick him lovingly with my free foot. He grabs it for its turn to be massaged. "We'll start with these plans and make adjustments along the way."

He stops massaging and lays his hand on my stomach, waiting for the baby to move. "Is Dr. Slocum concerned about this little guy being smaller than Logan was?"

"Yes. Right now, he weighs less than five pounds. And, this is a critical time for his lungs developing."

"That makes sense," Ronnie says, sighing heavily."

***

On January 26, 1997, Derek Anthony Farley arrives on his due date at 6 lbs. 2 oz. Two days later in my hospital room, the four of us wait for Dr. Slocum to come in and release me. I enjoy watching Logan squeezed into a chair beside Ronnie, helping hold his baby brother. Logan is telling Derek about the toys they'll play with when we get home.

Dr. Slocum comes in the door. "Hello everyone. Sara, how are you feeling?"

"Pretty good. The question on our minds is, how's Derek?"

Ronnie stands, comes over to me and lays Derek in my arms. He picks up Logan.

"The last test on his lungs came back, and he is a healthy baby boy." He glances at Ronnie and smiles at Logan. "I know the six weeks of bed rest have been difficult for all of you, but Derek's crying is so loud that he sometimes wakes the other babies." He pauses with a smile. "The nursery's ready for him to get out of there."

Ronnie and I sigh simultaneously. We look at each other and laugh in relief.

"Sara, you can get out of here today and get back to normal."

Chapter 2 – Abandoned

"Where's Daddy's car?" Derek asks, as we come out of McDonald's.

"Maybe he went to get gas or something," I answer. I feel the Big Mac in my stomach churn.

"Why didn't he wait for us?" Logan asks, looking anxious.

"I don't know. Let's go play on those big rocks over there." I need the boys to be busy while I jumpstart my brain.

Where else would he go without telling me? My breathing feels constricted. *Have to stay calm. Breathe slow, slow-ly. Is he following through with his many threats to leave us stranded some place? But 200 miles from home! He's a jerk sometimes, but this is just plain mean!*

The sound of one of the boys crying interrupts my struggle to plan for our impending survival. I brush the dirt off Derek's knee and kiss the boo-boo. Back to the rocks he runs. *The motel's paid up for two days. The boys playing in the pool will keep them occupied while I find someone to come get us and take us home. How do I explain this to Logan and Derek? I don't want them to know what a terrible father they have. Oh my God! Has he really deserted us?* My heart pounds and it seems I can actually hear it beating. *Have to keep my head and not panic. Money, how much do I have?* Recounting what is in my billfold three times doesn't increase the $15.28 that I have. *Can't waste any on a cab to get us back to the motel.* Frantically, I check each of my pockets for the motel room key and find it in my back pocket.

"Mommy, I gotta pee," Derek says.

"Okay, let's go back inside until Daddy comes."

I see tears filling Logan's eyes as he gets closer to me. "Did Daddy leave 'cause I'm bad?"

I kneel down. "Of course not. Why do you ask that?"

"'Cause he said he'd leave us some day if I'm bad."

Oh God! I didn't know they heard him say that! I wrap my arms around both of them. "Daddy was really mad at me when he said that yesterday. He sometimes says things he doesn't mean when he's upset." I stand and take their hands. "Come on, let's go inside." Just as we come out of the bathroom, Ronnie pulls into the parking lot.

Both boys run out the door asking, "Where'd you go? Where'd you go, Daddy?"

"To get these for you." Ronnie gets out of the car and pushes the driver's seat forward. He hands them each a new Hot Wheels car as they climb into the backseat. Nonchalantly, he leans against the side of the car with a half-smile, watching me closely.

When I see him pulling into the parking lot, I'm greatly relieved he came back for us. Just as quickly, fury replaces the relief. Out of nervousness, I brush my hair back with my hand and, through clenched teeth, I ask, "Why in hell did you leave us here like that?"

"To get gas," he answers. "Did you think I left you here or somethin'?" The corners of his mouth curves into a grin. He looks like a Cheshire cat with perfect white teeth.

I hurry around the car and keep going, intending to walk however far it is to our motel. My heart pounds, my underarms get wet, my mouth is dry. I know my hooker makeup that Ronnie demands I wear is streaking down my face with my tears. My mind feels stalled but races with questions at the same time.

Willing my legs to not tremble as I increase my speed to a near-jog, I intensely desire to outrun my thoughts. The physical exertion lessens my panic. When I pull my gaze up from the sidewalk to look at the horizon, I see hues of orange and pink dancing across the western sky, painting streaks of color in every direction. I slow my pace as I watch the changing shapes and colors of the sunset and feel it sooth my whole being.

"Hey, good looking, where ya going?" A wolf whistle follows, and I hear Logan and Derek laugh.

I look around and see the guys in the car trailing alongside me. Ronnie whistles again. I struggle to keep my face straight because I don't want Ronnie to think leaving us at McDonald's is okay. *If I don't get in the car, he could still take off again, leaving me stranded alone in Branson.*

I get in the car. Ronnie takes my hand. I don't jerk it away like I would rather. "Honey, I'm sorry if I scared you. I just thought you'd know I went for gas." He gently kisses the tears from my face. "Let's go have some fun."

"Yeah, Daddy, let's go ride the ducks," begs Logan.

"I don't wanna ride no ducks!" says Derek. "They'll bite me when I sit on 'em."

"No, little bro. These ducks are amphibious ducks. Daddy says they're left over from some war. They can travel on land AND water. It's going to be fun to ride 'em."

"How about it, Honey?" Ronnie asks, giving me an irresistible grin.

"Sure. Let's go."

"Hooray," the boys chime together.

After Ronnie pays for the tickets, we go through the building and out the back door. "Look! There's an army tank," Derek says.

"No, silly. That's the duck we're riding." Logan and Derek look at each other and run toward the amphibian.

After going up and down the Ozark Mountains through the brilliant fall-colored trees, the duck splashes off of land into the water. Over the PA system we hear an announcement by Captain Ducky asking if there are any passengers on board who wants to drive the duck. Logan's eyes light up. "Is he talking about this duck?"

"Hurry, go get in line," I say pointing toward the front of the vehicle.

He smiles wide, grabs Derek's hand and they are gone.

"Come on, Sara, you want to drive, don't you?" Ronnie asks as he stands to follow the boys.

"No, I'll stay here and enjoy the scenery while you guys drive."

"Party pooper," he says without a smile.

Can't stop thinking about whether Ronnie was leaving us or just went after gas. If I say any more about it, he'll be so enraged we'll be back in St. Louis within three hours. Don't want the boys to miss going to Silver Dollar City. Just have to keep my mouth shut and bring the subject up at a later time when he's in a good mood.

***

At home on Sunday afternoon, the boys rush to Zach's to show him their new Power Ranger vehicles – toy ducks. As Ronnie and I sit on the front step drinking iced tea, leaves flutter to the ground, splotching our grass with red, yellow, and orange.

"Looks like we can have our leaf party in a couple of weeks," Ronnie muses.

"I'll get the hot dogs and marshmallows the next time I go to the grocery store. Do we need to have the chimney cleaned before we use the fireplace?" I ask.

"No, I checked it last week and it still looks clean. We didn't use it much last year." He gives me a puzzled look. "How did this leaf-raking party thing get started?"

"Two years ago when the boys and I were raking leaves, I hid in a big pile of them. When they came looking for me, I jumped out at them. We spent the rest of the afternoon covering each other up and leaping out. It was a lot of fun, and we actually filled a few sacks with leaves."

He reaches for my hand. "Must have been while I was at work."

"Yes, you were." I take a sip of tea instead of adding "as usual" to the end of the sentence. "After that, we roasted hot dogs and marshmallows in the fireplace. And, voila, we now have leaf parties every year."

He puts his arm around my shoulders and pulls me close. "I love cozying up with you in front of that fireplace. Maybe we can light a fire tonight." The warmth of his smile sends a tingle all the way to my toes.

"Sounds good to me."

"You know, the boys were quite a bit of help with the leaves last year. Wonder how long before they'll start wanting hard, cold cash instead of hot dogs and marshmallows," he says with a big smile.

"Until they're teenagers?" I grin.

"Dream on, girl. Dream on."

We laugh happily together.

"There's something I want to ask you," I bravely say.

"Sure, Babe, what is it?"

"In the eleven years we've been married, you've never gone any place without telling me where you were going." I feel him bristle as he removes his arm from my shoulders. I hesitate to say more, but I need to know the answer. "What was different in Branson yesterday that you didn't tell me you were going after gas?"

He jumps to his feet. His eyebrows knit together, and his teeth grip hard. "I told you why – to get gas! You're so fucking stupid!

Always ruining our good times by asking stupid questions!"

The coldness in his eyes matches the temperature of the iced tea, which splashes onto my foot as he throws his cup to the ground. The nerves in my body jump to full alert with the staccato slamming of the screen and front doors.

Chapter 3 – Nice Daddy

My hand is shaking so much it is hard to turn the key. I pray for strength to cope with whichever man is in my house tonight.

"Mommy, my homework's in the car," Logan tells me. His voice sounds stressed. "I gotta get it."

Handing him the keys, I say, "Remember, keep these in your hand while getting your homework. We don't want Daddy mad because the keys got locked in my car."

From the small front porch, I watch Logan run with Derek on his heels. My smile turns into a frown as I wonder if I could survive as a single mom. At the sound of the front door opening, I jump. "Hi Sara, do you need help?" Ronnie asks, reaching for the grocery bags in my arms.

"Thanks." My tense nerves unwind some. I trail behind my husband through the living room and dining room, turning left into the kitchen. The chasm between us doesn't feel quite so deep and wide at this moment.

Ronnie sets the groceries on the counter. Crinkles appear at the corners of his eyes as he smiles at me. "I'll go see what the boys are up to."

"Great." I pull groceries from the bags and start putting them away.

Derek rushes into the room. Fear rears its ugly head momentarily until I notice Derek is smiling. "Mommy, Mommy, I gotta hide!"

I lean down and whisper, "Get in your cabinet."

He runs to the cabinet, opens the door, and squeezes himself inside.

As I put perishables in the refrigerator, I hear Ronnie and Logan come in the front door. When I turn around, I can see them through the spindles dividing the kitchen and dining room.

"Hey, Mommy, look at me flying." Logan says excitedly, spread-eagled on Ronnie's shoulders.

Ronnie swings Logan down to the floor when he gets into the kitchen. "Where's Derek?"

I point at the cabinet door that's ajar with Derek's pant leg hanging out. Ronnie eases the door open. Derek's face is alight with joy. Although he resists with all of his might, Ronnie and Logan pull him out, pots and pans trailing onto the floor. He is tickled until he becomes breathless.

"Okay, boys, time to settle down," Ronnie says as he stands up. "Do you guys have homework tonight?"

"Yeah, I've got dang math to do," answers Logan.

"Me too, but mine's dang spelling." Derek's tone of voice mimics his brother's.

"If you get it all finished while Mommy and I fix dinner, we'll play video games after we eat."

"All right," they say, racing to the living room for their book bags. Coming back into the kitchen, they hurry up onto the stools, open their books, and start working fast and furiously.

"I'll be checking your homework before any games are played," I remind them.

"Awww," Derek groans. Both of them slow their pace.

***

At bedtime, the boys are happy and smiling. I read Derek his favorite book and kiss him goodnight. When I go into Logan' room, Ronnie is sitting on the end of the bed, listening to Logan read from his library book. As I bend down to kiss Logan's forehead, I feel Ronnie's hand slide into mine, squeeze and release it.

"Goodnight, Logan, sleep tight."

"Good night, Mommy."

Ronnie follows me into the kitchen and fills the dishwasher as I wipe the stove off. I hear the whirring of the dishwater. He comes up behind me and puts his arms around my waist. "Are you feeling frisky tonight?" He brushes my hair away and runs a trail of kisses down the back of my neck, giving me shivers. "How about going to bed early?"

I turn and kiss him gently, then passionately. In a fluid motion, he sweeps me off of my feet to carry me up the stairs. Eager to get to our bed, he stumbles, almost dropping me on the creaky fifth step, setting us down on the steps. We laugh together.

Then I hear Logan asking, “What you guys doin’?”

Looking over Ronnie’s shoulder, I see Logan standing at the bottom of the stairs with his arm draped around Derek’s shoulder. They have mile-wide smiles. “We’re playing,” I say, motioning for them to join us. The four of us gradually bump our way down the stairs to the dining room floor, laughing, tickling, and wrestling.

Later, as I tuck Derek into bed for the second time, he says, “Mommy, I like Daddy tonight. I wish nice Daddy would stay here.”

“Me, too, Sweetie. Me too. Love you.” I blow him a kiss as I close the door.

Ronnie and I pick back up where we left off. In our lovemaking, he is passionate, so pleasing instead of his usual demanding, despicable self. Afterwards, I cuddle against him and pray the 9/11 nightmares won’t intrude into my sleep tonight.

Chapter 4 – Verbal Warning

At work, I listen to phone messages from workers' compensation claimants. My thinking is inhibited by the weariness and exhaustion of the 9/11 nightmares. I can't remember what to do next. Tears threaten to leak out of the corners of my eyes.

"Good morning," Nancy says from behind me. I grab a tissue from its box and pretend to blow my nose. I swivel my chair around toward the door of my cubicle.

"Are you okay?" she asks.

"Yes, allergies acting up."

"I'll be right back," my supervisor says and walks away. Momentarily she returns with a red folder in her hand. "The conference room is free right now," she says, motioning for me to follow her. As she closes the door, I sit down in a chair on the far side of the table. Sweat dampens my clothes, and forms on my brow.

Nancy drops the red folder, not too gently, on the table across from me, and sits down. "You seem distracted a lot lately. What's going on?"

"I don't . . . know."

"Are you having family or health problems?"

"No, nothing unusual. Why?"

She snaps the red folder open and lays a claim in front of me. "In reviewing your claims, I've found you are making way too many mistakes." The more sheets she lays down, the harder they hit the table. Finally, they stop. She leans back in her chair and folds her hands at her waist. "You're not following standard procedures."

"I know I've made a few mistakes." I try to control the quiver in my voice. "I thought I'd fixed 'em. But this . . ." I say, waving my hand above them. *Don't know what made me think I could succeed as an adjuster. Should've stayed unit secretary.*

"Now tell me what's going on," she says a little less terse.

"I'm having trouble sleeping."

She looks impatient as she asks, "Have any idea why?"

Maybe she'll give me some leeway if I tell her. "I'm having nightmares about what happened to the Twin Towers."

"Are you talking about 9/11? That happened over a year ago. Why on Earth would you dream about that?" she asks so loud, I wonder if people beyond the walls can hear her.

"I don't know. But since the anniversary last month, the nightmares just won't stop." I move my hands to the back of my neck, massaging the tightness.

"Too bad you're not sleeping well." She pulls a page from the red folder, leans forward and slides it across the table. As I stare at it, she says, "Because you've received two verbal warnings previously and have been resistant to counseling, you have to decide if you will go to counseling or resign from your job."

Oh my God, what will Ronnie do if I get fired? Breathing is a struggle. I move my hand away from my thigh, realizing my fingernails were digging in.

"Did you say resign?" comes out as a choked whisper.

"Yes, I did," Nancy answers without looking up from scribbling on paper. "I had to talk to human resources about your many absences and tardiness and they are the ones who said this is your last chance to keep your job." Her eyes are softer.

I slowly pull my hand through my hair, trying to get my voice back. *Have to do it. Just can't tell Ronnie about it.*

"Okay. I'll go to counseling," I say, resignedly. I slump lower in my chair.

Abruptly, she stands. "Good choice," she says in a flat, emotionless voice. "Call employee assistance to find a counselor and we'll readdress your performance in three months." As the door closes hard behind her, my chin quivers. I drag my numb body out of the chair. "Don't have time to cry. Pull yourself together, girl." I wipe sweat and tears from my face. As I walk out of the conference room, I force the corners of my mouth up into my usual pasted-on smile.

That interminably long workday finally comes to an end. *Have to pick up the boys and stop for groceries.* I push my weary body out of the chair.

Chapter 5 –Meeting Carol

Two weeks after my meeting with Nancy, I hand paperwork to a receptionist through a sliding glass window. I sit down and look at an outdated magazine. After flipping through several magazines, I feel an urge to move. I walk from frame to frame, gazing at unspectacular art on the walls. I hear a door open in the corner and turn to look. A woman, perhaps in her late forties, says, "Sara?"

"Yes, I'm Sara."

"Nice to meet you. I'm Carol." She motions me through the door as she holds it open. "My office is the last one on the right."

"Thanks." As I step into her office, right in front of me is a large window overlooking a wooded area of trees showing off their beautiful fall colors. I smile slightly. *Those will be comforting. They remind me of growing up on the farm.* I sit down in the chair with the best view of the window. Out of a nervous habit, I twist my wedding ring.

Carol settles into a rocking chair facing me, puts her feet on a low footstool, and places a folder on her lap. "I've reviewed the questionnaire you completed online about your difficulties at work, but first I'd like to hear about your family."

Thinking about my sons brings a smile to my face. "How about I show you my boys' pictures?" Without waiting for an answer, I pull them out of my purse and hand them to her.

"The little one is Derek. He's five and in Kindergarten." She writes a few words and looks back at the photos, apparently waiting for me to say more. "He loves reading and science and Spider-Man."

"He looks a lot like you with those hazel eyes and dark hair." She moves Logan's photo in front of Derek's. "My guess is that this one looks more like his dad."

"Yes, he does. Those beautiful sky-blue eyes are what first attracted me to Ronnie." I fidget in my chair. "Logan is eight and in second grade. His favorite subject is recess." I laugh nervously. "He loves all kinds of sports."

I wait as she writes on a yellow pad.

When she looks up, I add, "They both love Matchbox cars, Power Rangers, Yu-Gi-Oh! cards and video games. On evenings when Ronnie's working, we play board games. Ronnie hates those. My boys are such a delight."

"Personality wise, which parent does each of them resemble?"

"Derek is quieter like me and Logan is more rambunctious like his dad. But physically, Derek's stocky like Ronnie and Logan's thin like me."

She hands the pictures back to me. "And what does Ronnie do?"

"He drives an 18-wheeler for Royal Grocers."

"Does he drive over the road or locally?"

"Once in a while he'll make an overnight trip, but mostly he delivers to stores in small towns around St. Louis."

She looks at the questionnaire again. "Tell me more about the problems you're having at work."

I stiffly lace my fingers in my lap. "Sometimes, well actually often, I get confused and have to retrace my steps until I can figure out what I was doing."

"I see the nightmares you're having are all about 9/11. Do you know anyone who was injured or killed that day?"

"No, I don't. I've never even been to New York. That's what makes the nightmares so puzzling."

"How long have you been having them?" she asks.

"They started right after the first anniversary." Butterflies flutter around my insides.

"How often are you having them?"

"Four to five nights a week," I answer.

"Is it always the same nightmare or different ones?"

"Different. They change. Sometimes it's the same scene repeating over and over. In one of them I'm sitting on the couch pushing my TV remote to turn off the 9/11 scenes, but it won't work." I move around in my chair trying to get more comfortable. "They are chillingly realistic." I pull a tissue from the box sitting on a nearby table.

Carol turns a page of the questionnaire. "When did you start taking the antidepressant prescription?"

"About a year ago, and I was feeling better. But I don't think it's working anymore."

"What makes you think that?"

"Most mornings, I stand in my closet and stare at my clothes for several minutes before I can make a choice of what to wear. It's not like I have a lot to choose from, either. I just can't make a decision." I rub my eye that's twitching. "The other thing that happens is after the boys go to bed, I sit at the computer intending to play only a game or two of Solitaire. Several hours later I'm suddenly aware how much time has passed. It's almost like I go into a trance. Saying that out loud reminds me the same things were happening last year when my doctor put me on the medication."

"Sometimes our bodies build up immunities to drugs we're taking. And when this happens, it's time to increase the dosage or change it," Carol says.

"Guess I need to talk to my doctor about this."

"Yes, you definitely should."

"Has anything major happened in your life lately to increase your stress level? Perhaps a major illness, a death of a loved one, or a major scare of some type."

"No illness or death." I cross my forearms and slide them back and forth, rubbing them with my hands. "A few weeks ago, when we were in Branson for the weekend, my husband unintentionally scared me."

"Tell me about it."

I give Carol the details about thinking Ronnie was abandoning us in Branson.

"Have you come to a conclusion as to what he was really doing?"

"I guess he went after gas." I sigh heavily. "But when he exploded at me the next day . . . that's the frustrating part, not knowing for sure," I say sadly.

"How do you feel about what happened?"

"Feel? Uh . . . I have no idea."

"That's okay. Sometimes it's hard for any of us to know how we feel." She gives me an encouraging smile. "This is a safe place to express all of your feelings," Carol says. "I'm sure I heard anger as you were telling me about it."

"Oh! Yeah. I'm so angry I could spit nails!" I feel myself blushing and drop my eyes to my lap.

"Very good, Sara."

I look up. "That was unusually loud for me." I smile timidly. "Until you said anger, I only knew that I'm very upset about what happened."

"Anger is a strong normal emotion that we all have, and it can be negative or positive."

"How can anger be positive?" I ask in surprise.

"When there's an injustice happening such as child abuse, positive anger motivates people into action. I've seen abused women stay with their abusive partners until he injures one of the children. The mothering instinct creates a positive anger that motivates her to get all of them away from the abuser."

"But what if . . ." Carol waits for my question to form. "What if I allow myself to feel the anger and it turns me into another Ronnie?" I ask, fearfully.

"People with explosive tempers allow the anger to control them. I don't know you very well yet, but I'm sure your emotions aren't a driving force in you. In fact, I would guess because you are on the receiving end of Ronnie's verbal abuse, you have difficulty knowing what you are feeling."

I'm taken aback with a sensation that I've just been slapped in the face with the words "verbal abuse." Tears sting my eyes. I shift in my chair and pick at a hangnail. *How dare her call Ronnie an abuser! He just has a lot of frustrations he doesn't handle very well.*

"As difficult it may be to believe, everyone – including Ronnie – has the ability to choose how to manage our anger."

"I don't think Ronnie can control his. When he goes into a rage, I have to wait for him to vent so he can regain control of himself."

"Has the doorbell or phone ever rung when he's 'venting' his anger?"

"Uh . . . yeah. A couple of weeks ago when my brother and his family arrived early for a birthday party."

"Did his venting continue or did he stop?"

"He, uh . . . stopped, went to door, and let them in."

"Did he choose to control his anger or did he continue venting after they came into the house?"

I sit rigid, almost in a daze as my head starts hammering behind my eyes. "Of course he stopped." *Oh my God, he does have control.* I reach for the ibuprofen in my purse.

After swallowing the pills with the Coke I brought with me, I ask, "How do I help Ronnie understand he can control his anger?"

"That's his responsibility, not yours."

"But if I can just explain it to him so he can get a handle on it, we'd all be so much better off, including him."

"Would he be willing to go to an anger management class?"

"Absolutely not! He doesn't want anyone nosing into our business."

"Does he know you are coming to counseling?"

"No, and there's no reason to tell him because I'm only here until the nightmares stop."

"The only way you can help him manage his anger is by changing how you respond to him."

I straighten up in my chair, ready to spring into action to help Ronnie return to being the man I married eleven years ago. "Okay. What do I do?"

"There isn't a simple, clear-cut plan of do this and this and he'll change. Changing how you respond to him is your part of the dynamics of your relationship. How he acts is his responsibility."

I feel like a deflating balloon as I slump down into the chair. "So . . . what do I do when I feel angry? I sure don't want it spilling out onto the boys like Ronnie's does."

"I'm glad you asked about that. One of the best ways to defuse anger is physical activity."

"I did that in Branson. I walked several blocks when we left McDonald's. I wasn't as angry when I got into the car."

"That's a good example. As for me, I clean house like mad when I'm upset. We'll talk more about anger later." Carol makes a note. "Right now we need to discuss some strategies to reduce your nightmares."

"Okay. After all, that is why I'm here."

"Research has found caffeine has a detrimental effect on our sleep. It not only keeps us alert during waking hours but also hinders sound sleep at night. Do you know how much caffeine you drink per day?"

"Too much, I'm sure. But I know I'm not drinking any more than I was before the September 11th anniversary."

"That may be true, but our body chemistry changes as illnesses and stresses fluctuate in our lives. Since we don't know the causes of your nightmares yet, it seems logical to me to follow the experts' advice and change anything that might make a difference." I take a drink. "I guess I can reduce them to one per day instead of three," I say, holding my Coke bottle up.

"That's a good start. Do you also drink coffee?"

"Yes. I'll switch to decaf and hope Ronnie can't tell the difference."

She finishes a note. "When you go to bed at night, what do you think about?"

"I try to just rest. If I don't sleep, I can't have nightmares."

"But not sleeping builds more stress, physically and mentally. What do you enjoy most in your life?"

"My boys." I smile in relief. "You know – the cute, fun, silly things they do." The next several minutes are spent talking about my sons some more.

"Reminiscing about them will help your body and mind become more relaxed as you're falling asleep. This may reduce the number of nightmares some."

"Logan and Derek are entertaining. They've done enough funny things to help relax me for months."

"That's great. Another thing I think will be helpful is to keep a journal."

What if Ronnie finds it? That might make him hit me for the first time. "I don't want to do that."

"Why not?"

"I'm afraid of . . . my husband finding it."

Carol leans closer. "Would you say that again, please?"

"I'm scared what will happen if Ronnie finds it," I say louder.

"What do you think would happen?"

"I . . . I don't know." My voice strains and rises in pitch.

"Perhaps you could do it at work during your breaks and lunch hour."

"Maybe . . . How does this journaling thing work?" I straighten up in my chair.

"Put the date, what happens each day, interactions with Ronnie, problems you're having at work. Be as brief or prolific as you want. Also, when you have the nightmares, include those in your journal."

"Okay. I guess I can give it a try."

"Good. We've got a plan."

I feel a spark of hope, not sure for what, but it feels good. The depression doesn't seem to weigh quite as heavy.

"Per your employer's protocol, we need to schedule six appointments, two weeks apart. Does four o'clock on Wednesdays work for you?"

"It worked well today, but I was hoping for sessions every week," I say.

"That's my preference, too, but since they are giving you an hour off work to come here, we have to follow their guidelines." Carol and I agree on dates, and I write them in my pocket calendar.

> Journal Entry — 10/24/2002 — I'll just do this journaling thing and the counseling until the nightmares stop. Speaking of which, if thinking about the boys stops them, I won't need all those scheduled sessions. One of the information sheets the receptionist gave me suggests I think about what I want to get out of counseling. That's easy – for the nightmares to stop!

> Nightmare Entry — 10/25/2002 — Had one last night — I'm standing in our front yard watching Ronnie back out of the drive to go to the hardware store — the bright blue sky fills with millions of documents floating to the ground like glistening confetti, some of them on fire, others with scorched edges — Ronnie is running around snatching them out of the air and adding them to the collection of others in his hand — he's in my face, gigantic and menacing, yelling questions rapid-fire, asking why I've been writing down everything that happens in our lives for the world to see.

Chapter 6 – Hot Dogs and Fried Chicken

Ronnie hasn't been home two minutes when he yells from the kitchen door, "Why the hell you cooking hot dogs? I told you to fry chicken tonight."

I turn sideways to look at him. "I had a rough day at work and don't feel like standing over a hot stove."

"You didn't get fired, did ya?" he snarls.

"No! Why'd you ask that?"

"'cause I know you're stupid and always screwing things up."

I turn back to the stove and stir the macaroni. When he's this perturbed, he won't hear anything I say. I feel him grab my shoulders. He spins me around to face him. Bending down from his six-foot-two stature, he puts his nose about an inch from mine and screams. "Damn it, woman! You'd better tell me right now."

"Okay, okay." I yank myself out of his grasp and back up against the refrigerator. "I got a verbal warning for some mistakes. I'm exhausted from the nightmares."

"Well, the way to fix that is to stop having those damn things."

"I'm going . . ." *Can't tell him I'm going to counseling!* "I read stress causes nightmares. And right now you're pushing mine over the top!"

He smiles slightly. I breathe a small sigh of relief, thinking his anger is subsiding. In the length of time it takes him to move three steps closer to me, his grin is replaced with rage in his eyes. The line of his jaw hardens. "You damn well better start cooking the fucking chicken or you'll be picking yourself up off the floor."

I make the safe choice of getting the chicken out of the fridge. Ronnie moves around the counter to a stool and sits, watching my every move. I feel like a child being hovered over by a parent ensuring tasks are completed as instructed. I hear him draw on his cigarette and pour coffee into a cup. I feel his eyes boring a hole into my back.

As I flour the third piece of chicken, the sound of him standing to his feet chills my blood. His footsteps sound louder and louder until he is standing next to me. He pushes me to the side and grabs the heated pan of hot dogs from the stove. He goes across the kitchen to the sink and dumps them with the pan clanging as he drops it. "You're taking too damn long. Go get me KFC." He stomps into the living room and turns on the evening news.

The fear eases some because he is out of the room. I don't have enough money to buy chicken for all four of us, so I retrieve the hot dogs, rinse them off, and slam them and the pan back on the stove. Anger builds inside me where the fear has vacated.

***

With Kentucky Fried Chicken in the passenger seat, I pull into our driveway. The tears I am holding back flood to the surface. As the anguish subsides, I blow my nose, wipe tears away, and go into the house of anger.

While Ronnie eats KFC in front of the TV, the boys and I eat our dinner in the kitchen. "What did you guys do at Kyle's this afternoon?"

"Played catch," Derek says.

With a look of concern beyond his eight years, Logan asks, "Mommy, are you okay?"

"I'm fine. Why do you ask?"

"'Cause your eyes are so red and you look so sad," Logan says. I feel Derek's hand searching for mine under the counter, and I squeeze as I grasp it.

I smile weakly. "My allergies are acting up."

As the boys jam the last bites of food into their mouths, Ronnie yells from the living room. "I'm going to Chuck's for a beer." *God only knows when he'll be home.*

> Journal Entry — 11/1/2002 — From now on I have to make a last-second mental check of my words before releasing them to Ronnie. I'm so stupid for almost telling him I'm going to counseling. Could've avoided him yelling and threatening me if I hadn't changed the menu. Maybe Carol can help me figure out what I'm doing wrong that ticks him off so often. Maybe Carol can get us back to where we used to be. Sure miss that guy. Maybe this is how everyone's marriages go after being married eleven years.

***

Lying in bed, I feel my face relax into a smile. I start reminiscing about the afternoon I heard belly laughter waft into the kitchen from the living room. *When I peeped into the living room to check on Logan and Derek, they were sitting on the floor playing. As I walked in, I asked Logan how he managed to get Derek out of the playpen.*

Beaming from ear to ear, he said, "I didn't. He climbed over the top." I sat down on the floor to play with them. The three of us took turns cranking the Jack-in-the-Box, and clapping our hands when Jack popped out.

When I asked Logan to show me how Derek climbed out, he got up and went to the playpen, stood on his tiptoes and tried to reach the big blocks in the bottom of it. His arms were too short to connect. He turned around and said, "Derek put the blue one on top of the red one, cluummbed on top of 'em, then I helped him down so we can play." Logan sat down, still beaming.

I told him to come tell me when he sees Derek climbing on his blocks because we don't want Derek to fall and get hurt. At naptime, I kissed Derek and put him in the playpen with the blocks. I grabbed my camera from a shelf in the closet, stepped around the corner into the dining room, and waited. Pretty quickly, I heard his blocks rattling and him breathing heavy. I peeped into the living room. There he was, just as Logan described him, one foot on his stacked up blocks and the other stretching for the top rail. I snapped his photo. It's now in his baby album.

> Nightmare Entry — 11/1/2002 — I'm in the kitchen and can't believe what I see — an ant-like trail of hot dogs with arms and legs running up over the rim of the sink, down the cabinet, across the floor to the other side of the room, up the cabinet, and jumping into a boiling pan on the stove — the sight would have been funny if their panic-stricken eyes weren't darting in all directions looking for the monster — I go looking for the boys — can't find them — Ronnie is stomping the little hot dog guys and spraying them with hornet spray — he sees me and comes at me, spraying the chemicals — I can't run away.

Chapter 7 – Can't Be Domestic Violence

In Carol's office I look out the window while she reads my journal pages. *I sometimes wonder if I forget to do what Ronnie asks on purpose. I just have to try harder to be the kind of wife he wants.*

"Sara, you're doing a good job of journaling."

"Thanks." Uneasiness runs through me as I go sit down. "How's this going to stop my nightmares, though?"

"It may show us a pattern that will help us find the causes." She smiles slightly. "Does thinking about Logan and Derek help you relax before going to sleep?"

I giggle. "Yes." I tell her about the playpen escapade. "I don't think I had a nightmare that night."

Our conversation pauses as she reads and makes a checkmark on one of the pages. "Your journal shows you dreamed about hot dogs. Did something happen that day that isn't in your journal?"

I shift uncomfortably from side to side. "Oh . . . that must have been the evening I made the mistake of cooking hot dogs instead of fried chicken for dinner."

"Would you clarify that for me?" Carol's gray eyes are kind.

"Last Friday I had twice as many claims as usual. It was impossible to get them all done with Nancy's damn checklist; pardon my French. When I got home, I was cooking the simplest thing I could think of – hot dogs and green beans with macaroni and cheese – the boys' favorites. Ronnie was working overtime, and I thought he would eat with the guys at work, like he does quite often. But he walked into the house right after I put the macaroni in the water. He went ballistic. He wanted to know why I wasn't frying chicken."

"Did he specifically ask you to fix chicken that night?"

"He did the night before, but then in the morning he said he would be working overtime. I was going to cook the chicken on Saturday evening when I knew he would be home." My bottom lip quivers. "I tried to explain, but somehow he interpreted me having a rough day at work into asking if I got fired."

"Why would he do that?"

"Because I'm stupid and screw things up."

"Why do you think you're stupid?"

"Uh, I guess because of those mistakes Nancy showed me at work."

"Do you think everyone who makes mistakes is stupid?"

Carol waits as I try to figure out what to say.

"No . . . but I'm not like everyone else."

"Let me see if I understand you correctly. People like me, your coworkers, your family and friends, even your boys, make mistakes and are still of normal intelligence. But . . . when *you* make a mistake, you're stupid? Please explain that rationale to me."

My shoulders slump as I struggle to say, "I guess I believe I'm stupid because Ronnie calls me stupid so often."

"So . . . if Ronnie tells you something enough times, does that make it the truth?"

"I guess not." My throat tightens around the words.

Carol walks to a bookcase behind her desk, takes a book off the shelf, and returns to the rocking chair. She flips through it, stops, and says, "The dictionary defines stupid as brainless and dimwitted. Are you either of those?"

"No . . . don't think so." I straighten my posture.

"Even though we haven't done any intelligence testing, our conversations indicate to me that you're of average or above average intelligence."

"Really? I've always thought of myself as not being very smart. My sister made A's and B's in high school without cracking a book. Most of my evenings were spent studying to get B's, C's, and once in a while an A, if I was lucky."

"Perhaps she just retains information better or is able to put it back on paper easier."

"Oh . . . maybe."

"What other names does Ronnie call you besides stupid?"

"Um . . . bitch."

She flips toward the front of the dictionary. "This says 'bitch' is a female dog. We know that does not apply to you. A second definition of bitch is a lewd, immoral, or overbearing woman. Is any part of this definition true of you?"

"No. I have my faults, but I'm pretty sure I'm not any of those."

"From now on when Ronnie calls you a name, I want you to look it up in a dictionary for an accurate definition. This will show us whether what he says is fact or simply his opinion. These words can also go into your journal."

"Okay . . . I'll do that."

Carol pulls a sheet of paper from the folder on her lap. "This is a list of descriptions of how people treat each other," she says as she hands the sheet to me. "Do any of them describe how Ronnie treats you?"

I quickly scan the sheet. It is titled "Am I a Victim of Domestic Violence?" (Appendix A)

"I don't see any." I hand it back to her, letting go of it quickly.

She looks at the sheet. "I see one that says, 'does he call you names,' and another one of 'does he blame you for how he treats you.'"

My breathing labors. My heart races. *Ronnie's never hit me so I can't be abused.*

"Would you read this sentence out loud for me?" she asks me, pointing to the center of the page as she holds the page up in front of me.

"'If you find yourself saying 'yes, this has happened to me' to any of these, then you are at risk to become a victim of domestic violence.'" *If I tell her everything, she may tell me I have to leave him, but I can't make it on my own.* "But he's never hit me!"

"I understand that. At the women's shelter, clients told me over and over that the broken bones and bruises heal, but the words never go away. I know that's a cliché, but every one of them said it, without exception." (Appendix B)

"Really?" A chill ripples through me.

"You know how when someone gets shot in the movies, the body jumps." Carol pulls her footstool closer with her foot. "Many women that have experienced all forms of abuse have told me they actually hurt physically from their abusers' words."

"Oh… maybe that's why I feel like I have the flu or something after Ronnie rants and raves about something forever." It's difficult to get the words past the tightness in my throat.

I watch two cardinals through the window while Carol pulls out a sheet of paper and reads it. Sitting side by side, the birds take turns chirping as if they are having a discussion. Then they tap their beaks together, and the male bird flies away. Carol saying, "Sara?" draws me back.

I tell her about what I just saw. "My Aunt Lola says cardinals are unusual because the female and male both sing. In other species only the male sings."

"I didn't know that. Is Lola your mother or father's sister?"

"She's my mother's youngest sister. She's only eight years older than me, and we grew up in the same house together."

Carol writes a note. "Maybe we can talk more about that part of your family soon." She paperclips my journal pages together and slips them inside my folder.

"Sara, one of the difficult things about emotional and verbal abuse is that it doesn't leave evidence comparable to the bruises of physical battering." Carol pauses and blows her nose. She appears to have a cold. "How about describing a specific situation when Ronnie has gotten extremely angry?"

"Uhm . . ." I hear my voice crack. "He gets angry when I don't say something the way he thinks I should." I keep my eyes staring at my lap. "He rearranges my words. It isn't just what I say and how I say it. He even tells me what I mean by it. When he finishes his analysis, I'm so confused I don't remember what I actually did say. Then he calls me stupid because I'm confused."

"How do you respond?"

"I try to explain what I meant by what I remember saying. Then his volume goes up a notch or two with him cursing and yelling at me more." I pause to wipe my sweaty palms on my skirt.

"Have you ever thought he was going to hit you?"

She has some nerve asking THAT! "Absolutely not! He would never actually hit me!" I hear my voice waver. My whole body feels taut, like over–tightened guitar strings.

"How long has he been threatening you? Weeks, months?" Carol asks.

"Well . . . I know it's been more than weeks." I wipe sweat from my temple, soaking the tissue in my hand. "I guess it's been longer than months." *Oh my God, it can't be years, can it?* Perplexed, I ask Carol, "Why can't I remember when it started?"

"Stress affects all of our bodily functions, including memory. I would guess his threats have been intermittent and insidious which makes it difficult to pinpoint a specific time." She writes notes on the yellow pad for what feels like forever. "In my counseling experience, I have seen threats become physical abuse more often than not."

Silence hangs in the room. I pick at a hangnail. "Well, I *know* Ronnie will never hit me!"

Unexpectedly, my hands start to tremble. I fall silent. I interlace my fingers to stop the shakes. They shake in unison. I take several deep breaths. Tears well up in my eyes and fall on my blouse in erratic patterns, erupting like a volcano. *She's going to think I'm a blubbering idiot.* I pull tissues and more tissues from the box. I try in vain to dam up the river. Finally, it ebbs enough that I get my voice back. I whisper shakily, "I'm sorry."

Carol leans forward in the rocker. "This is a safe place for you to talk. Or cry. Or yell. Whatever you need to do." She sits back and covers her ears with her hands. "I'll do this if you yell too loud." She smiles.

I like this woman. I laugh tenuously at first. Then the laughter grows until I laugh as hard as I cried. The relief of being able to cry and laugh so hard is tremendous. "Boy, that sure felt good!"

"I'm sure it did." She pauses, writing a note on the pad. "I think the emotional release you just experienced may alleviate some of the nightmares."

"I sure hope so," I answer, wiping tears from my face.

"In case you ever need help, I need to tell you about 314-HOT-LINE. It is answered 24/7, and the volunteers are there to answer questions and listen to your problems. It's connected to all the battered women's shelters in the metropolitan area."

"I told you he never has and never will hit me!" Reluctantly I take a business card from her hand that has the hot line number on it that she is holding out to me.

Carol looks at me intently. "Sara, I was a domestic violence counselor at a battered women's shelter for seven years. Threats like Ronnie's almost always escalate into physical violence."

"But what I just told you about happened years ago!"

"As long as you are around Ronnie, there's a possibility he will resort to violence eventually."

I jump up and scream, "Ronnie is not an abuser!" I feel a fury I've never felt or shown before. Ashamed of my actions, I go to the window so I don't have to look at Carol. Silence. I stare at a rabbit zigzagging among the shrubs. *She may not be my counselor any more if I don't turn around and if that happens, Nancy might fire me.*

Soon as I move, Carol says, "Sara, I am not the one who has to decide if Ronnie is an abuser or not, you have to make that determination."

I push strands of hair back into the knot on top of my head as I walk back to my chair. My voice is quivery like a little girl's. "But I thought domestic . . . violen-ce is when a man beats a woman up."

"That's the part of abuse that shows visibly and that we hear about on the news. A lot of other abuses occur before and with the physical abuse."

"Oh." I feel unnerved and queasy.

"Sara, I can see how difficult it is for you to talk about your relationship with Ronnie. But with the things we've discussed so far, I can see Ronnie is a big stressor in your life."

"Yeah, he sure is." I move around in my chair, hoping to dispel the anguish building inside me. "But that was going on long before 9/11 happened. The nightmares didn't start until after the first anniversary. Why would they happen then?"

"Did you have any when 9/11 happened?"

"Don't think so." I stand and snatch my purse from the table. "I can't talk about this any more." I walk to the door. Starting to turn the knob, I hear Carol say in a kind voice that I don't want to notice, "I'll see you in two weeks."

"Yeah, I'll be here." And I walk out the door.

Journal Entry — 10/23/2002 — I tossed that dang business card in the trash on the way out of the counseling office. Don't know why she was so insistent I take it. Ronnie gets pretty angry sometimes, but I know without a doubt that he will never, ever hit me! I really don't want to go back to see that broad. Can't jeopardize my job.

Nightmare Entry — 11/3/2002 — Standing across the street from the World Trade Center. An overwhelming body odor stench assaults my nose — I look down and see a woman sitting on the sidewalk leaning against the wall — she sweeps her long, greasy black hair away from her face — IT'S ME! — my heart thuds and labors visibly, pushing my chest out by several inches — I see windows full of faces — THEY'RE TRAPPED! I point at the towers, yelling as I try to get someone's attention — some faces are deformed and distorted by people pushing on them from behind — I hear a voice call me stupid, then another voice repeats it — someone points their finger at me — now everyone is pointing and calling me stupid — I run in slow motion with the homeless ME hanging onto my leg.

Chapter 8 – Life Without Parents

Carol greets me at her office door. "Sara, how have things been?"

"Okay. Sorry I got so upset at my last session, but I just know Ronnie isn't the reason for my nightmares."

"I accept your apology even though it isn't necessary. Helping my clients see things they don't want to see is part of my job."

Sheepishly, I say, "I realized that after I calmed down."

"How have things been going?"

"Okay. Ronnie hasn't been on any rampages, and the boys are busy with school and church. We're doing the usual everyday things."

"That's good to hear. First, let's talk about the nightmares, then I'd like to learn more about how you and Ronnie met."

I hand Carol my journal pages, stand, and move to a sofa. It's soft and comfortable. After reading a few pages, Carol asks, "Are the nightmares as exhausting as they were in the beginning?"

"Not the ones that repeat. It seems about the time I'm sleeping better a new one happens and the exhaustion overtakes me again."

"Keep tracking them, and we'll continue looking for ways to reduce your stress level." She lays the pages in her lap. "Let's talk about your family."

The subject makes me squirm in my chair. I don't understand why. "What do you want to know?"

"The questionnaire says you grew up in Joplin, Missouri. Where is that? Did you live in town or in the country?"

"Well, Joplin is about a hundred miles straight west of Branson in southwest Missouri. I grew up on a farm there with my older brother, Jimmy, my younger sister, Annie, my Mom's six younger siblings and her parents." I shudder.

"What happened to your parents?"

"They got divorced right after Annie was born. Dad went to work for the telephone company in Kansas and remarried within a year. Mom remarried when I was four and moved about five miles away."

"Did you see either of them very often?"

"No. The first time I remember seeing Dad was when I was twelve. We saw Mom once a month, or thereabouts. It was very apparent to Jimmy, Annie and me that we're not, and never will be, as important to our parents as their new families."

"You didn't spend weekends or summers with your Mom?" Carol asks.

I drop my head and stare into my lap in silence. Pain inside me has a will of its own, wanting to be released. "Ummm . . ." I look back up. "I do remember one time when I wanted to go home with her really bad. I grabbed onto her pants leg as she was leaving. She kept walking, pulling me along the ground. By the time Grandma got to us, Mom had stopped walking and was prying my fingers loose. Grandma picked me up and said, 'Fern, just take her home with you for the night. Your dad and I will come get her tomorrow.' Mom didn't even answer her mother. She turned, ran to her car, and drove away." I'm shaking so much I can see the arm of the chair moving. "Grandma sat down on the ground, holding me close, started rocking, and sobbing a prayer." I feel thousands of volts of energy rush through my nerves and spill out of their severed ends. Tears burst forth, relieving pressure. I wipe my eyes and regain my composure. "Mom's house was cold and uninviting after that."

"Do you know how old you were?"

"Grandma says I was three or four years old. Aunt Elly says I was a very bubbly child before that and afterwards I was much quieter."

"I'm so sorry that happened to you, Sara. It had to be extremely hurtful."

"Yes, yes it was. I get more depressed if I think about either of my parents very much. So I focus on being so loved by my Mom's family. Now that I'm grown and have children of my own, I know growing up in my grandparents' house with God at the center of our lives was the best place in the world for the three of us." I smile. "There were 11 of us in the house until one of my uncles got married."

"That sure was a houseful. When did you move to St. Louis?"

"After I graduated from high school, I came up here to live with Aunt Lola. I stayed with her until I married Ronnie."

"How and when did you meet him?"

I relax more. "When Annie graduated from high school, she came to live with Aunt Lola and me. In the summer of 1990, Annie and I were at a Sonic Drive-in. A car pulled in next to us with these two good-looking guys in it, Ronnie and Brian. By the time we left, Annie and Brian had exchanged phone numbers. They both love dancing, and Ronnie and I didn't. That seemed to be the deciding factor of who dated whom. The four of us spent a lot of time together. Then in October, Annie and Brian got engaged. As they planned their December wedding, Ronnie and I spent more and more time together."

"What attracted you to Ronnie?"

I grin inwardly as I remember the first time I saw him. "The way his sky-blue eyes twinkle when he smiles at me. He was solid muscle, very sexy and had gotten out of the Navy a few months before we met."

"Sounds handsome. What drew you to him emotionally?"

"That's a lot harder to answer." The grin fades as I stand and walk to the window to get a better look at the few leaves still clinging tight to the tree branches. "We talked for hours. I hadn't dated anyone before who seemed so interested in me. He teased me a lot like Jimmy and Grandpa have all of my life."

"Teasing was familiar and made you feel loved?" she asks.

"I guess so. Hadn't thought of it that way."

"What didn't you like about him?"

I gain comfort from the beauty outside before answering. "Well, an example is one time when we were with Brian and Annie, the guys went inside Texas Tom's to buy food. He knew I always got a cheeseburger and Coke. When they came back out, Ronnie didn't bring me anything. Brian asked him why not. Ronnie said 'I don't know' and just kept on eating. Finally, Ronnie offered me a drink of his coke."

"Sounds pretty selfish," Carol says. "How did you feel about it?"

"Surprised. But he was tired and hungry from working a double shift the night before. We were running late for a movie, so I said I wasn't hungry."

"So all you felt was surprised?"

"Uhhh, no. I felt . . . hurt. But he did buy me popcorn and a soda at the movie."

"Sara, do you know what he learned about you that day?"

"I guess . . . that what he wants matters more than what I want or need."

"That, too, but mostly he learned he could get by with being disrespectful toward you and that you'd accept his bad behavior."

"Oh." I feel overcome with emotions.

"When did Ronnie propose to you?"

"At Annie and Brian's wedding reception the first weekend of December, and I said yes." I chew on my lip until I taste blood. "By the time Ronnie and I married, Brian and Annie were separated."

"Did they divorce?"

"Yes, and he's been married to Nicole about 5 years."

She pulls out the family tree I completed at the beginning of my counseling. "Is your brother married?"

"Yes, Jimmy and Earlene married in 1989 and had a son by the time I married Ronnie in 1991."

"Do you think both of your siblings being married influenced your decision to marry Ronnie?"

"Definitely. I was 22, struggling financially, tired of being alone, and Ronnie needed a roommate after Brian got married." I pause with a frown. "Lousy reasons to get married, weren't they?"

"Not the best, but I've heard worse." Carol smiles softly at me.

"Did you discuss your decision with anyone?"

I shrug after a moment. "Not really. For some reason, I thought if Grandpa liked Ronnie when they met, that would be a confirmation I was making the right decision." I rub a tissue between my palms to soak up sweat. "The two of them were instant friends."

"Does your Grandpa know about the problems you and Ronnie are having?"

"No because he passed away when Logan was seven months old." I feel my stomach do a flip-flop. "Grandpa was a big influence on Ronnie. As long as he had Grandpa to talk things over with, he was a great husband. One weekend every month, we drove five hours each way to and from Joplin, like clockwork."

"Sounds like Grandpa became a surrogate father to Ronnie."

"Exactly. After he passed away, Ronnie quit going down there as often. The only times he's been to Joplin in the last six years were for Grandma and Aunt Elly's funerals." I let out several sighs. "Aunt Lola and Uncle Steve still go every month. Three of my aunts and uncles still live in Joplin. Most of the time, the boys and I go with them. Once in a while, Aunt Lola and Uncle Steve take the boys without me so Ronnie and I can have a weekend to ourselves."

"In what other ways did Ronnie change after Grandpa's death?"

"When the boys and I are gone, he spends most of his time at Chuck and Amy's – Chuck is his oldest brother. There are always cases of beer stacked in the corner of their kitchen."

"Do you think Ronnie has a drinking problem?"

"He says he can quit any time he wants to – that he just doesn't want to."

"Do *you* think he has a problem?"

"Definitely. Almost every place we go, he drinks excessively."

"When did you first think his drinking might be a problem?"

"When he was late for our wedding rehearsal dinner. He'd bought a jug of Arkansas Hillbilly Moonshine when we went to Joplin. We were there to pick up my grandparents so they could be at our rehearsal." I smile as I say, "Because Grandpa raised me, I chose him to walk me down the aisle instead of my dad."

"Sounds like a good choice to me."

"How did you feel about the reason Ronnie was late for your rehearsal?"

I shrug. "I was embarrassed. When he got there, he told everyone he'd worked a double the night before and had overslept. I accepted his little white lie because I didn't want him to look bad in front of everyone. I briefly thought about canceling the wedding, but I ignored it and married him."

"What were the other reasons you went through with the wedding?

"One of them was that it felt so good to have someone love me so much that he wanted to be with me all the time. I didn't want to give that up."

"When did the drinking become a major problem?"

"After his brother Harry passed away with an aneurism last summer. I think Ronnie is drowning his sorrow in alcohol. He won't even talk to me about the good memories."

I go to the window to watch a small black bird flapping light rain from its wings. "The first three, four years of our marriage were so great. I ache for that man!"

Nightmare Entry — 11/23/2002 — I'm in a coffee shop — I run to some stairs — with my bloody hands I'm clawing at concrete and debris blocking them — emergency lights throw off eerie shadows — I pick myself up off the floor and run through debris — I'm looking at a postcard with the skyline of New York City including the Twin Towers — my legs tremble — I can't see through grey dust — something mushy in my hand — diamond wedding rings shimmer at me from a blackened hand severed at the wrist.

Nightmare Entry — 11/26/2002 — A drunk pushes and staggers his way through throng of people, stopping right in front of me — a man with liquor-glazed eyes stares at me — cold wraps around me like a crude blanket — a faceless man yelling at Logan and Derek to get their butts in their rooms and stay there — eyes with fire in them, yells 'You're the worst wife in the world!" — me running away from the crashing tower debris that is hitting me in the back like waves at the beach, but this one is hot glass, cement and metal.

Chapter 9 - Shattered

Ronnie gets up from Brian and Nicole's dining table and goes to the kitchen for another beer. From the TV in their living room, I hear, "Here's Pat Sajak and Vanna White."

Brian grabs his tea, and says, "Come on, girls. I want to show Ronnie and Sara how good I am at solving these puzzles." Nicole and I follow him.

Ronnie comes into the living room from the kitchen and sits down on the sofa. "Wheel of Fortune, huh? Sara's pretty good at solving these damn things."

Brian scoots forward in his chair, takes out his wallet, pulls out a dollar bill and lays it on the coffee table. He smiles at me confidently. "Put your money out here, Sara. We'll see who's the best."

"I'll bet my money on Sara," Ronnie says, reaching for his pocket. He adds one dollar to the betting pool.

I frown at Ronnie for butting into our conversation, and then look at Brian. His chest is puffed out. "Okay, champ, I'll gladly take your money."

Ten minutes later, there are three dollars in front of me. "Ronnie, get me a beer, will ya?" Brian says. "Maybe that will get my brain in gear so I can beat Sara." Brian strokes his trim black mustache and taps a one dollar bill on the table as if that will change his luck. Ronnie returns from the kitchen with a beer for Brian and a new one for himself. Anger simmers within me at the sight of Ronnie drinking two beers to each of Brian's.

"Computer keyboard," I yell.

Brian jumps up. He looks mad but a slight curl at the corner of his mouth betrays him. "Dang you, Sara! You could've been nice and let me have one of 'em."

"Nope, that would've made you feel like a chump, instead of an ex-champ." I laugh as I pick up my winnings from the table, snapping each bill. "I'm ready for a rematch any time."

As I stand up, Ronnie attempts to grab my money but only gets one dollar bill. I pull my hands and money to my stomach. "You're not getting these," I say.

"I want all of it because I staked you!" Ronnie yells at my back as I walk away.

"Ronnie, you're such a jerk sometimes," Nicole says.

Nicole and I spend the afternoon scrapbooking, enjoying each other's company, and taking turns checking on the kids. Brian and Ronnie talk and watch sports.

When the evening news comes on, Ronnie stands to his feet, stumbles, and catches his balance before he falls. "Sara, it's time to go."

I look at Nicole. "We should have left before he drank that last six-pack." As I walk past Ronnie, I tell him, "I'll get the boys."

***

As the six of us walk down the sidewalk, Ronnie drops his car keys. Nicole grabs them without him noticing. "Here, you're driving home," she whispers, pressing the keys into my hand. *Ronnie will be raging tomorrow when he sobers up. This isn't a good idea!*

Before I can say anything to dissuade Nicole, she walks forward and takes Derek's hand, leads him to the passenger side of the car, and opens the back door. "Brian, come here a minute," Nicole says. "I need your help."

Brian leaves Ronnie stumbling around, digging in his jeans and jacket pockets, and still looking for his keys. Nicole closes the car door and says a few words to Brian.

"Hey, Ronnie, did you find your keys yet?" Brian asks as he walks back toward him.

"Hell no. They can't just disappear."

Standing in the open driver's door, I watch Nicole open the front passenger door and wait. Quietly across the roof of the car, she says, "It's going to be all right, Sara. I've got a plan. Okay?"

I am terrified of Ronnie's drunk driving. Reluctantly, I nod and sit down in the driver's seat. I hear Logan click his seatbelt behind me.

I watch Brian grab Ronnie by the arm and guide him to the passenger side. Then Nicole takes charge. "Ronnie, sit down here for a minute, and the rest of us will go look for your keys."

He sits. "Hey. . . wait a minute, where's the damn steering wheel?" He looks to the right and then the left and sees me. "Damn it, Sara, you know I always drive." He starts to get out.

In a stern voice, Nicole says, "Ronnie. Stay right there. Sara is driving home. Brian and I will find your keys and bring them to you tomorrow."

All Ronnie gets out is, "But I –" when Nicole interrupts him.

"No, Ronnie. Stay there. Brian will fasten your seatbelt."

He leans back in the seat like an obedient child, and Nicole steps back. As Brian leans down, he winks at me and I give him a look of relief. I hear the seatbelt click. "We'll see you tomorrow, ole buddy."

Ronnie complains and curses all the way home about his keys being lost. As I'm unlocking our front door, I remember some overdue bills that desperately need to be mailed. Going back toward the car, I meet Ronnie at the edge of the drive, still trying to make his way to the front door. "I'll be right back," I say as I pass him. "I have to go mail some letters."

"Derek, race you back to the car," Logan yells.

"Soooooo," Derek answers.

Ronnie mumbles something, waves his hand at me, and continues stumbling.

The boys are buckled in by the time I get there. At the end of the driveway I am waiting for a car to pass when I hear the sound of shattering glass. By the time I turn my head, Logan is asking, "Why'd Daddy break our bay window?"

"I don't know." Ronnie is swaying from side to side, muttering something. I notice the coffee cup isn't in his hand any more that he took with him from the cup holder. "I just don't know." I pull the car forward a few feet. Ronnie hasn't moved. I stop the car. *Ronnie might break me next if I get out. Can't let the boys see that!* Ronnie stumbles to the porch and trips as he steps up.

"Mommy, we gotta help him," Logan says as he unlatches his door.

"Don't get out!" I yell. Derek is down on the floorboard behind me. "It's going to be okay, Logan. We're going to sit here until Daddy gets inside the house." Logan reluctantly closes the door. "I'm sure he'll lie down and go to sleep."

Ronnie finally maneuvers himself through the front door and closes it behind him. I hold my breath for a drawn-out moment before exhaling slowly. White-faced, Logan sinks in the seat. I put the car in reverse and back out of the drive.

I feel a whole new fear, an all-consuming fear different from any fear I've ever felt before. *Maybe Carol is right about him!* As I hear my heart beating, sweat pops out on my forehead. I grab a napkin from the door pocket to wipe it away. I force myself to pay attention to the street. I need to think but it's too painful to think about what Ronnie just did. I feel so alone.

After dropping the envelopes in the mailbox, I see the golden arches come into view. I know we have to stop while I piece myself back together. "Hey, boys, how about we stop for an ice cream cone?"

"Yeah," says Derek. Soon as the car stops, he loosens his seatbelt and opens the door.

"What about Daddy?" Logan asks.

"He's fine. Probably watching TV. Take your brother inside to the playground, and I'll be there in a minute."

"Okay," he says and gets out.

I let the tears loose. The hard weeping washes away enough of my fear that my mind starts connecting again. I know it isn't safe to go home. I don't have enough money for a motel. I wish I had a cell phone to call Aunt Lola, but Ronnie says it isn't in my budget.

Realizing it's been several minutes since the boys went inside, I force myself to stop crying and take deep breaths.

Inside McDonald's a half-hour later as we are finish our cones, I ask, "Logan, Derek, would you like to go see Aunt Lola?"

They respond, "You bet!" and "Yeah!" together.

Journal Entry — 11/30/2002 — Aunt Lola kept the boys entertained while Uncle Steve took me home to get Derek's asthma medicine. We're spending the night with them. Ronnie must have found his spare truck key. Probably at Chuck's drinking more. I was going to clean up the broken glass and put plastic on the window, but Uncle Steve said Ronnie needs to see what he did when he sobers up. When he remembers he didn't drive home tonight, we're not going to see Brian and Nicole for a long time. Last time he got angry, it was at least a year before we saw them again. Wish I had the courage Nicole has! The worst part of it is he won't allow me to talk to her because they're *his* friends, not *ours*. One time when he caught me talking to her, he pulled the phone jack right out of the wall.

Nightmare Entry — 11/30/2002 — I'm at the Statue of Liberty — sea gulls feed on a man's hairy leg severed above the knee — ship horns blast the air — everyone's heads tilt back in unison, thousands of eyes stare up — an airplane hits the side of a Twin Tower, ejecting fire out of the wound — people run, I join them — debris pounds the ground — people bleed — taste metallic dust on my lips — eyes sting — I inhale a gray cloud, which sets my chest on fire.

Chapter 10 – Can't Believe It

"How was your Thanksgiving?" Carol asks as I lay my coat on the sofa and walk straight to the window. I'm going need all the help I can get to make it through today's session.

"We had Ronnie's Mom over, ate a good dinner, then the boys and I took her home." I take a couple of deep breaths, building my courage.

"How was the rest of the weekend?"

"Horrible. Absolutely horrible."

"What happened?"

Out of the corner of my eye, I see several leaves fall from their branches on their way to join the leaf carpet below. "On Saturday we went to Brian and Nicole's. Brian and Ronnie have been friends since they were teenagers." As I turn around, I see Carol pulling my family and friends pages from the folder in her lap.

I reiterate Saturday's events, and then ask, "Is there a water fountain close by? My mouth is really dry."

Carol walks to her desk, opens the door of a mini-fridge next to it, and brings a bottle of water to me.

"Thanks." I take several shaky swigs. My breathing rate speeds up. My hands and face tingle in several places, especially around my mouth. The room starts to rotate.

I hear Carol calling my name through a fog. "Sara? Sara?"

My legs are shaky. I feel Carol's arm go around my waist, guiding me until my knee brushes against a chair.

"Sit down," she says.

I sit.

Carol squats in front of me. "Breathe slowly through your nose, not your mouth – slowly – through your nose. That's it."

The circling room slows. I wipe sweat from my brow. "What happened?"

"You hyperventilated." Carol stands and keeps watching me as she goes back to her chair. "Have you ever done that before?"

"No." I open and close my hands trying to get the tingling to go away.

"Stress and anxiety sometimes cause over breathing. Did you feel light-headed and tingly?"

"Yes . . . I felt like I wasn't getting enough air."

"That's a common thing people say when hyperventilation happens, but actually your body needed more carbon dioxide. The method we just used has replaced the old time remedy of using a brown paper bag."

"Hopefully it was a one-time thing and won't ever happen again."

"If it does, you'll need to talk to your doctor about it."

"Okay, I'll do that." I groan. "I still can't believe Ronnie broke the living room window." I drum my fingers on the arm of the chair.

"What did you do after going to the post office?"

"Ummph . . ." I say, clearing my throat. "Went to Aunt Lola's and Uncle Steve's. The three of us decided the boys and I should spend the night at their house, but I had to go home for Derek's asthma inhaler. If he misses one dose, we're in the emergency room. Uncle Steve drove me to the house."

"Was Ronnie home when you got there?"

"No . . . he was out drinking and driving."

"Didn't you say he was already staggering drunk and you had his keys?"

My hands feel cold and are trembling. "Yes, but nothing stops Ronnie from drinking and driving when he's in the mood. And he used the spare truck key from a kitchen drawer."

"Has he ever gotten a DUI?"

"No, and he's never wrecked, either. One moment I worry he's going to kill himself. And the next moment, I'm angry he's willing to risk everything we have."

"What do you mean risk everything?"

"Getting a DUI means he loses his job and we'll be in money trouble with the first missed paycheck."

"When he's sober, have you discussed you doing the driving when he's been drinking?"

"Several times. And he agrees but always changes his mind after a few beers. He's convinced he's a better driver drunk than anyone else is sober. I've also refused to get in the car with him when he won't let me drive. Then he tells the boys to get in, and they're afraid to not do it. When the car starts moving, the boys are yelling, 'Come on, Mommy' or 'Daddy, don't leave her.'"

"That's a tough situation to be in."

"I've thought about calling the police and giving them his license number. But that takes me back to worrying about a DUI. It seems I'm damned if I do and damned if I don't."

"Alanon is a family support group that's associated with Alcoholics Anonymous. Have you considered going to some of their meetings?"

"Are you kidding? Ronnie would absolutely explode!" I shift back and forth in the chair, feeling like I am wearing holes in my skirt. I massage knots out of my neck and roll my shoulders to loosen them up.

"When did you next see Ronnie or talk to him?"

"He called Aunt Lola's, wanting me to meet him out on their front porch to talk. I agreed so I could find out why he broke the window."

"What did he have to say?"

"Not much. Everything I ask, he kept saying 'I don't know' or 'I just did' or 'I am really sorry.' There were long silences. Finally, he asked me to get the boys and go home with him. I told him we were spending the night. I went inside and left him sitting there."

I stand to pace. I press my hand to my chest because it feels like my heart is pounding against my chest wall. "When I got inside, Uncle Steve let loose of Logan and he ran into my arms shaking and sobbing." I gulp. "He had been crying and talking at the same time. All Uncle Steve could understand was something about me, Ronnie, and someone getting hurt."

"Did you find out what he was talking about?"

"Not really. I held him tight until he calmed down. Then I couldn't get him to talk about it any more." I stop pacing and stand still looking at Carol. "My whole world is crashing down around me and it seems I can't do anything to stop it!"

"Sara, I see you're breathing fast. Let's talk about something pleasant for a little bit so you don't hyperventilate again. Tell me why Logan and Derek love being at Steve and Lola's."

I sit again. "They have a pool table that the boys love rolling the balls around on. They eat whatever is in their cabinets." Long sigh. Short sigh. "Once in a while they will come home with new toys too expensive for me to buy." My heart rate decreases. "I'm so thankful to have an aunt and uncle that are so generous."

"Are you feeling better?"

"Yes. Thanks. What am I going to do?"

Carol walks to a file cabinet and pulls out sheets of paper. When she sits back down, she holds one of them up and says, "This diagram shows cycles of domestic violence." (Appendix C)

"But–"

Carol raises her hand. "I understand he's never hit you. But these cycles are happening in your marriage without the physical violence." She points to the right of the diagram with her pen. "This is the Honeymoon phase when things are normal and stress levels are low." On the bottom is the Tension Building phase that she describes as when victims feel like they're walking on eggshells.

I nod my head. "I definitely felt tension building in me as I watched Ronnie getting drunk at Brian's."

"At the top are violent events like the broken living room window. At this level, victims' fears escalate, emotions go numb, and thinking ability is almost non-existent. The whole thing seems unreal."

"That's exactly how I felt Saturday and Sunday."

"I'm sure it was. When a couple has come full circle back to the Honeymoon phase, abusers apologize profusely, promise it will never happen again, and beg forgiveness."

A dull, steady pounding starts behind my eyes.

"Victims are so relieved to get back to normal, they accept the apologies. And once again, they hope the Honeymoon phase will last forever."

I sit staring at the diagram. My mind resists what my eyes are seeing.

"Did you go home on Sunday?"

"Yes. The boys had school and I had to go to work on Monday. We couldn't do either of those from Aunt Lola's. When we got home, Ronnie had cleaned up the broken glass and put plastic on the window. The boys went to Zach's house for the afternoon. I did laundry, and Ronnie watched TV. In the four days since then, the wall of tension has diminished to the usual level."

"Which phase does that fit into?"

I didn't need to look at the sheet of paper to know the answer. "Honeymoon." *My God, what now? Can I make it on my own? Oh my gosh!*

"Sara? Are you okay?"

"I . . . What do I do now?" I ask with resignation.

"You don't *have* to do anything. I've just given you a lot of information, and I suspect you are feeling pretty overwhelmed."

I nod and blow my nose.

"But before our time is up, we need to discuss safety planning." (Appendix D) She picks up another piece of paper she had gotten from the file cabinet.

"What's safety planning?"

"A Safety Plan is a list of recommendations and questions to help you think about and be ready for future emergencies. For example, one recommendation is to pack a suitcase with needed items such as Derek's inhaler and a change of clothes for each of you." She offers the pages to me. "When Ronnie does something violent again, you will be ready to react, whatever the circumstances."

I reluctantly take the pages and try to focus my eyes on the words. Tears sting my eyes. "Oh . . . if I had done this before last weekend, it sure would have simplified things." I hand the pages back to Carol.

"I know you want to believe nothing like this, or worse, will ever happen again. And I hope so, too. But we can't count on it, can we?"

Softly, I say, "I didn't think he'd ever do something as stupid as this. I just want to ignore the whole thing and get back to where we were before Saturday." I choke in great gulping sobs. "But I feel like . . . if I do the safety plan, I'm expecting something else to happen."

"I prefer to think of it this way; it's better to be prepared and never need it rather than have another situation like Saturday and not have Derek's medication."

"I guess that's true. I'll do it, but I sure do hate it!"

"I understand." She puts the Safety Plan back in the folder. "The sheets of information I've shared with you before today didn't need to be readily available to you. But the Safety Plan is different because you will need to refer to it while preparing your emergency suitcase. I recommend you not take it home with you or leave it in your car. It isn't safe for Ronnie to see it."

"What do I do, memorize it?"

Carol smiles slightly. "No. I recommend you keep it at work. Is there a time during the day when you can be close to the fax machine for our receptionist to send it to you?"

"I guess lunch time would be best when there are fewer people around."

"Good. How about calling our office on Monday when you go to lunch and she will fax it to you while you're watching for it at the machine?"

"Okay."

Chapter 11 – Emergency

"Thanks, Carol, for getting me back in for a short session," I say as we walk down the hallway to her office."

"What's the emergency?" Carol asks while closing her office door behind us.

"I want to . . . I need your help to . . ." I stammer. "I need a separation."

"What brought you to this decision?"

"While the boys were at their Christmas party last night at church, I went to the library. I got online and learned a lot more about domestic violence." I wrap my arms around me, tight. "The more I read, the more sure I am that my marriage is a ticking time bomb. I thought about waiting till after the holidays, but Ronnie will be drunk again on Christmas Eve and New Year's. I still can't believe he threw that cup through the window."

"Carol writes on a yellow legal pad, and then looks up at me. "The broken window is visible evidence that Ronnie's behavior is escalating."

"The internet said violence goes up when victims attempt to leave. It seems I'm in danger no matter which I choose."

"That's true. Do you still have my business card with the emergency number on it?"

I smile sheepishly. "I have to confess I threw that away."

"That happens a lot." Carol smiles slightly. "Do you remember the number?"

"Yes. I'm glad it's easy to remember, 314-HOT-LINE."

"Do you know how you're going to approach Ronnie about a separation?"

"Yes. I talked to Aunt Lola. Uncle Steve is out of town this weekend. She said, she'll be glad to have the boys for company Saturday night." I realize I'm holding my head at an awkward angle when the left side of my neck hurts. I rub it. "I can talk to Ronnie on Saturday evening, and he can move some clothes and stuff this weekend."

"Where can he move so quickly?"

"His brother, Chuck's. They have an empty bedroom because their oldest son quit high school and moved out."

"Might work, short-term anyway."

My mouth suddenly feels dry. I get a breath mint out of my purse.

"Will you and Ronnie be going out to dinner?"

"Yes. Why?"

"Because people, even abusers, are less likely to make a scene in public."

"Really?" *Wait a minute, he only rants and raves at home.* "Wow, that's a good idea. He won't want his public image tarnished, even in front of strangers."

"That's why it works. Another thing that helps is to use 'I' messages."

I frown at her.

"That means saying things like, 'I was really frightened when the window got broken.' 'I' messages aren't as likely to put him in a defensive position."

"That makes sense. Also, knowing he won't be yelling at me will help me remember what I've said so he can't twist my words and me get confused."

"Something else to discuss is how and when he'll see the boys. From what you've told me I'd guess that Chuck's house isn't a good environment for Logan and Derek to spend weekends with their dad."

"You're right about that," I reply, thinking about the continuous drinking they do. "I guess he can come to the house on Saturdays while I do errands."

"How are you feeling about all of this?"

"Scared . . . hopeful that a separation may make a difference in my marriage."

"Have you thought about the possibility that a separation won't make a difference or it might make things worse?"

"A little. But I really think he's ready for things to change. He hasn't had anything to drink since Saturday. It's been a long time since he's gone six days without a beer."

"That's a start."

"I think he's going to be willing to separate because he's apologized to me twice. I can't even remember the last time he apologized to me even once, much less twice about something."

"If he agrees to the separation, when will you tell Logan and Derek?"

"I guess when we pick them up on Sunday."

"And what will you say?"

I stare at Van Gogh's *Starry Night* on the wall as I think. "Maybe that Daddy and I are confused about why the window got broken. And that he's going to stay at Uncle Chuck and Aunt Amy's while we figure out how to stop such scary things from happening again."

Carol smiles. "What I like about that is it's the truth. You being the good Mom that you are, I'm sure you'll be giving them reassurances and answering all their questions."

"That sure warms my heart, 'a good Mom,'" I say, putting my hands to my chest. "Until I started coming here, Ronnie had me convinced I was the worst Mom in the world."

"Sara, you are a strong, resourceful woman. I'm amazed at how on a daily basis you can do all the normal things we women do plus use your ingenuity to handle all the things Ronnie throws your way."

"Thanks for saying those nice things. I feel like you're talking about someone else. Maybe I'll believe those words about myself some day."

"We'll keep working on it."

> Nightmare Entry — 12/6/2002 — I'm in a 9/11 video of people walking down a stairway in one of the Twin Towers — bodies everywhere, whole ones and pieces of others — Ronnie rips at a tailor-made blouse my mom made for me, "Bet you'll never wear any homemade shit again!" — the building sways so much it bounces us from side to side and knocks us to our knees — I scream "Oh

God" — I duck behind a car thinking I'm going to die — I think, at least that would get me away from Ronnie.

Journal Entry — 12/7/2002 — Hopefully, I'll be sleeping in this king-sized bed by myself tomorrow night. I'm petrified at the thought of asking Ronnie for this separation. BUT, thinking about me or one of the boys getting broken instead of windows is too scary. What if he goes berserk and hits me? He wouldn't do it in public, but he might when we leave the restaurant. Wish I had talked with Carol about what to do if he hits me. I'd guess she'd say to call the police, but can't do that because he might hit me a lot more after the police leave. Good thing Carol gave me the hot line number and it's so easy to remember. I'm *so* afraid to talk about a separation! And *so* afraid to *not* do this! Just have to live with whatever the consequences are.

***

While Ronnie works overtime Saturday morning, the boys and I go the library. With shaking hands I make copies of my driver's license, my car registration, all three of our birth certificates and social security cards. I keep telling the boys to be quiet over and over.

Driving to the hardware store, I pray for strength to follow through with my plan. I haven't talked to God this much since the complications of my pregnancy with Derek.

Rowdiness intrudes into my thinking from the backseat. I bark a flustered, "Be quiet!"

"Sorry, Mommy," Derek says.

"You're sure a grouch today," Logan adds, sounding like his dad.

My ire rises but resends quickly as I remember whom I'm talking to. "You're right, Logan. I'm sorry."

"Okay," Logan says in a kinder voice.

A few minutes later with new keys in my pocket, I park in Hillridge Bank's parking lot. "You guys can stay in the car this time. I won't be but a couple of minutes," I say as I open the car door. "Remember, don't unlock the doors."

"Yeah," they each say without looking up from their Power Rangers game.

Standing at the teller's window, I'm so close to vomiting that I can barely say, "I want to set up a savings account."

The bank teller points at a couple of people sitting at desks in the lobby. "That has to be done by the account representatives."

I sit down at a desk, pull $10 out of my pocket, and lay it down.

"I want to open a savings account," I say, swallowing several times keeps my breakfast down.

"Is this for one of your children?" he asks as he picks up the money.

"No, it's for me."

He places the $10 back in front of me. "You have to have one hundred dollars to open a savings account unless you are under 15 years of age." He pushes the "ignore" button on his cell phone.

"But I have to have it for safety reasons."

"Doesn't matter. Can't do it." He is now texting a message.

Trembling with anger instead of fear, I stand. He gives me a self-satisfied, smug smile.

I place my hands on his desk, spread apart and lean forward like a bulldog about to attack. "Mr. Whatever-your-name is …"

"Is there a problem here, Jeff?" a man with a bass voice says, walking up to the desk.

Oh! I sounded like Ronnie. I pick up the $10 and walk away, very ashamed.

"Ma'am, I'm the bank president," says the deep voice as I push on the front door. "Please come to my office. I think I can help you."

I turn. "But your bank policy . . ."

He offers his hand. I ignore it. "Because you said 'for safety reasons' I think I can be of assistance. Please come to my office."

Reluctantly I follow him. "Do you have any accounts with our bank," he asks while shutting his office door.

"Yes, a checking account."

He offers his hand again as he walks behind his desk. "I'm Jeff Brown."

I shake his hand. "Sara Farley." I plop into a chair.

"Mrs. Farley, if I'm off cue in what I'm about to ask, please forgive me. " He puts his elbows on his desk with his hands folded. "Do you need to open this account because of domestic violence?"

How does he know that? I stare at him.

"My mother became a victim when she remarried after my father passed away. As I helped her escape that horrible situation, I learned symptoms to watch for in victims. I have been able to help several women save money in small savings accounts so they can leave their abusers."

My anger changes to tears of relief. "But your policy . . ."

As he turns to type on his computer, he says, "I'm overriding policy."

"Thank you so much," whispers out of my mouth. I pull the $10 out of my pocket and hand it to him. With MY savings account book in hand, he walks me to the front door.

As I push the lever into Park in front of Aunt Lola and Uncle Steve's house, I hear Derek's seatbelt unclick. "Finally!" he says. He bolts for the house.

As Logan and I walk across the yard, Logan asks. "Why do you have a suitcase? Are you staying too?"

"No, Aunt Lola's keeping some things for us in case we have another emergency."

"You mean like when Daddy broke the window?"

"Yes."

He takes my hand and squeezes it. "Love you, Mommy."

Chapter 12 – New Beginning

"Let's go to Red Lobster tonight. I'm in the mood for shrimp," Ronnie says, while backing out of our driveway. "You're going to try the lobster this time, aren't you?"

"No, but I like their steaks."

"Steaks! Are you kidding me? Try the lobster. After all it is a seafood place."

"I know it's a seafood place. But I'm not taking a chance lobster will make me throw up like shrimp does."

"I still say this stupid allergy thing's just in your head. Wish you'd eat seafood like normal people."

Stay calm, girl. Don't want to tick him off before talking about him moving out.

***

Soon as we walk in the door at Red Lobster I grab a seat on a bench. Ronnie checks in with the hostess then comes and plops down beside me. "Can you believe it's going to be twenty minutes?"

"That's not long for a Saturday night." Minutes drag by as I fleck my nail polish. Ronnie's body stiffens beside me each time someone else's beeper goes off. Ours finally buzzes and blinks red.

The hostess leads the way to our table. After we place our order, the silence between us is loud as I try to think of something, anything to talk about. Finally, as the waiter sets our salads in front of us, I ask, "Remember bringing the boys here for Logan's birthday? They both started eating their shrimp without peeling it."

His eyes sparkle. "That was funny."

"I almost couldn't hold in the laughter at the amazed looks on their faces when you showed them how to peel the shells off. Which one decided he liked it better with shells on?" I ask.

"I think it was Logan," he says, scrunching up his face to imitate the boys.

I giggle, relaxing a little.

Our dinners are placed in front of us. I take a bite. Ronnie loads his baked potato with salt. "How's your filet mignon?"

"Really good." *Is it time yet? Or do I wait until we're about finished eating?* To bolster my courage, I have to believe this evening will turn out well.

"Which of our favorite video stores do you want to go to when we're done eating?"

"Blockbuster."

"You know what kind of video stores I'm talking about," he says quietly.

"Twenty-four hour porno stores are your favorites, not mine," I say in my normal voice.

"Shh, don't talk so loud," he says through clenched teeth. He gulps down a long draw of beer. "You sure liked that little red silky outfit I bought you the last time I went."

"You like that tight skimpy thing, not me. Maybe we should discuss this when we get in the car."

He nods.

"Thanks for getting the glass replaced in the window this week."

"You're welcome," he answers, not looking up.

A deep breath boosts my courage. "I still don't know how to answer the boys when they ask me why you broke the window."

He continues peeling shrimp and eating, then he says, "I don't know what to tell them, either."

"They've asked me about it every day since Saturday. I finally told them that maybe your coffee cup slipped out of your hand and accidentally hit the window."

"Yeah, maybe it did." He leans back and folds his arms, staring at his plate. "All I can say is I'm sorry, really sorry." Barely audible, I hear him say, "I'll admit I was too drunk. I didn't know where you were going when you backed out of the driveway." He still doesn't look at me.

"As I passed you going back to the car, I told you I was going to mail bills."

I see his jaw clinch.

"I've told you over and over that I can't hear you when you talk so damn quiet."

I pause to stay focused and refuse to let his blame game upset me. "I know I was more frightened than I've ever been before in my life! And since we don't know why it happened, I think we should separate for a while."

His head jerks up. "I don't –" His sky-blue eyes darken with anger, piercing me with a stare. "You're –" His volume rises. He glances around from table to table, a muscle jerking at the corner of his mouth. His Adam's apple bobs as he looks back down and starts peeling and eating again.

Concentrating on cutting my next bite of steak, I look up and see a baby smiling at me from the table next to us. I return her smile.

Ronnie raises his head and stares at me strangely. His lips are thin as he asks, "Why in hell do we need to do that?"

I glance at the baby and other people while I fortify my courage. "Because the boys and I are afraid of you. Logan is wetting the bed again, and Derek is stuttering."

Cold, hard looks grip his features. He peels and eats so long I think he hasn't heard me. My steak has lost its flavor, so I pick at the potato peel, waiting for time to crawl by.

"That's because you baby them all the time."

I respond firmly, "No, it's because they're afraid of you." The people in the next booth look at us. I don't care anymore if we are overheard. I have to protect myself and the boys.

As I lay my silverware across my plate, I see perspiration beads forming on his forehead. "How long a separation are you talking about?" He wipes the sweat away with his napkin. He scoots shells in circles on the plate.

"I don't know. But what I do know is that neither of us has been happy in a long, long time. I think we've got several problems that need to be worked out."

Now he's circling the potato peel on his plate with a fork. "Yeah."

"Maybe you can stay with Chuck and Amy for a while since Cody moved out."

"I guess that's a possibility," he says, finally looking at me.

"May I take your plates?" asks our waiter.

"Uh, yeah," Ronnie says, looking at me in an almost normal way.

"Did we save room for dessert?" the hovering waiter asks.

"No. We don't want any," Ronnie tells him.

The waiter places the bill tray on the table.

Ronnie reaches for my hand. "Can't we just work things out? Separating seems so extreme."

I lean back so he can't touch me. "I think a shattered window says it is time for something drastic!"

Ronnie fumbles for his wallet. Two twenties shake as he pulls them out and places them on the money tray. He slumps back into his chair. "I'm all torn up by what I did. I wish I could take it back." His pleading puppy-dog eyes tug at my heart. "But I guess you're right."

"When do you want this to happen?"

"The sooner, the better. Maybe you can talk to Chuck and Amy in the morning while I get your laundry done."

He slaps his hand on the table. Immediately, he looks down, appearing to remember where we are. His anger makes his handsome face ugly as he struggles to keep from erupting. He runs his hand through his thinning hair. Like a bulldog with all of its teeth bared, he asks, "Are you telling me you want me out tomorrow?" He glances around the room.

"Yes, before we pick the boys up. I don't see any reason to delay this." I lean forward, offering my hand. "Ronnie, I love you. I want us to get back to like we were when we first got married. Those were such wonderful times."

I'm hoping my quick-change of our topic has taken some of the power out of his anger. I see his color shading down as my open hand patiently waits for him.

"Yes, they were." He takes my hand. "I want you to know the only reason I'm doing what you want me to is because I screwed up by breaking that damn window. I'll talk to Chuck and Amy in the morning." He stands up and puts a small tip on the table. "Let's go."

> Journal Entry — 12/8/2002 — 3:00 am — I HATE SEX! Hate it. Hate it. HATE IT! Took two hours to get him finished this morning. Are all men as insatiable as Ronnie? What is wrong with me that I can't satisfy him? Have to continue having sex with him while we're separated. Couldn't stand being responsible for him

going to some other woman's bed. That would be the end of my marriage for sure. I'd be the one who failed. And, *that's* not an option! Won't be sharing this journal with Carol – too many other things to talk about.

* * *

"Thanks for taking us to the movie," says Derek, smiling from ear to ear as he squeezes her neck too tight. "Love oo, Aunt Lola." Hopping down the steps like a bunny rabbit doesn't slow Derek much. He runs across the yard to catch up with his Daddy. Logan and I give Aunt Lola quick hugs and walk hand in hand toward the car.

"Hey, Daddy, you missed our street," says Logan.

"I did? You're kidding."

"Yeah McDonald's," cheers Derek.

"No, where's your other favorite place?" I ask them.

They look at each other puzzled. Then their eyes light up as they say together, "Fun House!"

Derek's face goes solemn. "But we only go there when it's dark."

"We've never gone there on Sunday afternoon before," Logan adds.

"Tomorrow's Mommy's birthday and we're celebrating today since we'll all be busy at school and work tomorrow," Ronnie answers, looking at me forlornly.

"How old will you be, Mommy?" asks Logan.

"Boys, you might as well learn right now that you never, ever ask a woman her age." Ronnie instructs them.

"Not even a Mommy?" Derek asks.

"It's okay to ask this Mommy," I say, patting his hand. "Just don't ask any other ladies. I'll be 33 tomorrow."

"That old?" asks Logan.

"Yes, and your Daddy is older than me."

"Daddy's so old, he musta' seen dinosaurs," whispers Derek loudly to his brother.

* * *

"Okay, guys, settle down, settle down," Ronnie tells them, glancing at me. They are anxious to watch the pizza-making process and play video games. "We need to talk about something," Ronnie tells them as we sit down at a table.

I take a deep breath. "Logan, Derek, remember how scared we were when Daddy threw his coffee cup through the window?"

"Can we go play videos?" asks Logan.

"Not yet," Ronnie answers, picking at a hole in the tablecloth. "Sometimes, we adults do things we're sorry for immediately. I wish I hadn't broken the window."

I swallow hard. "Daddy moved his clothes to Uncle Chuck's today so he can stay with them for a while." I hope they haven't noticed my shaky voice.

Four little eyes fill with tears. "How long you staying at Uncle Chuck's?" Logan asks, chewing on his already down-to-the-quick fingernails. He immediately stops and shoves his hands under the table when he sees Ronnie's frown.

"I don't know. Just till we can figure some things out," Ronnie says while enlarging the tablecloth hole.

"Are we getting a deevorce like Kyle's Mommy and Daddy?" asks Derek.

Ronnie jerks his head up, watching me closely.

"No, we're not," I reassure everyone. "Sometimes grown-ups can think better when they're not living in the same house."

"Can we go play now?" asks Logan.

"Yeah, I'm missing seeing our pizza cooked," says Derek.

"Yes, you may. We'll talk more later."

They both jump up, holding their hands out to Ronnie. He counts out quarters. "Save a few for after we eat."

They run to lose themselves in their child-world. Logan will have quarters left for more video games after eating. Derek will stand on a stool, watching pizzas until he's sure he's seen "our" pizza go into the oven. The video games will eat up his quarters in no time. Then he'll ride the free mechanical horse until it's time to eat.

"Why'd they want to go play when we're telling them I'm moving out?"

"Because they're little kids. If whatever is going on doesn't affect them at a particular moment, it's outside their scope of vision and doesn't matter to them." *Just like you.*

"Oh."

Journal Entry — 12/8/2002 — Thank you, God, for helping everything go so smooth in talking with Ronnie about the separation. I thought I might be depressed about him moving out, but, instead, I feel hopeful that we can retrieve our marriage from the ash heap. In all the years we've been married, I don't remember him being so sorry for anything that he has done. Hopefully, breaking the window will be a good thing in the long run. It may be the key to us working things out. Talking to Carol gives me new ideas of how to respond to him. Ronnie hasn't been in a rage for 2 weeks. My trust is rebuilding, I have faith things are getting better. It's so much easier to do my journaling here at home after the boys are in bed.

Nightmare Entry — 12/11/2002 — Me sitting at a table doing scrap booking of the boys — I'm staring at a New York driver's license of someone I don't know — next is Logan's first grade picture and a picture of Derek hugging his Jack-In-the-Box — ashes are dumped on the table — I gag on the dust — now me and the table are in the middle of Ground Zero with the bucket brigade close to me — I smile as I look at a photo of Poppa and Granny with three-day-old Logan — someone yells, "It's collapsing!" — I can't move to run away — I see a photo of Ronnie and me when we were dating, I shake ashes off of it — parts of the photo disappear with the ashes.

Chapter 13 – Shopping with Daddy

Everyone, including Pepper, our dog, seems more relaxed with each passing day that Ronnie is gone. Even the furniture and the house itself seem tranquil. The boys play rambunctiously in every room without being commanded to go to their rooms.

On Monday evening, I am surprised when Ronnie calls, asking to take the boys Christmas shopping Saturday afternoon.

Logan and Derek are doing their homework in the kitchen. As I sit down with them, Logan wraps his arm around my shoulders.

"Mommy, what's wrong? You look funny."

"Oh . . . um . . . that was Daddy. He's coming over Saturday afternoon to take you and Derek Christmas shopping."

"Why? He's never done that before," Logan says, disinterested. He knows Daddy is not dependable when it comes to following through with plans and promises.

"I know, honey." *Can't believe Ronnie even thought of this.* "We need to give him a chance." I fake a big smile for their sakes.

"He even said he would take us out to eat and let us pick the place."

"Really?" ask Derek.

"You're kidding!" Logan adds. "But he's always telling us where we're going to eat." A smile brightens his face. "Can we go to that fun place with the playing cards on the ceiling?"

"Yeah! Kyle says. "They have two really old video games – Miss Patch Man and Alleger."

"No, they're Ms. Pacman and Galaga," Logan corrects his brother.

"Well… Daddy did say we can choose. What's the name of this place?" I ask them.

"Pizza at the Arch," they chime together.

***

On Saturday afternoon, Ronnie picks the boys up, and they are gone for a couple of hours. Then, true to his word, we actually go to

Pizza at the Arch to eat dinner. I see him clinch his jaw when the check arrives, but he doesn't complain.

In the car on the way home, Logan says, "Hey, Daddy, tell Mommy about your Matchbox cars."

"Do you mean the ones you play with at Grandma's?"

"Yeah, yeah, those."

"When we saw them at the store today, I told the boys how I got the ones at Mom's for my seventh birthday." His voice sounds sad. "That's the only time I remember actually getting a present. All of my other birthdays, I got a dollar or two in a card that Mom had made herself."

"Sounds like you guys had fun today." I attempt to suppress the hope growing within me until I see more changes.

"Sure did," Ronnie says. "Don't know why I've never taken them shopping before. The boys said their school Christmas play is Thursday. What time does it start?"

"Seven. Why?"

"Because I want to go. It's too late to get a vacation day, so I'll see if I can trade with someone."

"I didn't know you could do that. Is this a new policy?"

"No, I've just never done it before," he answers. A chill goes up my spine when he takes my hand and caresses my palm with his thumb. "Sara, I really miss you and want us to work things out." His voice catches.

I squeeze his hand. "Me, too."

***

With the boys in bed, I go into the living room and sit down on the sofa. Ronnie is standing at the bay window, staring out into the darkness through the replaced glass, seemingly deep in thought.

Nervously, I say, "I thought you might be meeting Chuck and Amy at the bar tonight."

"Suppose to later." He turns and says, "I'm going to get a glass of iced tea. Do you want one?"

"Sure. Thanks."

I caress my wedding rings. *Do most people take these off when they're separated or does that only happen with divorces?*

When he comes back, he hands me the ice tea and sits down in the middle of the sofa. His eyes look unhappy and his face is haggard as he looks at me. "First of all, I want to thank you for jolting me into reality by asking for this separation."

I am so shocked, I almost spew the tea in my mouth at him. I wipe it from my chin. I try to make my voice light to dispel the intense nervousness I feel. "You're welcome," is all I can think of to say.

He looks away from me and leans forward with his elbows on his knees. "I've been trying to figure out why I broke the window." Nervously, he scoots his tea glass back and forth about an inch on the coffee table. "I've realized my drinking has increased a lot since Harry died, so I'm cutting it back to two six-packs on the weekends and only one or two beers during the week."

I can't count the number of times you've cut back before. I'll believe it when you go longer than a week. "I know his death has really been hard on you."

"Let's change the subject. Talking about him makes me miss him even more." He turns sideways on the sofa and reaches for my hand. "I've been thinking about nothing but you since I've been at Chuck's."

Journal Entry — 12/14/2002 — Seems like Ronnie and I both are more relaxed with each other than we've been in a long, long while. We reminisced about the little apartment we lived in as newlyweds. He even teased me today, sneaking up behind me quietly to tickle my ribs. He used to tease me every day. This was a good day.

Nightmare Entry — 12/17/2002 — Ear-splitting sound like a locomotive that lasts for a long, long time, making me cover my ears, followed by silence — thick stream of eerie, glowing, molten pieces of the tower drop in five- to six-foot-long droplets. One of them hits a fireman rescuing a woman — Ronnie says "the Pentagon is on fire" — American flags wave in the wind – a radio commenter says "This can't be happening here in America." — terrorist photos flash on TV, one of them kind of looks like Ronnie.

Chapter 14 – Homeless?

As I walk into Carol's office, snow flurries stick to bare limbs outside the window. As we settle into our chairs, she says, "I am anxious to hear how your conversation went with Ronnie."

"Talking to him about the separation at Red Lobster worked. Wish I'd known about talking to him in public a long time ago." I feel more relaxed today than usual.

"Tell me what happened."

"He reluctantly agreed to the separation, and he moved to Chuck and Amy's on Sunday."

Carol appears either pleased or surprised, maybe both. "Wow. That was fast!"

"Some people would say Chuck and Amy having an empty bedroom at the perfect time was coincidence. But I believe God had a hand in arranging this."

"Is God a big part of your life?"

"Not as much as when I was growing up. The boys and I go to church Sunday mornings and rush straight home. Ronnie demands we do family things on Sunday afternoons."

"What family things?"

"Taking a drive in the country – the boys hate that one. If they make too much noise in the back seat, Ronnie yells and orders them to enjoy the scenery. We go see his mom every other weekend and quite often we end up at Chuck's so Ronnie can have more beer."

"How are you and the boys doing now that he's been out of the house a few days?"

"Me, I'm lonely, but it was lonely with him there, too . . . less stressed, more relaxed." I stand, stretch, and walk to the window. "I think our separation is like these trees." I turn sideways so I can see Carol. "We're going into a dormant state to regain strength and renewal of our relationship." I give Carol a confident smile, but she doesn't return it.

"I hope so," she says, "but Ronnie has to work as hard at changing things as you are."

"I believe breaking that window was a wake-up call for him," I say, returning to my chair.

"How are Logan and Derek doing since he moved out?"

"Good. It seems they're getting along better. Last night, we started giggling about something. I haven't laughed that hard since I don't know when. We laughed and laughed until our sides hurt."

"That's great! Have there been any other changes in the boys?"

Emotions well up in me so unexpectedly that I bite my lip to stop the tears. "Derek's stuttering has lessened, and Logan has only wet his bed one time since Ronnie moved. It's amazing and exciting that changes are already happening."

Carol looks through the folder in her lap, pulls a sheet of paper out, and hands it to me. "This is a list of behaviors commonly found in children who live in homes of extreme anger or violence. Do you see any other problems either of the boys is experiencing?" (Appendix E)

I stop reading at the third paragraph. "Logan has temper tantrums sometimes, usually about something Derek has or wants. Don't normal kids do that?"

"Yes, but how hard is it to get him settled down or distracted with something else?"

I swallow. "Very hard most of the time. I send or carry him to his room until he calms down."

"That sounds pretty stressful," Carol says as she goes to the file cabinet.

"Logan has always been a difficult child to correct. I'm ashamed to tell you I got so frustrated with him last week that I picked up a little paddle that used to have a ball attached to it and spanked him with it."

"How did you feel after that happened?"

"A little less frustrated and wished I could think of some other way to have handled it."

"I just happen to have some ideas for you." She hands me a sheet of paper on the way back to her rocking chair. "As you were growing up, were you allowed to be angry?"

"No, it was considered disrespectful."

"As I told you in our first session, anger is a normal emotion we all have. Because Ronnie demonstrates the wrong ways to express anger and you suppress yours, Logan and Derek have no idea what to do when they become angry."

"That makes sense. I like the stress ball."

"I had a client who bought several rubber balls. Then she cooked her kids their favorite meal and, instead of dessert, she gave each of them a rubber ball as a present. She explained they were to carry the "stress balls" in their pockets to squeeze the heck out of when they get angry. A year later, the event was repeated with a twist. The children gave their mother a present with a pink stress ball inside. The last time I spoke with her, this tradition continues even though the kids are in high school."

"I love that! And I like the counting to 10 or singing the ABC song because those can be done anywhere."

"Yes, those do work well in public. There's probably another eight or ten ideas on that page that you can experiment with."

"I'm anxious to try some of them."

"How does Derek act when he is angry?"

"Occasionally he shows his anger like Logan does, but more often, he's quiet, sulks, and goes to his room. He handles anger more like me.

"And Logan lets it out like Ronnie does. Is that correct?"

"Yes he does." I grasp the arms of my chair, repositioning myself. "I've just been glad Derek wasn't as hard as Logan to get calmed down. But I guess I need to help him talk about his anger."

Carol smiles that comforting smile she has. "Yes, you do."

"Okay, I'll give it a try." I smile a mile wide. "Wouldn't it be something if Ronnie learned a new way to handle his anger?"

"Yes, it would. When Ronnie sees you teaching the boys new ways to handle their anger, he may pick up on some of it. But I wouldn't count on it because it's gotten him what he wants for a lot of years."

"Yeah, I guess it has."

"Have you had many nightmares since Ronnie moved out?"

"A few." I go to the window again.

"Sara, you've been coming here long enough that I know when something is difficult for you to talk about because you move to the window. What is it this time?"

I turn around and smile weakly. "In one of my nightmares, I'm in New York, looking at the Twin Towers. Suddenly, two hands grab my leg. Then there's an awful, awful smell. When I look down, I see a homeless woman sitting on the sidewalk." I lean back against the window sill. "I try to walk away from her, but she holds on tighter. As I demand she let go, she brushes black, slimy, greasy hair out of her face and – and – it's me." I sit. "Why would I dream that?"

"Are you worried about a possibility of you and the boys becoming homeless if Ronnie doesn't give you support money?"

I burst into tears. "Oh my gosh . . . yes, I am."

"I'm sure that's a very scary thought, but you would be eligible for food stamps and I'm sure Lola and Steve will be there to help you."

"Yes, I know they would," I say. "But I don't think Nancy would let me take off work to go apply for help of any kind. I'm out of paid time off, and I sure can't afford to miss any money."

"Sara, whatever happens during this separation, you and the boys are going to be okay. I've watched and admired the courage and ingenuity of women I've seen in similar situations. You have a great family, and there are a lot of resources available."

"I know." I straighten up in my chair and smooth my skirt. "It's encouraging that we've found one of the nightmare connections. Now if we can just figure out the rest of them, I'll have more energy for everything."

"We will do our best to figure out the rest of them. Since you've accomplished the separation, what's next?"

"I'm so relieved the separation happened, I haven't thought much about what's next. A lot depends on Ronnie – what he does and doesn't do."

"How about starting a list of changes you want to happen?"

"I can do that. Since I'm not walking on eggshells 24/7, my thinking seems a little more coherent."

"I need to let you know I'm going to spend some extra time with my mother over the holidays. She's having some health issues."

"I'm sorry to hear that."

"Thanks, Sara." Carol seems apprehensive instead of me. "I'm taking three weeks of vacation."

Three weeks! Who will I talk to if Ronnie does something else as stupid as breaking the window? My heart beats faster.

"Melissa is another counselor here in our office and has a counseling style similar to mine. She has agreed to work you into her schedule if you need someone to talk with while I'm gone."

Settle down, girl. He's really changing since he moved out. Have confidence you won't need Carol while she's gone. My heart rate slows.

"Okay. But if things continue the way they've started, I won't need her."

Chapter 15 – Hot Tub

Derek's Power Rangers relocate to a secret place, the bay window in the living room, mid-morning on Saturday.

While cleaning the bathroom, I overhear a conversation between the boys. "Hey, bro, why'd you move your base so far away from me?" Logan asks.

"'cause they're on a secret mission. Go away."

"I'm going to put my base at the other end of the bay window."

"No! Not till my secret mission's done!"

I step into the hallway just in time to see Derek move into a boxer's stance, his angelic face trying to look mean. "Go away!"

"All right, all right," Logan says, backing away. "How'll I know when the mission's done?"

"You'll know," he answers, taking a step toward Logan.

For the next two hours, Logan repeatedly maneuvers too close to the secret base. Derek growls and scowls. Logan walks away, sulking and complaining that Derek is being selfish.

From upstairs around noon, I hear Derek announce, "Daddy's here! He's here!" By the time I get to the top of the stairs, I see Logan slide around the corner from the hallway into the living room.

"I beat ya. Ha!" Derek beams at his big brother.

"Secret mission, huh?" Logan says, cuffing Derek on the shoulder.

Soon as Ronnie closes the front door, he squats down to their level. "You guys must be ready for Christmas shopping since you're both waiting at the door. Where's Mommy?"

"She's upstairs. How can we shop for her when she's coming, too?" Logan wants to know.

Quietly Ronnie answers, "It's too big to go under the tree, so she gets one of her presents today. I see Ronnie put his finger to his lips. Both boys giggle.

***

"Why are we going into a swimming pool store in the winter?" I ask, as Ronnie holds the door open for me. He has a mischievous gleam in his eye.

"Yeah, Daddy, it's too cold for swimming," Logan says.

"This place sells other things."

"Hey, I see pool tables! Are we getting one like Uncle Steve's?" asks Derek excitedly.

"That sounds like fun, but not today." Ronnie puts his arm around my waist, guiding me toward a hot tub. "Hey, look at this one. Isn't it a beaut?"

"A beauty is right. Look how high those jets are. *They would feel wonderful on my knotted muscles after long days on the computer.* Wistfully, I add, "Maybe some day." I walk around the tub, running my hand along the top and enjoying the smoothness.

"Welcome back, Mr. Farley," a salesman says. "I have the paperwork ready. All we need is a color choice."

I look at Ronnie for an explanation.

His eyes brighten as he pulls a wad of bills out of his pocket. He holds it up in the air, and I see a $100 bill on the outside. "Honey, I've been saving overtime for two years to see that look on your face. What color do you want?"

I run into his arms. He sweeps me off my feet, swinging me around and around.

"They've been acting weird like that a lot lately," Logan explains to the salesman, embarrassed.

"Oh, honey, this seems too good to be true." Back on solid ground, I feel my heart pounding. My imagination goes into overdrive at the thought of sharing the hot tub with my husband when snow's turning the world white. Without looking away from Ronnie, I ask, "What colors does it come in?"

"Mrs. Farley, your choices are gray, blue and green. There's a green one over here with water in it if you'd like to see it."

"No, I'll take blue," I say, gazing into my husband's eyes.

Ronnie counts out the hundreds to the salesman and settles on the Friday after Christmas as the delivery date. *Wonder where he's been keeping that extra money for two years. But, wow, he's buying this for me!*

"Sara? Honey?"

"What? Oh, are we ready to go?" He takes my hand. *For years, he's told me how he hates holding hands. But, now he's the one initiating it.*

***

"Mommy, are you and Daddy happy?" asks Derek as I kiss him good night.

"I'd say we're happier than we've been in a long time."

"Is Daddy coming home now that you're happy?"

"Maybe. Do you want him to?"

"Yeah, but I only want the nice one. The mean one has to stay at Uncle Chuck's."

"I hope that's possible. Good night, big boy."

"Night, Mommy."

When I walk into the living room, Ronnie says, "Come, sit by me."

As I sit down, I feel like a teenager about to launch into my first romance. He puts his arm around my shoulder and strokes the length of my cheek with his fingertip. Then he takes my hand. "Sara, I want to spend the night here so I'll be here for Christmas morning." His eyes beg me to agree with him.

I move away from him a few inches, physically and emotionally. "I'm glad you mentioned Christmas. The boys and I won't be at Chuck's on Christmas Eve."

He lets go of my hand and slumps into the corner of the sofa. "Why not? It's tradition!"

"I know it's tradition but I'm tired of hearing Jason's filthy mouth. And Derek wants to go to bed early for Santa to come."

"Mom will really be hurt if the three of you aren't there, especially since it's the first Christmas without Harry."

"Oh . . . yeah, that's true. I definitely don't want to make the holidays any harder on her." I notice the black screen of the TV and wonder how long it's been since we sat on the sofa together without our attention glued to the boob tube. "I guess we can come, but we'll be gone by ten."

"Great! But why leave so early?"

"That isn't early for two little boys waiting for Santa Claus. And I usually have a few gifts left to wrap."

"Oh . . . I see," he says as he sits up tall and leans closer to me.

"One thing I know for sure, this Christmas morning will not be like the last several years," I tell him with assuredness in my voice.

"What do you mean?" he asks defensively.

"Whatever time the boys wake up is when we'll be opening presents. I refuse to make them wait until nine or ten when you can finally drag yourself out of bed."

"I don't remember it being that late," he says, looking sheepish. "How about I leave Chuck's at the same time you and the boys do on Christmas Eve?" His eyes soften.

"We'll have to see how things go between now and then."

Ronnie stands and pulls me up into his arms. My promise to myself to not let him back into my heart too fast melts like a glacier in July. My eyes close with the pleasure of his touch. "You look lovely tonight," he says, caressing my forehead with kisses. My spirit, soul, and body ache for the good times. He steps back and slides his hands down my arms to my hands. He leads me to the door. "I'll call you tomorrow." As the door closes behind him, loneliness thunders in like a herd of wild horses.

> Journal Entry — 12/21/2002 — Can't believe Ronnie spent so much money on that hot tub today, on something I've wanted for a long time. Must be because he's feeling guilty about breaking the window and drinking so much. It feels strange for him to just up and leave like he did tonight. I was preparing myself mentally to endure sex with him – or, I might have enjoyed it for a change the way his touch was making me feel. Hard to believe he's cutting back his drinking so much. Time will tell how serious he is about it. My longing for my dream marriage is so intense I often ache physically. Wonder if people can be addicted to other people like drug addicts are to drugs.

Chapter 16 – Best Christmas Ever

"Do we have to go to Uncle Chuck's tonight?" whines Derek as the three of us get into my car.

Rather than starting the motor, I turn around so I can see both of them. "Yes we do. It's everyone's first Christmas without Uncle Harry. Grandma needs us to be with her tonight."

"Why'd Uncle Harry have to go dying?" Derek asks.

How many times do we have to have this conversation? "He didn't want to die. God wanted him to go live with Him and Jesus."

"Yeah, it was an anpherism," states Logan.

"Aneurism. Hard word to say, isn't it?"

"Uh-huh," he says, going back to playing with his Power Ranger.

I look at Derek. "Remember when we put water in a balloon and pricked it with a pin. Then the water came out faster and faster."

"Yeah. That's how the vein was in Uncle Harry's head." He picks at loose button threads on his coat.

"Yes, that's right. But the doctors didn't know about the hole in his brain until it was too late to fix it."

"Can we go see Grandma now?" interrupts Logan. "Will Daddy be here in the morning when we open presents?"

"Yes, he's going to sleep here tonight."

Logan looks deflated. "Are we going to have to wait for hours and hours to open presents – again?" he asks in a shaky voice.

"No, absolutely not! Daddy promises he'll get up when you guys come to wake us in the morning."

"But what if he doesn't?"

"If he doesn't, we'll open presents without him," I answer decidedly.

"Yea! Sure hope Santa got my letter," says Derek.

"Don't worry, Logan. We're going to have a great Christmas because your dad's changed a lot."

"Okay, Mommy," he says, wiping away tears on his coat sleeve.

***

"Merry Christmas, darling," Ronnie says, meeting us at Chuck's front door. He gives me a quick kiss. "More of that later." His voice causes a shimmering inside of me and a warning of danger that I choose to ignore.

"Merry Christmas, boys." He picks Derek up and tousles Logan's hair. They say Merry Christmas to their Grandma and give her hugs. "Let's go say hello to everyone else, then you can go play," Ronnie tells them. My heart swells with joy watching him.

"Merry Christmas, Mom Farley. How are you?"

She reaches up from her stature of almost five feet and pats my cheek. "Fine, dear. I don't have to ask how you're doing. I can see the happiness on your face."

I give her a hug and keep my arm around her shoulders. "Let's go see if dinner's ready."

"Hey Sara. Wanna beer?" Chuck asks as we get close to him.

"Merry Christmas, Chuck. Apple cider sounds better today." I stop at a small table beside the refrigerator that divides the open dining/kitchen areas. While I dip hot cider into a mug, I say "Merry Christmas, Amy." She waves a hand at me from where she stands looking at a recipe on the kitchen counter.

Without walls between the three rooms in a L-shape, it's easy to see and hear everyone. Mom Farley is sitting at the dining room table with Ronnie and Chuck who are teasing her about watching *It's a Wonderful Life* every year. Her sky-blue eyes sparkle when Derek runs into the room, gives his Grandma a hug, and runs out again without saying a word. He tells me he likes hugging Grandma because she's squishy like his teddy bear.

Amy looks like she's lost more weight. I bet she barely weighs a hundred pounds and that's paper-thin on her five-foot-eight frame. I worry about her health because she drinks and smokes so much.

"Anything I can do to help?" I ask as I walk over closer to her.

Amy turns around. "Hi. You can make the gravy."

"Okay, glad to. How are things going with Ronnie living here?

"Great. Reminds me of when he stayed with us for a couple of months after he came home from the Navy." I move out of her way so she can put the rolls in the oven. "Ronnie sure wants to come home. I can't believe he's only drinking on the weekends."

"Really?" *He really is cutting back. What a relief!*

"He told me, if that's what it takes to work things out with you, it's worth it."

The doorbell rings. One of the kids opens the front door. "Hey, it's Jason and Maria."

"Come on in here," Chuck yells through the house. "You're just in time to eat."

When I try to squeeze past Jason to go greet his family, he catches me off guard and gives me a too-close hug. As I get loose, I smell his beer breath and almost gag at the site of his mossy teeth.

I hurry into the living room. "Hi Maria. How are you?"

"Doing good," she answers. She's bent over, taking two-year old Tyler's coat off. "Would you please take Rosa's snowsuit off?

"Sure, love to."

Rosa's black eyes brighten up as I sit down on the couch beside her. "You're sure growing fast, baby girl." With the snowsuit off and folded on the back of the sofa, I take Rosa in my arms and stand to go to the kitchen. When I look at Maria, she looks worn and haggard. "I'm surprised to see you with makeup on."

"I don't like wearing this stuff so heavy but Jason insisted I wear it like this today." Her left eye is partially covered with her long black hair.

"Come on, everyone. Fill your plates!" Amy hollers from the kitchen.

***

After dinner, the men sit around the kitchen table talking about fishing boats, old acquaintances, and whatever else men talk about. Meanwhile in the living room, I deal cards for our traditional ladies game of gin rummy, Mom Farley's favorite. Within minutes, Mom says, "Gin." She gives us a broad, beaming smile. Maria deals another round of cards.

I feel someone looking at me, and, when I raise my eyes, I see Ronnie gazing at me tenderly. I feel fluttery as I return his smile.

"Mommy, when are we getting our outside bathtub?" asks Derek, as he runs into the living room from the basement.

"Friday. And it's called a hot tub." Derek runs back downstairs.

Mom, Maria, and Amy look at me wide-eyed. I feel a blush warming my cheeks. "Ronnie bought it for me last Saturday. I've wanted one forever but didn't think it could ever happen."

Mom and Maria smile. Amy looks down at her cards with a solemn expression.

"He's been saving his overtime for two years to buy it," I volunteer. It feels great to have something positive to say about Ronnie.

"How long have you two been separated?" Maria says. "If you don't mind me asking."

"It's just been two weeks, but things are getting better pretty fast."

"That's wonderful." Maria lets out a heavy sigh and leans closer to me. "I'd like to ask you some questions later." She looks desperate.

"Sure, maybe after this game."

She attempts a smile.

"Sara, you'd better ask Ronnie to come home soon, or some other woman's going to snatch him away from you," Amy says.

I stare at her. *That's a strange thing for her to say. Hope I can talk to her later, privately.*

As we play cards, we talk about Christmas presents we've bought for various people and how much we miss Harry. The children come and go in and out of the room, enjoying the holiday.

"Looky here, everyone. It's snowing for Santa Claus to come," Derek says while jumping up and down at the front window.

Several of us join him. I feel a familiar hand on my shoulder. "I love you," Ronnie whispers in my ear. I catch a whiff of his spicy after-shave — the one he wore when we were dating. He hasn't worn it for years.

"Kids, are you ready to watch Christmas movies with me?" asks Grandma.

"But we haven't finished our game," I protest.

"Yes we have. I'm beating the socks off you girls 'cause you're jabbering too much." She laughs, and we join her.

"Okay, Mom," I say. "Some Christmas you're going to lose at this game."

"Promises, promises." She flaps her hands at us. "Go join your husbands in their poker game. Shoo, shoo, go on."

***

"I don't know why I even bother playing poker." I rearrange the three coins lying on the table in front of me. "After I win one hand, it's all downhill from there."

"Here hon, I'll stake your losing endeavor," Ronnie says. He holds his beer bottle up in the air like a trophy. "Only my second one tonight," he brags. He scoots several coins over in front of me.

I nod my head, smile, and move my chair closer to his.

"Come on, you love birds. Save it for later. Damn it, Ronnie, it's your turn," says Jason.

Ronnie puts his arm around me and gives me a long, passionate kiss just to aggravate his nephew. "How much to stay in?" Ronnie asks as he turns back to the table.

"We're up to a quarter," Chuck slurs. From a cigarette stub in his hand, Chuck lights another cigarette to keep his chain smoking going.

By 9:30, I've lost my money and the money Ronnie gave me. He glances at the clock on the wall. "Honey, are you ready to go home?" He tosses a nickel on the table. "We'll go soon as I win this hand."

I feel my heart pitter-patter. "Yes, I am. I'll go get the boys."

As I walk back into the dining area, Ronnie asks. "Are we ready?"

Jason points to the clock. "Ronnie, ole buddy." He stands, staggers around the table and slings his arm over Ronnie's shoulder. "You've barely drank any beer. What the hell's wrong with you?"

Ronnie looks up at him. "Nothing. My family's more important than staying here for beer and poker," Ronnie answers. He pushes Jason's arm off of him and picks up his winnings. As Ronnie gets to his feet, Jason shoves him from behind making him stumble a step.

"Stop it Jason!" Amy yells.

By the time Ronnie regains his balance, Jason is in front of Amy. He leans down, and wags his face in hers. "Stay out of this, you damn bitch!

"Jason! Your Grandma's gonna hear you," Maria tells him.

He whips around and raises his hand in the air. "Shut the fuck up, Maria! Or I'll be straightening you out when we get home." She cowers in her chair.

Oh my God, there's a shiner on her left eye! I know Jason is a pig but hitting Maria is unbelievable!

Ronnie grabs Jason from behind pinning his arms to his sides. "Jason, you are out of control." Jason struggles to get loose but Ronnie hangs on. "You're going to either leave right now or sit down and behave yourself. Which is it going to be?

I feel a tug on my pants leg. I look down. "Mommy, can I ride with Daddy?" Derek asks.

Ronnie walks Jason around the table to the dining room chair he had been sitting in earlier. "Jason, are you going to spoil everyone's Christmas or are you going to behave yourself?" Jason has quit trying to get out of Ronnie's hold on him and is quieter.

"I'm okay now. " Ronnie lets go and Jason sits down. "Sorry everyone," he says as he picks up his beer for a drink.

"Mom!" Derek says, pulling on my hand this time.

I feel good saying, "Sure you can, Derek," because Ronnie's only had two beers tonight. "And Logan can ride with me." Everyone exchanges hugs, goodnights, and holiday greetings.

As I hug Maria, I whisper, "If I can ever help you with anything, *anything*, don't hesitate to call me. Anytime, night or day." When I step back, I see tears in her eyes. She nods.

When Ronnie closes Chuck's front door, a snowball hits his back. Whap! "Why you little . . ." Ronnie says as he grabs up some snow. Logan jumps into my car and locks the doors. When he sees his Daddy smiling at him, he puts a thumb in each ear, waving his fingers, and mouths, "Na na, na na na."

Ronnie scoops Derek up in his arms. "Race you home," he says, running for his car.

***

"We beat 'em! We beat 'em!" Logan announces as our empty driveway comes into view.

"Sure did!"

"Here, Mommy, I'll hold the door open for you like Daddy does now."

"Thank you, sir." I smile at him.

Logan comes into the kitchen where I'm putting water in the coffee pot. He is tossing his Rubik's Cube in the air. "Derek's always liked this thing, and I solved it a long time ago. Would it be okay if I wrap it up to give to him?"

"Sounds like a great idea to me. There's paper and tape by the blue rocker." *Wonder what's taking them so long. If he stopped to buy beer, he can just go right back to Chuck's tonight.*

Waiting for the coffee to finish brewing, I watch Logan do an eight-year-old wrapping job at the counter. "Where's Daddy and Derek?" he asks, adding unnecessary tape.

"Don't know. Just hope they haven't had an accident or something."

"I'll go put this under the tree and watch for them," Logan says with concern on his face.

"I'll be there soon as I get a cup of coffee."

As I walk toward the living room, Logan announces, "They're here!"

Coming in the front door, Derek is talking as fast as he can. "You shoulda' seen the bunches of police car lights. No sirens, just lights." He works his way down the hall toward the bedroom as he talks. "And Daddy kept saying 'I can't believe this. Gotta get home. Can't believe it.'"

Ronnie looks flustered and nervous. "It was a sobriety check point." He keeps looking at me, then the floor, back at me, and finally adds. "All those years of driving home from Chuck's hammered, there's never been one of those."

He smooths his hair, or lack thereof, and lets out a heavy breath. "Then, this time when I've only had two beers, I get stopped. I can't believe it."

Sure hope this scares the hell out of him as much as it looks like it did. Maybe he'll stop the drinking and driving.

"I can't, either. Did you get a ticket?"

Before Ronnie can answer, Derek says, "Hey, Mommy, Daddy. I'm ready for bed. I don't even want a bedtime story. I just want to go to sleep so Santa can come."

"Sounds good to me," says Logan. "'sides, I'm getting too big for stories."

"We'll see about that," I say, walking toward Derek's room.

I hear heavy footsteps behind me. When I turn to look, Ronnie is following me with his hand on Logan's shoulder. "I'll tuck this one in, then come say goodnight to Derek."

"Ahhh, Daddy, I'm too big to be tucked," Logan informs him.

"Guess maybe you are," Ronnie answers and boxes Logan on the arm lightly.

Really want to know if he got a ticket or not. Will he get mad if I ask about it? He didn't give in to Jason's harassment and sit back down for more beers like he did last year. And the way he took control of Jason was pretty amazing! So many holidays have been ruined through the years because of so much drinking. If this separation is going to change anything, I have to ask about it.

"There . . . last Power Ranger wrapped," I say, scooting packages around under the tree. I look at Ronnie sitting on the sofa. He beckons me. When I sit down next to him, I feel him trembling slightly. "Did you get a ticket tonight?"

"No, but when I admitted I'd been drinking, they asked me to take a Breathalyzer test. I passed it."

I'm surprised by how long he looks at me.

"Did you drive home from Brian's that night with my keys or yours?" He hesitates. "And if mine, how did you get them?"

Before answering him, I prepare myself mentally in case the monster suddenly appears. I lean sideways away from him. "It was your keys. When you dropped them, Nicole picked them up and put them in my hand."

"Oh." He's quiet. "From now on, I'm letting you drive when I've had anything to drink."

I snuggle up next to him. "That's a good decision." *Another problem solved.*

"Thanks for letting me spend the night. I promise I'll get up when the boys wake us in the morning." He grimaces and adds, "Whatever time it is."

We laugh.

"Thank you so much. It's great to have back the man I married . . . no, you're better than that guy because you're being such a great dad."

"That's the best thing you've ever said to me," he says, a possible tear in his eye. He pulls me close as our hearts beat in sync.

> Journal Entry — 12/24/2003 — 1:00 am — Can't sleep and want to get this on paper while it's still so pleasurable. Our feverish lovemaking transported me into another world tonight! For the first time in years, I was relaxed enough that I could play the temptress and be aggressive with him – that's what he likes. Holding his hand against my cheek and feeling its solid strength made me feel secure – the way it used to years ago. He said I'm everything he's ever dreamed of and that he loves me beyond measure. Those are romance-novel words that swell in my heart and give me chills. Then afterwards, as he held and cradled me, I brought myself back to reality by remembering how the changes that are so wonderful these last few days can go pffft in a split second and be gone.

***

"Mommy, Daddy!"

Derek's voice rouses me. "Mommy, Daddy!" Logan's hand is pushing on my shoulder, and Derek is pulling on my foot. "Santa came!"

"What the . . ." says Ronnie, rolling away from me.

He promised! What now? I sit upright in bed, looking at four frightened eyes staring at me. *Either he gets up as promised to open presents, or he can just leave for good when he crawls out of bed.*

I hold my arms out for the boys to scramble onto the bed. Ronnie rolls over in our direction, pulling the covers over his face. Suddenly he springs up, smiling from ear to ear. The tickle monster, wriggles his fingers. Squeals of delight come from the boys as they scurry under the covers. "Good morning, honey," Ronnie says, giving me a kiss. "Do I smell coffee?"

"Sure do. I remembered to set the timer last night. Why don't you . . ." I say, pointing to the giggly blanket bumps. He nods.

My legs shake as I step to the side of the creaky fifth step out of habit, going down to the kitchen. Collapsing onto the stool, I pour myself a cup of coffee, hoping the caffeine will calm my quivering innards. *Okay, Sara, calm down. He's up. No hangover this year. Gotta talk to Carol about these old reactions when things are going good with Ronnie.*

I hear footsteps hurrying down the stairs. "Don't you guys peek inside any presents before Mommy and I get in there," Ronnie says as the boys rush for the living room. He pulls me out off the stool into his arms. "Are you okay? You're shaking," he says, pushing me back to look at my face. "Why are you crying?"

"Tears of joy, honey. I didn't think we'd ever see a Christmas like this again."

"Come here, sweet one. This is only the beginning of our new life. Thank you so much for letting me be here this morning."

Wow! What a kiss! Then, with his arm around me we walk to the living room.

> Journal Entry — 12/25/2002 — What an absolutely marvelous day! Ronnie getting up like he promised started our day off right! Best Christmas I remember since Derek was maybe two! I'm really missing Ronnie tonight with him back to Chuck's after dinner. He surprised me by not asking to stay another night. I'm so glad God has helped me through so many tough times with Ronnie so I don't have to break my wedding vows. Of my many fears, it appears the worst one isn't going to happen – the boys growing up without their Daddy in the house. Divorce isn't going to happen. Hallelujah!!!

Chapter 17 – Together

From the kitchen, I hear Ronnie ask, "Honey, is lunch ready?" as he comes in the front door.

"Almost," I answer, sliding a pot roast back into the oven.

"Beginning to think Chuck's boat motor isn't worth the thirty bucks I paid him," he says, setting a bag on the counter that clinks.

I feel his arms slide around my waist from behind. He nuzzles the spot where my neck and shoulder joins, giving me shivers. I turn around and kiss him the way he likes to be kissed – tight lipped.

"Got strawberry wine coolers for you." He moves away, putting the drinks in the fridge, then goes to look out the window. "Sweetheart, come look at this," he croons.

"How long has it been snowing?" I ask when I see large snowflakes falling fast and heavy.

"Started a couple of hours ago when Chuck and I were outside trying to start that damn boat motor. Wanna skip lunch and get in the hot tub?"

"Ummm . . . how cold is it?"

"Thermometer said 23 when I came in."

"Going to be bone chilling cold getting from the back door to the tub."

He gets a cooler out of the fridge, opens it and hands it to me. "This will help warm you up."

I take a long drink. "Haven't had one of these in a long time. Hope we don't get frostbite!" I say, sprinting to find my bikini.

Ronnie is already lounging in the hot tub by the time I get back to the kitchen. When I open the back door, cold air whooshes in. I hold my breath, steel my will, and make a wild dash, jumping into the 102-degree temperature.

Ronnie starts laughing. "I think that's the fastest I've ever seen you move." He hands me another cooler.

"Ahh . . . this feels so good. It was worth the trip to get in here," I say moving closer to him.

"Would you like bubbles, jets, or a combination, my dear?"

"Bubbles and jets, please."

"Your wish is my command," he says, pushing a couple of buttons on the console. "It was nice of Granny and Poppa to meet you in Collins yesterday to pick up the boys."

"Yeah, it was. But if it snows like this all week, it's going to be a long trip to pick them up next weekend."

I kiss my new husband gently and position my right shoulder in front of a massage jet. His breath brushes my cheek, causing me to have chills even though I'm sitting in hot water. *Wonder where he was hiding that overtime money. Stop it! No negative thinking.*

"Sara . . . honey . . . things are different, will be different. Don't you think it's time for me to come home?"

Need to talk to Carol. He has made some very good changes. "I don't know. Why do you think it's time?"

"He pulls me close and looks at me with a gaze that melts my resistance like snow touched by the sun. "I miss you so much. I ache to be here with you and the boys – in our house."

He did buy me this wonderful tub, went to the boys' Christmas program, and didn't get drunk Christmas Eve.

"It's only been three weeks," I respond.

"True . . . but look how good this feels, us being together."

I feel my top loosen. I jump up out of the water into the freezing temperature and right back down. "Haven't lost my touch, have I?" He laughs heartily.

"Guess not. Reminds me of when we were dating," I say, reconnecting a hook.

He stops my hands from moving. "Please leave it off."

"But it's daytime and the neighbors might see me."

"They can't see under the water."

"Guess that's true," I reluctantly agree.

"In fact . . ." he said, moving my hand into his lap showing me he's naked. He nods to me to do the same. I slip my swimsuit bottom off as I glance at the neighbors' windows.

"Remember that time we were going to make love on the tenth green at Rockaway Golf Course?" he asks.

"Sure do. Took a week for my butt rash to go away," I say. "They must use strong chemicals to keep the grass so green."

"I'd forgotten about that. You did have a baboon red butt for a while."

Our laughter sounds light and free. "I was thinking more about the car lights flashing across us. Then me trying to get my panties on as we made a run for our car."

"Yeah, then when we were almost there, we saw a couple putting a blanket into the trunk of their car."

"Guess we're not the only ones who think golf courses are too beautiful to just knock those little balls around on."

He pulls me close. "What happened to us? We used to have such good times."

"Life happened. We bought this house, had two kids, and became responsible."

"That's true." He sounds regretful.

"Now my good times come in the enjoyment of Logan and Derek. And especially with you, like right now."

"Yeah, but I miss the good ole days. Come here, you. Let's see if we can screw in the water."

Journal Entry — 12/30/2002 — Sure glad Carol's back next week because I can't wait to tell her how well this separation is working, how I have my real Ronnie back, and to ask her how we will know it's time for him to come home. Maybe things are moving too fast. I don't know how, and I'm not sure I want them to slow down. Won't need counseling any more with the nightmares not happening. I'm sleeping sound and getting my energy back.

Nightmare Entry — 1/4/2003 — Amazing that I'm still not having any of them.

Chapter 18 – Full Closet

"This trip to Joplin would have been a lot better if Uncle Steve could have gone with us," I say to Aunt Lola as we approach St. Louis from the south.

"Yeah."

"Does he ever consider changing jobs so he can be home more?"

"We discuss that once in while, but he loves the challenges he has with this company. He knows I won't get too lonesome with you and the kids around." She smiles at me.

As I turn onto my street, I see Ronnie's truck parked in the driveway. "Did you know he was going to be here?" Aunt Lola asks with bits of ice in her voice.

"No, sure didn't."

"Hope it's not going to be a problem," she says.

I bristle. "Don't be so negative. He's changing for the better since we've been separated." I answer brusquely.

"Takes longer than four weeks to know if he's really changed or not."

I don't respond. As we pull into the drive, Ronnie runs out the front door . "Hi, honey. How was your trip?" he asks as I get out of the car.

"Good. No weather problems."

He gives me a light kiss. "Glad to hear that." Both boys run to Ronnie, vying for his attention. "Logan, Derek, how was your stay with Granny and Poppa?"

"Great," answers Derek as he grabs Ronnie's hand.

"We made snow people like we did here Christmas day but Granny wouldn't let us put boobs on any of them. "She said it isn't proper to do things like that."

"Really. Well, she's old-fashioned."

I walk to the back of the car where Aunt Lola is pulling suitcases and Christmas presents out of the back. Ronnie follows me with Derek riding on his shoulders. "I knew you'd be worn out when you got here, so I made chili," Ronnie says. He smiles proudly.

"Wow, thanks, that's great." I glance at Aunt Lola. She shrugs and pulls the last gift from the truck. "Would you like to stay and eat with us?" I ask.

"No thanks." As she walks around me and goes to the driver's door, she whispers, "Call me if things aren't okay here. I still don't trust Ronnie."

"I'll talk to you soon," I say as she closes the car door. She doesn't even look at me.

Ronnie puts his arm around my waist, and we walk to the house together with both boys chattering.

Maybe it really is time for him to come home.

***

Soon as the four of us are seated at the dining room table, Derek announces, "Logan broke Poppa's window."

Logan frowns at Derek with a look of anger that says "I'll get you for that later."

"How'd that happen?" Ronnie's voice sounds stern.

I see Derek grimace and look into his chili. Out of habit, all of my body tenses as I wait to see if Ronnie's going to explode.

"Accident," Logan answers, not looking up from his bowl of chili. "Are you gonna be mad at me?" he asks timidly.

Ronnie reaches over, raising Logan's chin. "Was Poppa mad? It's his window." Ronnie gives him a gentle smile. "No, I'm not going to be mad. Just tell me what happened."

Derek regains his excitement. I breathe again.

Logan looks up, studying his daddy's face. He lets out a big sigh. "We were in the woods helping load firewood in the pickup. Poppa told us to not throw wood on the spare tire 'cause it might bounce and break the back window." Derek and Logan look at each other. Derek snickers. "The very next piece I threw hit the tire and broke the window just like he said it would," Logan says, still looking apprehensive.

Derek can't stay quiet any longer. "Yeah, and Poppa looked real mad." Derek lowers his voice. "Poppa said, 'Logan, I told you to not . . .' then Poppa started smiling and laughed so hard he had to sit on the ground."

Ronnie puts his hand on Logan's shoulder and gently rocks him back and forth. "Things happen, and we have to make the best of them," he says, looking at me strangely.

After eating, Ronnie and the boys clear the table and then play video games. I unpack the boys' suitcases, putting away their clean clothes. I can always count on not having any laundry to do when Logan and Derek come home from Joplin, thanks to Granny.

Upstairs I put away bathroom items and then open the full-length mirrored closet door. Impacted by what I see, I feel like an exhausted mountain climber within inches of the summit whose foot has slipped, leaving me dangling on a rope 50 feet above ground. I fall to the floor. His shirts, pants, and shoes are all in place, as if never gone. "Oh my God!" I sit there in pain so intense, I barely notice it as it gradually retreats into numbness. Like a robot, I stand and mechanically unpack a few things. Then I check the closet again to be sure it's not my imagination. I unpack a few things, check the closet, unpack a few things, and check the closet. *I CANNOT believe he's done this!*

When I go into the living room, the Cheshire Cat grins at me, nervously.

"Come on boys, bedtime. Christmas break's over," I say, surprised at the anger in my voice.

"But I want to play more Zelda with Daddy before he goes back to Uncle Chuck's," Derek whines.

"Hey, little buddy, we'll play more tomorrow evening. Off to bed with you, like Mommy said."

With teeth brushed and no bedtime stories read, I say, "Goodnight, boys. Love you." I close both bedroom doors. I don't want them to overhear Ronnie's voice if he gets loud.

Ronnie's loading the dishwasher when I walk into the kitchen. "We've gotta talk," I say, plopping down on a stool. My head aches and my shoulders sag, heavy with the invisible weight pressing down on me – HARD.

"I know," he says, reaching for a soda in the fridge. "Want one?"

"No. When did you move your clothes back?"

"Saturday." He sits down and slowly drums his fingers on the counter. "Cody moved home and is going back to school. Had to get my stuff out of his room."

"It's good he's going back to school," I say because I'm so unsure of what I really want to say. My fists clench and unclench under the counter. My mind battles to deny this is happening. "I wish you'd told me! I was shocked to see your clothes in the closet!" My voice sounds uncommonly loud for me.

"I've been trying to find a way to tell you ever since you got home but haven't had a chance." He leans forward, and I lean away from him.

"Why didn't you call me at Poppa's on Saturday to discuss this?" *I'm angry with him for moving back while I was out of town, but angrier with myself for being suckered into believing he's really changing.*

He lights a cigarette and inhales deeply. "It seems like something we should talk about in person, not on the phone," he says.

"Not when it's something that needs to be decided before I can get home!" I stand suddenly, causing the stool to scrape the linoleum. "You could have slept on the couch or something at Chuck's until I got back so we could talk about this." I'm shaking all over, and my legs feel unsteady.

"Sara, I'm really sorry I've upset you so much," Ronnie says with love in his eyes. "Please calm down so we don't wake the boys."

He stubs out his cigarette, stands, and walks to the end of the breakfast bar. He stops and reaches for my hand. I ignore it. "With the conversation we had in the hot tub last weekend, I'm hoping this is going to be okay with you." He comes closer, sits down on a stool, and takes my hand.

His touch pulls sadness back into my awareness. But, the anger stays sucked far down into my swirling vortex of emotions, shrouded in darkness.

"Sara, honey, if you really don't want me here yet, I'll look for some place else to stay. It'll take a little while and lots of money to get an apartment."

"I just don't know what to say or think. I'm too tired after the trip home today. I'll have to talk to Carol about this on Wednesday."

He lets go of my hand and jumps to his feet. His face darkens as a muscle jerks in his left cheek.

My whole body goes into full alert as I say, "Oops!" out loud to myself.

"Who the hell's Carol?"

I stand and move backwards against the outside door. "Remember that verbal warning I got at work last fall?"

"Don't change the subject." He's three feet in front of me now. "Who in the hell's Carol?"

"Let me finish," I say firmly. "When Nancy gave me that warning, she insisted I go to . . ." I swallow hard. ". . . counseling."

His cheek jerks again. "Counseling? You've been going there all these months, telling this Carol person all of our business?"

"Yes, because Nancy demanded I go," I say strongly.

His face is livid. His mad eyes glaring at me gives me chills. I wait for him to say something, anything. "Another damn woman supervisor." He rubs his face with both hands. He turns and walks around the counter to the utility room door and then back and forth several times. He stops and looks at me – almost normal "You're not telling Carol any more than you absolutely have to, are you?"

"I've told her enough that I haven't had any nightmares for two whole weeks."

His eyes soften. "Oh . . ." He steps closer and stops. "So . . . you've been talking to this Carol person about me?"

"Yes. No more than I have to, but it's impossible to talk about my life without talking about you, me, and us."

"I guess so." He reaches out and pulls me up into his arms; his magic touch melts my resistance. "Please, please let me stay."

> Journal Entry — 1/5/2003 — Can't sleep. Carol will be asking me how I feel. Umm . . . angry that he did it without talking to me first, hurt that he's willing to risk the recovery we've made. Hope he's changed as much as I tried to convince Aunt Lola he has. She is so lucky to have a good man like Uncle Steve. Now that I've had a little time to calm down, I've decided to make the best of Ronnie being home. By concentrating on the positives and with God's help of loving him unconditionally, the changes will become stronger and life will be good. I'm not even going to tell Carol he moved home without me knowing it. That would be hanging onto a negative instead of clinging to the positives.

Journal Entry — 1/7/2003 — It's marvelous having Ronnie here. Don't know why I was so worried about him moving home. The separation did the magic of saving our marriage. He's working nights now, which is good in two ways – no childcare to pay and the boys have their homework done by the time I get home. He plays video games with them instead of vegging out in front of the TV all evening. Dinner has been ready two nights this week when I got here, and he helps me clean up the kitchen before he goes to work. He read Derek his bedtime story one night. I'm choosing to stay focused on the positives. Can't wait to tell Carol the good news tomorrow.

Chapter 19 – Facing Reality

In Carol's office I stand at the window and watch sleet collect on the tree branches. Crumpling the sheet of paper in my hand, I arch it into the air. It lands in the trashcan. "Two points." The door opens and Carol walks in while I'm retrieving my "ball" from its basket.

"Sorry about making you wait," she says.

"That's okay. " I uncrumple the letter from Human Resources. I hand it to Carol as I pass her to sit down in my usual chair.

"I think I need to be coming here every two weeks until the nightmares are gone for at least a month." I notice I'm teetering on the edge of my chair and scoot back.

"I received the same notice. We'll talk more about this later." She opens my folder in her lap and reads a note. "I see you didn't keep your appointment with Melissa while I was on vacation."

"No, I didn't need to." I pick my purse up from the floor and get out a sheet of paper. I start smiling. "So many good things have happened while you've been gone."

"You have a list?" Carol asks, looking surprised.

"Sure do." I shake the folds out of the paper. "Change #1. Ronnie went to the boys' Christmas program at school. He even traded nights with someone at work in order to be there."

"That's great. Is going to their activities one of the changes you had in mind?"

"Definitely. I've tried to get him to go to their events dressed in his work clothes so he can go straight to work afterwards. But he always has to be dressed up to go anyplace but work."

"Interesting."

"Change #2 – Ronnie only drank two beers at Chuck's on Christmas Eve. These were the best holidays we've had in years." I smile excitedly. "Christmas Day, we not only started out like a normal family by opening presents at seven a.m., but the boys wanted to stay home until mid-afternoon."

"Wanted to stay home instead of . . .?" Carol asks.

"Last year, they wanted to go to Kyle and Zach's as soon as the presents were open. They didn't want to deal with their Dad's bad mood and hangover, or have him yell at them for making noise with their new toys. I wished I could go with them."

"So, what did they do at home this year?"

I feel warm and fuzzy inside. "The four of us played Sorry, even though Ronnie hates board games. Then we took turns playing their new video games. After brunch, we went outside. We made snow angels and built a family of four snow people, including one that Ronnie put boobs on."

"Wow, sounds like a great day. Is there a Change #3?"

"Sure is! I finally got a present that isn't a kitchen appliance or clothing that makes me look like a hooker."

"Almost anything would be great compared to those two things. What is it?"

"A hot tub." I beam from ear to ear.

"Do you mean one of those portable Jacuzzis you use in the bathtub?"

"No! A real stand-alone hot tub with jets and everything. It's sitting on our patio right now."

Momentarily, Carol seems speechless. "I'm amazed."

"Ronnie's been saving his overtime for two years to buy it for me," I say proudly.

Carol looks through her notes. "Please correct me if I'm wrong, but I've gotten the impression that your finances are pretty tight."

My joy plummets. "You're not wrong," I say, quietly.

"Would you repeat that a little louder?"

"Our finances are tight," I answer, almost too loud. "My check goes for babysitting and groceries. He gives me $250 a week for the house payment and utilities. He saves the rest."

"What happens when you have an unexpected bill?"

"I give it to him, and he pays it out of his savings."

"Did you say *his* savings?"

"Yes." Feelings of resentment packed away deep inside me rumble and start inching their way to the surface. "My name isn't on that account."

"Do you remember tight control of finances being listed as one of the abuses of domestic violence?"

I nod my head. As anger rises out of the shrouded darkness within me, my face feels hot. "I do – now that you mention it."

"Do you think he actually saved his overtime to specifically buy you the hot tub? Or did he just decide to buy it out of his savings to impress you?"

"I hate these reality checks." I stand and walk to the bookcase, glancing at book titles on the spines. None of them register in my mind. "It's so much more romantic to believe he saved the money to buy me this present."

"I know it feels better, and I understand how badly you want it to be that way. But that isn't the truth, is it?"

"I guess not." I shift my weight back and forth to expend my growing agitation, and then I wander to the large bookcase in the corner, around her desk, and back to my chair. I feel Carol watching me.

"Are there more changes?"

"Yes, but I don't want to talk about them." My enthusiasm is gone. I look at the sheet of paper lying in my lap. *Changes? He's fooled me again!* I pick it up and give it a tear, a small one, then a larger one, then rip after rip, faster and faster into smaller pieces until it looks like it has been through a shredder. "Damn you, Ronnie! You've duped me again!" I dust the paper bits off of my lap into the trashcan.

"Sara, what else is going on?"

"Just a minute. I need to take some ibuprofen?" I take a deep breath as I get the pills out of my purse. "Last weekend, Aunt Lola and I went to Joplin to pick up the boys from Christmas vacation. Ronnie couldn't go because he had to work Friday night." Another drink barely dampens my dry mouth. When we got home on Sunday, Ronnie had dinner ready. After eating, he played video games with the boys while I unpacked."

I get up and move to a red chair that Carol has added to the décor since my last session. "When I turned the light on . . . in my closet . . ." My lip quivers. I bite it until I taste blood. "Ronnie's clothes filled the other side of it."

Carol looks sad. "Your expression tells me you didn't know he was moving back home. Is that true?"

I barely nod. "He moved his stuff back while I was in Joplin."

"Really? Had you and he talked about him moving home?"

"Very briefly. His nephew came home, and needed his room. There wasn't any place else for Ronnie to sleep at Chuck's."

Carol writes while I struggle.

My mind is empty, drained. "How do I get him out of the house again?"

"He could move a twin-sized bed into his nephew's room at Chuck's."

"Oh, he'll really be pissed if I ask him to do that." My energy drains as I resist the temptation to ignore my emotions so I won't feel them "He thinks everything's just hunky dory. I guess it is for him – as usual."

"Or he could move to an apartment," Carol says.

I brighten up a little. "He did say he'd get an apartment if I really don't think it's time for him to be home yet."

"Maybe it's time for another public discussion," Carol suggests.

My spirits lift. "Good idea. I can talk to him about it this next weekend. Friday is Derek's sixth birthday and the boys are spending Saturday night with Aunt Lola and Uncle Steve."

"I think another public discussion would be very beneficial. Now, let's finish talking about the three weeks between your appointments. I think a support group can be a very helpful resource for you."

Apprehensively, I ask, "What kind of support group?"

"First, let me say it's free and meets weekly. It's the battered women's support group at Rose Brooks."

"But– " I walk to the window. A few snowflakes are now mixing with the sleet. "I still have trouble accepting I'm a battered woman because he hasn't hit me."

"I understand. But think about how traumatized you and the boys were when Ronnie broke the bay window."

I turn around and face Carol. "I guess the only thing *missing* is the visible bruises on my skin." Tears moisten my dry eyes.

Carol goes to her desk. "With Ronnie moving home the way he did, I think it's imperative you go to the support group between our sessions." She flips pages in her planner. " It's been a long time since I've seen Monica, the facilitator of that group. Would you like for me to go with you to the meeting next Thursday, the 16th?"

I am amazed. "You'd do that for me? What about your family time?"

"It just so happens, my husband and son have Boy Scouts that night." She picks up a sheet of paper, walks over and stands beside me. "How about meeting me here at 6:45?" she asks, pointing to a spot on the map in her hand.

"All right. I'll give it a try, but I have to be home by 8:30. Ronnie has to get to work. He's on the night shift now."

"We make sure the meetings only last one hour."

I feel myself getting panicky. *Going there isn't concentrating on the positives! But the changes aren't real. I'll have to lie to Ronnie; no other choice.* I lean down and pick up a stray piece of my changes list and drop it into the trashcan. "I usually attend a Scout leaders meeting on the third Thursday of each month. And since none of them talk to Ronnie, I think its safe to let Ronnie assume that's where I'm going when I leave the house."

"So — is it a date?" She smiles at me, tapping the map with her pen.

"Yes . . . it's a date." I return her smile.

Chapter 20 – Derek's Birthday

> Nightmare Entry — 1/9/2003 — They've started again — had the "homeless" one last night.

With family and friends gathered around our dining room table, Derek rips open his birthday present from Aunt Lola and Uncle Steve. His eyes light up at the sight of a Scooby Doo Detective Kit. "Thanks you, guys," he says with his best smile.

"You're welcome," Uncle Steve tells him. "I found it in Chicago last week when I was there."

"Hey, Bro, can I see that?" Logan asks.

"From Mommy and Daddy," Derek reads from the tag of the next gift and tears into it. "Wow! My blue Power Ranger I didn't get for Christmas." He hands it to Logan and digs for the bottom of the box, anticipating cash, and he finds a $20 bill. "Just what I wanted!" He looks like he's about to burst with excitement. "How 'bout keeping this?" he says, shoving his money into my pocket. "Don't want it lost."

"Sure," I answer as I pass by him going to the kitchen. With candles glowing on top of the Spider-Man cake, I place it in front of Derek.

We sing "Happy Birthday" to him with the kids continuing, "and keep watching Scooby Doo on channel two." That puts a bigger grin on his six-year-old face because Scooby Doo is his favorite this week.

"Mommy, can we go spend my money tomorrow?"

"That's the plan," interjects Ronnie. "Then you're spending the night with your favorite aunt and uncle." Ronnie winks at me like he has special plans. Whatever they are, mine will override them.

> Journal Entry — 1/10/2003 — Things are going surprisingly well with Ronnie back home. The thing that really infuriates me is his assumption that I would accept his coming home without resistance. Wish I were strong

enough to physically pick him up and set him outside with all his stuff and change the locks so he can't get back in. That vision makes me giggle. Maybe I can sleep now.

***

On Saturday morning, as we walk through the bookstore toward the children's section, a 9/11 book display catches my eye. *Maybe one of these can help me keep the nightmares away.*

"Logan, would you help Derek look at books? I'll be there in a minute."

"Sure, Mommy." Logan slings his arm around Derek's shoulder. "Come on, little buddy, let's find you a real Power Rangers book."

My pulse speeds up as I read bits of survivor stories in a book titled Before and After Stories From New York. *This could give me some answers. Can't let Ronnie see it though. He'll be accusing me of wanting to keep having the nightmares.*

"Look, Mommy! Logan found me a *real* Power Rangers book! He's a great brother."

"Yeah. I found it behind the baby books." Logan grins from ear to ear and stands taller.

On the way to the car with his hand in mine, Derek says, "I'm so happy, my inside kitty is purring."

***

Standing on Aunt Lola's front porch, I tell her, "Thanks a bunch for keeping the boys tonight."

"My pleasure, Sara. We'll bring them home tomorrow around four."

Aunt Lola takes my hand and pats it. "Good luck talking with Ronnie."

"Thanks. Talk to you later."

Before the car door closes, Ronnie not too gently pulls me over to him for a kiss. "You sure look gorgeous tonight. How about the Red Lobster?" He gives me a seductive smile.

***

"I like sitting side by side in a booth," Ronnie says, indicating he wants me to scoot over.

I smile weakly and move over. *I don't like being cornered in here.* "What are you having tonight?" I ask.

"Think I'll have shrimp and then you for dessert." He puts a couple of tender kisses on my cheek.

"How about ordering the blackened catfish, baked potato, and salad with honey-mustard dressing for me?" I nudge him to move out of my way. "I've really got to go to the bathroom – right now!"

He stands up. "Hurry back, my sweet. I'll miss you," he announces very loud.

Leaning against the stall door eases my nervousness. *Gotta move away from him. Too hard to talk about him getting an apartment with him being so close.* I take several long, deep breaths. *God, I'm counting on you to help me choose the right words. Give me courage.*

"I love their cheese biscuits here," I say, as I sit down on the other side of the booth.

"Why are you sitting way over there?" he asks, as I pull my silverware and napkin across the table.

"More elbow room," I say, flapping my arms like a bird. "Wouldn't want to give you a shiner with one of these." I give him my best smile. I don't have any small talk in me.

Ronnie looks around the restaurant and says, "Look at that big, fat woman over there. She must weigh 400 pounds. How can someone let themselves go like that?"

"Some people do have medical conditions that cause weight gain. Remember Aunt Elly taking Prednisone for years. That caused her to look fat."

Instead of responding to me, Ronnie drones on and on about overweight people as if he hasn't said any of it before. I close the sound of his voice away slowly until the waiter sets our food in front of us.

After several bites, Ronnie asks, "How's your catfish?"

"Good." I can almost feel my blood pressure soar as I say, "Ronnie, we need to finish talking about you moving back home."

He slams his fork down on his plate, popping a knife into the air, which clanks loudly to the floor. He smiles through gritted teeth. People in nearby chairs turn their heads to stare at him. "We already talked about it, and you agreed." Customers look at us curiously.

"We *briefly* talked about it, and you said you'd find a different place to live if I'm not ready."

"Damn counselor's idea. Isn't it?" His chin juts out.

"I won't lie to you. I did discuss it with Carol, but– "

"I knew it!" His fist pounds the booth seat where I had been sitting earlier. Heads turn again. He stares at his platter.

"Since you moved back home, the boys are fighting more. You and I aren't talking as much as we were. I feel we're losing the ground we've gained."

His jaw softens as he scoots shrimp around on his plate.

"We have made some good changes, and I'd like to keep them," I say. "Don't you?"

A devious smile slowly spreads across his face. "It's your turn to move out."

The fine hairs on the back of my neck rise. I cross my left knee over my right and swing my foot to dispel my nervousness. " I guess I could stay with Aunt Lola and Uncle Steve for a while." I squirm in the seat, which suddenly seems hard. "Let's see . . . you could get the boys up and off to school when you get home from work in the mornings. But who would be with them through the night?"

"They should go to Aunt Lola's with you."

"They'd have to change schools."

"No, they wouldn't if you drop them off at the sitter before you go to work, like you do now."

"I'd have to get them up at 5:30 to drive the extra twenty miles and me get to work on time."

He stares into space.

I pray.

"Guess you moving out won't work." He lets out a big sigh. "It's going to take time and a lot of money to find a place. Is that what you want me to do?"

"Or . . . you and Cody could sleep shifts in his bed," I say with a broad smile, trying to lighten the charged atmosphere.

He tries to hide his amusement. "That would be impossible on the weekends." His smile slowly dissipates as he stares into my eyes. "It definitely will take a while to find a place."

"I really hate to ask you this, but . . ." I scrunch up my face as if in pain. "Can we take the hot tub back?"

"You don't like it?" he asks, looking shocked.

"I absolutely love it! Best present you've ever given me. But that money could be a deposit and several months' rent on your apartment."

He sits back in his side of the booth. "Sounds like you've thought this all through."

I move around the table and scoot him into the corner. "Honey, I want things to work out between us so badly, I'm willing to do whatever it takes. You and our marriage are so much more important than the hot tub. My heart swells with joy every time I think about you saving overtime to buy it for me."

"I'll call the salesman tomorrow or next week," he whispers in my ear. "Let's go play naked in the hot tub."

> Journal Entry — 1/12/2003 — I'm proud of myself for going through with the talk. I'm surprised Ronnie didn't resist another separation any more than he did when he moved to Chuck's. If he'd ever been unfaithful, I would suspect he has a girlfriend, but he's never given me any indications of being unfaithful. He did start fishing more last summer and has only caught fish one time. He says just sitting on the bank watching the bobber reminds him of when he and Grandpa used to fish together. And they didn't catch fish very often either. What really matters is that he is going to be out of the house again soon.

Chapter 21 – Other Women Like Me

I wait at the intersection Carol pointed to on the map at my last counseling session. Shakily I turn the radio knob, scanning for music to calm me down. I pause on a classical station and decide if she isn't here by the end of the long sonata, I'll leave and go home.

As I start my engine, I hear a car horn honk. I look around and see a car going the opposite direction, but stopped. *That's not the back of Carol's head. Hair's too short.* The driver turns to look at me. Reluctantly, I roll the window down.

"Sara, I'll wait while you turn around so you can follow me," she says and gives me a big smile.

"Okay . . ." I look down the empty street, thinking of escape as I put the car in drive. Instead I say, "I'll be right back."

A half-mile from our meeting spot, I see a large compound surrounded by a ten-foot-high iron fence. Driving by, I've often wondered what this place was. Now it makes sense why there are no signs identifying it. Carol stops at the large front gate and says something into a speaker box on a post. She puts her arm out the window and motions for me to follow her. I almost rear-end her when she stops as soon as the back of my car is clear of the gate. When it closes, we park our cars.

Walking toward the building, Carol says, "We pause like that at the entry so no other cars can sneak through behind us."

"That seems a little extreme for a battered women's shelter."

"There was an abuser who found out his wife was here and managed to get through the gate behind someone. Thank goodness the security guard saw him and called the police. The locked doors of the building kept him out until the police arrived. Then a few days later he shot and killed his wife when she was picking their children up at school."

I shudder.

At the main door of the building, Carol pushes a button and a friendly woman's voice from the speaker box says, "May I help you?"

Carol answers, "This is Sara and Carol. We're here for support group." The heavy lock clangs loose and Carol opens the door.

As we enter a small conference room, a woman flies out of her chair and gives Carol a hug. One of two women seated at a round table smiles at me. The other one keeps her head down. Carol and I sit down at the table, which has a few bottles of water and a tissue box in the center.

"Hello, Faith. How are you?" Carol asks looking at the woman who hasn't looked up yet. She slowly raises her head and her face is drawn and haggard.

"Hello, Carol," she says without expression. "I'm okay . . . I guess."

"I'm glad to see you and am anxious to find out how things are going," Carol says.

A thirty-something woman with waist-length blonde hair and green eyes enters as I write my name on a sign-in sheet being passed around the table. "Hello, everyone," she says, exchanging smiles with Carol as she sits.

"First, we have a couple of business items to attend to," Monica continues. "I'd like to tell Sara and remind everyone else about maintaining confidentially of the group. Anything said in this room stays in this room. This ensures everyone can speak freely and say what needs to be said." Everyone else is nodding their heads and I join them. "Also, no one is required to talk. It's okay to just listen."

That's good 'cause I'm not talking to these strangers. I slip my shoes off, rubbing my feet against each other.

"Carol, please tell us who you are and why we have the pleasure of your company tonight."

"Okay. I used to be a counselor here at Rose Brooks, and I facilitated this group before Monica." Carol turns towards me. "But tonight, I'm here as support for Sara."

I look around the table. None of the women look like domestic violence victims. A heavy sigh escapes me.

"Nice to have you here tonight," Monica says. She turns her focus to the woman who had hugged Carol "Kristen, how did your court date go?"

Kristen runs her fingers through her short, spiked, dark hair. "I got my restraining order renewed another six months. (Appendix F)

But like the two previous hearings, Judge Hamerle ordered me to show him the pictures of my injuries – again. And . . . I had to remind him Michael is out on bail until his assault trial. I couldn't keep doing this if my court advocate wasn't with me for moral and legal support." She rubs her hair and it sticks up more.

"Due to my experiences in Judge Hamerle's court, I've changed my major to law instead of business," Kristen says. "I am going to be an attorney and help women in abusive situations." Everyone congratulates her.

Monica nods at Carol.

"Faith, how about an update?" Carol asks.

She looks up and clears her throat. "Tavio is still calling me every day and night multiple times, begging me to bring Lily and come home. One night last week, we decided to not answer his calls. Then the doorbell rang and the banging on the door was so loud I thought he was going to break in. I was afraid the neighbors would call the police, so I unlocked it. Soon as it unlatched, Tavio shoved his way in, yelling obscenities and calling Lily and me awful names." Tears flow. Someone scoots the tissue box closer to her.

"I'm pretty much numb to the name calling and horrible things he says to me." She blows her nose. "What really hurts is him calling his own 17-year-old daughter a slut and whore. Before leaving, he threatened her with physical violence if she doesn't answer her phone every time he calls."

"Have you considered a restraining order?" someone asks.

"Yeah, I have, but I just don't have the energy." She slumps down in her chair like a deflating balloon.

"Faith, it may seem as though you're treading water waiting for graduation, but you're not," Carol tells her. "When you first came to the group, you wouldn't do anything to stand up for yourself. I'm impressed that you and Lily have gained the courage to make a stand against Tavio." Faith straightens up slightly.

Carol continues, "Soon as Lily is handed her diploma in May, I'm sure the strategies you've learned here, as well as the strengths you've gained, will come to fruition and Tavio will be history."

"Thanks, Carol." She semi-smiles as she stares at her lap.

Smiling at a young woman who looks like she's still in her teens, Monica says "Julie, we've not seen you for a long time."

"I know. It's been a little more than a year. Things were going so well with Dr. Jekyll. I believed Mr. Hyde would never come back again, but he did just like I was warned he would. Then, the abuse started again a little over a week ago." She clamps her lips tight and swallows hard. "He didn't want me to go out to dinner with my sister. As I was walking out of his apartment, he kicked me in the back of my calf." Julie gingerly stands and pulls her long skirt up above her knee, revealing a large, deep purple bruise.

I draw in a startled, smothered gasp.

"Is your leg going to be okay?" Carol asks. "It looks pretty serious."

"Yes, but it'll take a while. Nolan's steel-toed boot caused a bone bruise. I went to the emergency room with it." She smiles slightly. "When I told the doctor what had happened, he asked if I wanted to talk with a domestic violence advocate. I told him 'no, thanks' because I would come back to the support group here at Rose Brooks. The doctor wrote detailed descriptions of my injuries and took a lot of photos documenting everything for Nolan's assault trial."

"I'm so proud of you for pressing charges against him," says Monica.

"Thanks," Julie answers. She sits down gently.

"When my sister took me to his apartment to get my things, Nolan kept apologizing and trying to make it sound like an accident. I didn't say a word. Just laid his apartment key on a table and walked out of Mr. Hyde's life forever."

"Sara, you look confused. Is it Julie's referrals to Nolan as Dr. Jekyll and Mr. Hyde?" Monica asks.

I nod.

"Women who are abused often use the terms Jekyll and Hyde to differentiate between the two men they live with." (Appendix G)

"Oh. I recently heard a woman at church say that about her husband. But I couldn't figure out what she was talking about because I know their last name isn't Hyde," I tell them.

"I saw the Jekyll and Hyde musical about a month ago," Kristen says. "The play ends with one half of the actor's face made up as Dr. Jekyll and the other half as Mr. Hyde's. By flicking the stage lights and quick turns of his head, Jekyll's face appears less and less often until Hyde was all that was left. It was a great visual of how our men can change from the man we love to an abuser in the blink of an eye."

"So what makes them switch?" I ask.

"Their need for power and control," answers Carol.

I take a bottle of water. "I thought I was the only woman living with two men in one body."

"You're definitely not the only one," says Julie. "My sister suggested I refer to Nolan as Jekyll and Hyde when I'm talking about him because that keeps the reality of what he actually is in the forefront of my mind."

"How have you been doing since you ended the relationship?" Carol asks.

Okay . . . mostly." Her bottom lip quivers. "Sometimes it takes all the strength I have to not answer his calls. I really miss the good times with him."

Monica gets up and walks to a large flip pad on an easel in the corner of the room. "Ladies, do you have any suggestions of how Julie can resist answering Nolan's calls?"

"Go for a walk and leave your cell phone at home," says Kristen. "I've had to do that myself."

Monica writes ideas on the flipchart as they are mentioned. The pros and cons of each idea are discussed.

"Take pictures of that bruise," Carol recommends. "Put them by every phone in your house. And, use one of them as his contact photo on your cell phone."

After more discussion about the ideas, Monica tears the sheet of paper off of the pad. "These are some good ideas. Julie, do you think any of these might work?" Monica hands the page to Julie.

"Yes, especially the bruise photo on my cell phone. I'll probably have to use all of them to resist talking to him and going back again. Thanks."

"You are welcome," everyone says together.

Monica pulls pages from her briefcase and hands the stack to Julie, who takes one and passes them on. When Carol hands them to me, she softly says, "I'd recommend you leave these at work where Ronnie can't see them." I see the title is "Why Women Stay." (Appendix H)

"Sara, just a FYI," Monica says, "as various subjects are discussed in our group, I have information sheets in my brief case to pass out. If you have a safe place to keep them, please take one. If not, please call the 314-HOT-LINE with your questions. It is answered 24/7."

Julie holds her page up in the air. 'These and the hot line have really helped me refocus and remember why I'm no longer with Nolan."

All eyes turn toward me.

"It's okay to not share your story if you'd rather not," Carol says.

Guess I'll tell them a little bit. I shift around and straighten up in my chair. "I'm okay and talking a little might be good for me." I smile at Carol. "I've been married 11 years, have two sons, six and almost nine. I was so scared of coming here tonight I was chickening out and leaving when Carol arrived."

Faith rejoins the conversation. "I drove away from the gate three times. Finally, a friend brought me and waited outside the gate until the meeting was over. You're in the right place." She keeps her head up and finally seems interested.

"I thought you looked pretty panic stricken," Carol says, looking at me. "How are you now?"

"Ummm . . . not as scared." I smile weakly. "When I came here tonight, I was sure I wouldn't talk, but my curiosity about Jekyll and Hyde got the best of me. It's comforting to know I'm not the only person living with two men in one body." I frown. "I've never been hit by my husband. But his threats that he's going to hit me are happening more often. Our discussions, as he calls them, turns into filibusters by him about everything he hates – blacks, illegals from Mexico living on our tax dollars, women's lib, and anything else he happens to be mad about. I don't dare walk away from him during these tirades."

"You've come to the right place," says Monica. "Please continue."

"We've been separated once before, and everything was going great." I pause, sigh and notice I've slumped. I straighten up and finish with, "He moved back, but has agreed to move out again because I'm not ready for him to be there."

Monica looks at her watch. “Sara, I’m sorry to interrupt you but it’s time to end our meeting. We hope you’ll come back. Everyone gathers their things.

Women give each other hugs and chitchat on the way out the door. Some leave quickly; others linger. Carol visits with Monica.

“Sara, I’m so glad you came tonight,” Faith says from behind me. “Sounds like our situations are similar, except my daughter is a teenager. I think we can be good for each other. Please come back next week.”

“I’ll try.”

> Journal Entry — 1/21/2003 — Ronnie’s drinking is still limited to mostly weekends, and he isn’t getting hammered. That sobriety checkpoint on Christmas Eve has stopped his drinking and driving. Me going to a support group is something I didn’t think I’d ever do. Ronnie’s always been so against counseling and sharing our problems with anyone else that I assumed he was right. Also, I thought I had been doing my own thinking, but journaling and counseling are showing me I don’t do anything without first trying to anticipate what Ronnie’s reaction is going to be. That in itself is very stressful. He controls way too many areas of my life. I can only read one or two survivor stories at a time in my 9/11 book because they generate such intense emotions in me. The question is still “Why?” I have learned from Carol that stress, emotions, and nightmares are intertwined, but what is the thread that runs through them? Almost midnight, have to get to sleep.

Chapter 22 – Pinewood Derby

I pour myself a cup of coffee and sit down on a kitchen stool on the opposite side of the counter from Ronnie. He has a stormy look on his face but I'm running out of time. My choices are to either ask him to help Logan with his Pinewood Derby car or use Ronnie's jigsaw. The boys and I have been forbidden to even touch any of his tools. He says we lose them but he's the one that doesn't put them back where they belong. I gulp down a swallow of coffee that burns my tongue. I go to the sink for cold water to cool it down. I hear Ronnie laugh under his breath seeming to enjoy my pain. *Rather than talk to him, I'll chance using the jigsaw.* I walk past him and go to wake the boys.

As I walk back into the kitchen, Ronnie has the rectangular wooden block in his hand turning it over and over. "Looks like Pinewood Derby time."

"In one week." I sit and take a sip of coffee. "I've been wondering if you'd help Logan saw that into a facsimile of a car. Maybe you can do it when he gets home from school today."

"Yeah, sure." A sadness steals some light from his eyes.

"What's wrong? I thought you'd enjoy doing this."

"Just wishing my Dad had helped me with my car the short time I was in Cub Scouts." A smile returns as he says, "It'll be fun doing this with Logan."

***

"After working so hard on my car, I want two Happy Meals," Logan announces as we walk through the front door of McDonald's.

"Hey, Squirt, what do you want?" Ronnie asks Derek.

"I'll take nuggets. Slides, here I come," Derek squeals as he runs toward the playground.

After eating, the boys climb and slide. I struggle for something to say to ease the heavy tension hanging between Ronnie and me. When I return from the restroom, I sit down beside him. Being close to him doesn't feel as good as I was hoping for. "Looks like you and Logan have a good design on that derby car." I'm having trouble giving up on the idea that if I give him unconditional love, and forgive him enough times for his bad behavior that he'll have a light bulb turn on above his head and magically return to the wonderful man I married.

Ronnie brightens. "He wanted a big windshield cut into it. But after scratching out some designs and talking about aerodynamics, he chose sleek and fast over having a windshield. It'll be interesting to see if it wins any races."

* * *

"Daddy, Daddy, look, look. I won!" Logan struts into the living room holding his first place trophy in the air.

"Congratulations. Let me see," beams Ronnie. "We did it son; we did it together." He puts his arm around Logan's shoulders as he sits down on the sofa.

"Wish you'd been there tonight, Daddy."

"Me, too, but I've got to go to work."

"But you're still here," Logan says, frowning. Ronnie glances at me as though I am supposed to answer Logan's unasked question. I shrug my shoulders, leaving Ronnie in the hot seat.

"I know . . . but I had to get rested."

"Oh . . . I guess," Logan says sadly. "Where's a safe place to put my trophy and car? The car has to stay exactly the same for the big race at the mall!"

Ronnie looks at me perplexed.

"A week from Saturday Logan's pack is racing against the Raytown pack at Blue Ridge Mall."

"Oh." Ronnie looks at Logan. "What do you mean the car has to stay the same?"

"It's one of the rules. The only thing we can do before the race is put more graphite on the wheels – after we get to the mall."

"How about putting them on the divider shelf?" Ronnie suggests.

The four of us go into the dining room. Ronnie lifts Logan up to put the car and trophy between spindles. "They outta be safe here." The two of them look as though they've just won the Indy 500.

Ronnie grabs me with one arm and with the other one around Logan, pulls us into a group hug. Derek squeezes into the middle saying, "Hey, let me in here." As I step back to make room for Derek, I notice dark circles under Ronnie's eyes that are a testament of his increasing drinking.

Chapter 23 – Out of Control

"Has Ronnie ever followed through with any of his threats?" Carol asks, as we start our session.

"Uhm, I'm not sure."

"I know he threatens to hit you, but hasn't – yet. Do you remember a specific time when you believed he was going to?"

"Yeah . . . one time when I told him I wasn't going to continue our conversation until he quit yelling at me. When I started to walk out of the kitchen, he jumped off the stool and blocked the doorway." I wring my hands. When I realize what I'm doing, I pull them apart and make them lay in my lap. "Then he poked his finger on my chest, saying, 'Bitch, you're not leaving till I'm done talking.' I backed around the counter and sat down. Leaning over me, he added, 'You damn well better never, ever try walking out on me again.' Then, he walked out of the room." I wait while Carol finishes writing.

"How long ago was that?"

"Years, I guess. I must have gone into shock because all I could do was sit there for a long, long time."

"I can hear in your voice how much that still frightens you. Has he ever tried to stop you from leaving the house?"

"Yeah. About two years ago, he had been tolerating me going to a weekly Bible study. One night when I came down the stairs to leave, he was standing by the front door. I thought he wanted a goodbye kiss." I shiver. "I picked up my purse and Bible from the end table, expecting him to move out of the way. As I walked toward him, I saw the veins in his neck were pumped out and his eyes were full of anger. Cautiously, I backed myself away from him inches at a time. He said, 'I'm damn sick and tired of the idiotic ideas those bitches are putting in your head.' He snatched my Bible from my hands, opened it, ripped several pages out, and threw them into the air." I pause to take deep breaths. "A hard, terrible grin spread across his face as he held my Bible out in front of him with both hands, and his face contorted as he struggled to rip it in half."

Carol waits, then asks, "Did you go or stay home?"

"I went. I don't know if it was the physical exertion or the failure of his attempt, but he threw my Bible on the floor, walked away, plopped on the couch, and started flipping through channels as if nothing had happened." I walk to the window to absorb peace from nature before I tell Carol the next part. "I was so upset and exasperated that I didn't think I could handle living with Ronnie anymore and started thinking about . . . suicide."

"What stopped you?" I hear gentleness in Carol's voice.

"I tried to remember a road high enough to run my car off of so it would look like an accident. Then I thought about the possibility of it not killing me. What if I became paralyzed or something awful like that, then the boys and I would be at Ronnie's complete mercy, of which he doesn't have any." I turn toward Carol. "Next thing I know, I'm parking in front of Naomi's house."

"Did you tell your friends what happened?"

"Yes. We discussed my options, prayed, and, I guess out of instinct, made a safety plan. Tracy's husband is a police officer. I was to call her when I got home and, if things were okay, we'd just say goodnight. If they weren't, I was to tell her I couldn't make the meeting and that was a signal for her husband to come check on me." I sit down on a couch instead of my usual chair. "When I got home, my Bible was laying on the end table again with the ripped out pages back inside it – in the right order. I took that as Ronnie's apology, and we moved into the honeymoon phase for quite a while."

Carol studies my face for so long, I start to feel uncomfortable. "These two incidents are good examples of resetting boundaries with Ronnie," she says.

"Boundaries?"

"When you're in a crowded elevator and someone gets off, do you stay in the same spot or shift positions?

"If there's space, I move, even if it's just a little bit. I like elbow room."

"That's called personal space, and we all need it. People shift positions to reset physical boundaries around themselves." Carol smiles mischievously. "I've purposefully not moved as elevators empty of passengers, and it's amazing to watch the looks on people's faces. They range from no expression at all to anger.

"That sounds like fun. I'll try it sometime."

"Fun aside, everyone also needs emotional boundaries. In domestic violence relationships, abusers and victims tend to have weak or no boundaries at all."

"Can they be reset like physical boundaries can?" I hear aggravation in my voice.

"Yes, emotional boundaries can be reset." Carol's face is more serious than usual. "You trying to leave the kitchen when Ronnie was yelling at you was a good attempt at resetting a boundary."

"But it didn't work." I feel exasperated.

"True. But when you went to your Bible study despite Ronnie's bullying, it was a start. Did you keep going each week thereafter?"

"Yes, yes I did." I glow inside. "I was successful that time, wasn't I?"

"Yes, you definitely were. You also succeeded in setting several boundaries when you asked for each of the separations, and those succeeded. I am proud of you!"

"Thanks, Carol."

"Are you ready to retry setting the boundary of not listening to his yelling?"

"That seems impossible!"

"It may seem that way, but think of how many things will change if you succeed. Let's break it down into steps to see what we can come up with."

Carol's smile encourages me. "Okay. What's first?"

"Which do you think will work best – stating your boundary to him or writing it in a letter?"

"Since the verbal attempt didn't work before, I want to try doing it in a letter."

"Good choice. And what will the consequences be if he continues yelling?"

"I'd like to walk out, but that didn't work before either."

"Isn't it the kitchen where he yells at you most often?"

"Almost always."

"If you position yourself close to the back door, you can make an exit to a different room or out of the house."

I brighten. "Hadn't thought of that."

"If Ronnie continues yelling, you calmly and strongly restate your boundary and leave."

"I don't know, Carol. This seems like something that might make him hit me."

"You are right. It could. But I think you have great instincts and will know when and if you should attempt to set this boundary." Carol pulls several stapled pages from the folder in her lap and hands them to me. "Here are some guidelines for writing a letter. If you consistently react with the response you state in your letter, Ronnie will see that his tactics and intimidations aren't working, and I believe he will gradually quit yelling at you."

"This sounds like training a child," I say, half joking because this conversation is making me so uncomfortable.

Carol's seriousness does not waver. "In a lot of ways it is, but the difference is that abusers are grown men who can injure you, so caution and planning are essential in setting boundaries with them."

"That's true." I feel embarrassed by what I said.

"Sara, I see this is getting a little overwhelming for you. You don't have to do this now or ever if you don't feel safe doing it. Take a look at the information, and we can talk about this again if you decide you want to follow through with it."

Chapter 24 – A Spaghetti Ladle

Alarm didn't go off! When my bare feet touch the hardwood floor, the coldness jars me awake. Then I remember – it's Saturday! No noise is coming from downstairs, so I snuggle back under the covers for a little more sleep.

Logan yelling "Daddy's home!" from downstairs rouses me out of my dream-state.

Later in the morning at the Blue Ridge Mall, twenty-one pinewood derby cars of imaginative designs and paint jobs line up on a table in front of the trophies. After a feast of hot dogs, chips, and drinks, two boys at a time restlessly stand at the starting line, waiting to hear the Cub Master say, "Gentlemen! Start your engines!"

I feel a tug on my shirt sleeve. I look down at Derek. "Mommy, I don't hear any engines. Why did that guy say that?"

"There aren't any engines because the cars are made of blocks of wood. But the Cub Master saying, 'Start your engines,' is his way of telling the scouts to be ready."

"Oh," Derek says. "Rrrmmm, rrrrrmmm" he adds under his breath.

I smile as I look back at the race. The green flag drops and each boy releases a lever that allows gravity to pull their masterpieces down a sloped ramp toward the finish line.

Some of the cars zip to the checkered squares, others creep, a few stall at various points along the way. Moans move through the crowd as losers are handed back their cars. Cheers liven up the crowd as the winners' cars are placed closer to the trophies setting on the table.

Joyfully, Logan's #8 outpaces its competitor by a full one and a half inches. After several more rounds of races, #8 has only raced once. Suddenly the Cub Master announces, "Race fans, we're ready for the finals!"

Ronnie jumps up. "Wait a minute! Wait just one minute. My son's car has only raced one time."

"What? Are you sure?" asks the Cub Master.

"I'm absolutely sure," Ronnie says as he jogs to the scorekeeper's table joining the Cub Master and judges.

I see tears building in Logan's eyes as he sits on the edge of his chair on the other side of Derek. He looks panicked as he glances back and forth between his Dad and me. Derek reaches over and hooks his finger in Logan's front pocket. "It's going to be okay. Daddy's gonna fix it." Time stands still as we wait, wait, and wait for a whole minute.

When the men come out of their huddle, the Cub Master announces, "Mr. Farley is right. Car #8 has run only one time. Because of our limited time here at the mall, it's been decided that #8's running time would have put him in place to race the top three cars."

Logan wipes away tears on his shirtsleeve as he runs to the starting line. Car #8 outpaces the 4th place car by two inches. Logan gives us a thumbs-up sign.

The 3rd place car bites the dust with #8 leading by one-half inch. I scoot to the edge of my chair. Logan is bouncing on his toes. Derek sits beside me with all of his fingers crossed and probably his toes, too. Ronnie is standing as close to the finish line as he is allowed.

Logan and Ronnie's forgotten car is now racing for the first place trophy. Logan and his opponent stare each other down for a moment like gunfighters before a shoot-out. The crowd of Scout families and a few mall shoppers is quiet.

"Gentlemen! S-t-a-r-t your engines!" The green flag drops.

Car #8 moves slightly ahead. Car #12 moves up even, right before the finish line.

Puzzled looks on the faces of the judges at the finish line silences the cheers. They and the Cub Master lumber over to the scorekeeper's table, talking quietly as they go. Ronnie starts to follow, but the Cub Master waves him away. Ronnie comes to sit with us, a stormy look on his face.

With everyone back in their places, the Cub Master tells us, "The judges say it was a tie. We're going to race for first place one more time."

Cheers start for #12 as it moves ahead. Number 8 catches up, and simultaneously they hit the checkered squares. The judges and Cub Master confer again while the crowd murmurs.

As the men turn toward the race fans, they are all smiles. "Ladies and gentlemen, we are proud to announce we have two first place winners this year!" The crowd goes wild.

***

"Can we have spaghetti tonight, Mommy?" Logan asks as we walk in our front door.

"Sure. And ice cream to celebrate."

The boys play in Logan's room. Since Ronnie didn't get any sleep when he got home from work at six a.m., he naps on the sofa. From the kitchen, I hear his cell phone ring. When he answers, his voice is groggy. I hear him say, "What the hell …" as he goes out the front door. I figure its Chuck calling to see if Ronnie's going to their house to drink tonight. He's been doing that more the last couple of weeks. Doesn't make sense though that he went outside to talk to Chuck. Wouldn't be Brian because Ronnie's mad at Nicole for "interfering" in our business. Ronnie says if Brian had kept Nicole in line that day, the bay window wouldn't have gotten broken.

With Italian sausage browning in a skillet, I pour spaghetti seasoning into the tomato paste bubbling on a burner. "What the hell are you doing?" Ronnie yells at me from the kitchen door.

I jump. I accidentally touch the heated pot with my finger. "Fixing dinner. What do you think I'm doing?" I answer sternly. I suck on my burned finger.

"You're supposed to put the seasoning in the meat, not the sauce!" he says in a thunderous voice.

"The spice goes in the meat for chili and the sauce for spaghetti," I answer strongly.

Is he right? Am I doing it wrong? Too late, it's already in the sauce.

With my back turned to him, I hear him pull a stool from under the counter and sit down. Suddenly I feel a rush of air and hear something whiz past my ear. WHAM! Out of the corner of my eye, I glimpse the spaghetti ladle careening off the cabinet and smashing into Logan's newest trophy, sending it and the championship car crashing to the floor.

Derek and Logan come running. My mind goes numb. I spin around. Ronnie glares at me. "Woman, you'd better start doing what I say or you'll be picking yourself up off the floor."

I run past the monster into the dining room and drop to the floor between the boys. The upset inside me is great, too great for anger or tears, so my emotions transform into numbness.

"It's broken!" wails Logan. "My big trophy is broken."

Ronnie stomps past us with his focus zoomed in on Logan. "Shut up, brat. It's only plastic."

"Mommy, can we paste it together?" Derek asks, with sympathy tears coating his cheeks.

"Yes, we can glue it back together." I pick up one of the pieces but it slips from my fingers. Derek picks it up and hands it to me as I fumble for the other half. Shakily I hold them up. "Look, see how the pieces fit back together."

"But it's broken. It'll never be the same. It's a trophy, not just plastic," sobs Logan.

"You're right! It is a first place trophy! We'll fix it right after dinner," I promise him.

Sitting in front of the TV in our usual places, the boys and I eat almost nothing as Ronnie gorges himself. Logan gags on his spaghetti a couple of times and looks at me helplessly. We both know we dare not say anything because it might ignite Ronnie's fury again.

After eating, the boys and I sit at the kitchen counter and glue the trophy pieces back together. But it has a chink out of the side of it – just like our hearts. "Why don't you go play in your rooms?" I tell them as I pick up our repair supplies.

"Okay," Logan says as he hugs me and whispers, "I want Mean Daddy to go back to Uncle Chuck's."

His words jolt my mind back into gear. *Oh my God, he's right. Why hasn't Ronnie moved out like he agreed? I can't just let this slide. He actually threw something at ME!*

I go upstairs where I won't be overheard. I dial the number at Zach's house. "Joyce, this is Sara."

"Hi Sara. That sure was an exciting win today."

"Sure was. I have something I have to go do tonight. I'm wondering if the boys can spend the night with Zach and I'll pick them up at church in the morning."

"Zach would love that. Bring them on down."

"Thank you, Joyce. I really appreciate this."

"Sara, are you okay? Your voice sounds funny."

"Yeah, I'm okay. Just allergies acting up. "We'll be there in a few minutes."

When I go into the boys' room, they are absorbed in racing Matchbox cars against the wooden block of #8 without any wheels. "How would you two like to spend the night at Zach's tonight?"

"That would be great, Mommy," Logan smiles with his eyes still red.

"Yeah! Logan won. Logan won," Derek practices cheering.

"I'm going to pick you up at church tomorrow, so get clean clothes to take with you." They scramble, throwing clothes into their backpacks.

As I open the front door, Ronnie glances away from the TV.

"I'm taking the boys to Zach's."

"Yeah, fine," he says, glaring at the three of us.

* * *

After dropping the boys off, I go sit in a small neighborhood restaurant. I can't stand being in the same house as Ronnie while I pull myself together. I shake so badly I spill hot chocolate on my hand. "Damn, that's hot," I mutter to myself. *Have to get his attention diverted from the TV long enough to talk to him about what he did. How can the man who says he loves me THROW something at me? What do I say to get him to understand how upsetting this was for the boys and I? If I have to leave suddenly . . . I'll put keys, license and money in my pockets. Might need a coat since it's February.*

"Ma'am, ma'am," says a voice.

"Huh, what?"

"Is this your scarf that was on the floor?"

"Oh, thanks."

Where was I? A coat. I look at my watch. *Game should be about over. Don't think I can do this. Was he aiming for my head? I have to do this.* I walk out of the restaurant with a resolve to confront Mr. Hyde, who has reappeared in my house.

* * *

"What took ya so long?" Ronnie asks as I walk through the front door.

"Talking to Joyce," I answer, heading to the kitchen on shaky legs.

Wish I had that safety plan that's in my drawer at work . . . coat, have to put a coat in the car without him seeing me . . . confronting him in the living room gives me an escape route out of either the front or back doors . . . gotta feed the dog . . . ten minutes left in the game.

I get a coat from the bedroom closet, walk down the stairs, stepping to the side of the creaky step, and go out the back door and around the side of the house. I lay my coat on the hood of the car. I don't want to chance Ronnie seeing the dome light go on and off through the new glass in the bay window. As I retrace my steps into the back yard, I call for our dog. "Pepper, where are you?" Shortly, she appears out of the darkness under the porch light as I sit down in a chair. "There you are, sweet thing," I coo while rubbing her inch-thick, black, curly hair. "Girl, tonight I wish you were a Doberman so you could protect me from Ronnie if he hits me." I walk to the food bin, scoop dog food out, and place it in her food bowl. I check to be sure her water isn't frozen. "God, in Jesus' name I ask you to help me say and do the right things as I confront that man in my house . . . that man I don't know any more."

Inside the kitchen, I sit on a stool, listening for the end of the basketball game. I force myself to breathe deeply. *Gotta do this. Carol says I'm a strong woman. Have to do it for the boys.* I feel a resilience growing in me that builds my courage.

I hear the announcer on the TV say, "Final score, 74 to 71 with KU winning this one." Propelled by sheer will power, I go into the living room and turn off the TV.

"What the hell?" the tyrant asks, as I turn to face him.

"We're going to talk about that ladle and the broken trophy is what the hell."

His Cheshire Cat grin appears, which, for a change, increases my resolve instead of irritating me. "Oh, that," the Cat answers.

"Why'd you throw that ladle at me?"

"'Cause you didn't stop putting the spice in the sauce like I told you to."

"That's no reason to throw it at me."

"I threw it at the cabinet, not you!"

"Why get violent about how I'm cooking?"

"Violent? You think that was violent?" he asks, standing up.

I move closer to the front door. "When are you going to get an apartment like we agreed?" I try to keep the shakiness out of my voice.

He comes two steps closer. "Agreed? I never agreed! *YOU* told me to move out."

"No, I didn't. When we talked about another separation at Red Lobster – we both agreed."

"It's bad enough I have to put up with that butch, lesbo dispatcher barking orders at me so I can keep my job." He stands right in front of me with a blackness about him.

My heart races wildly.

"I'm sure as hell not going to let a bitch like you tell me when to move out of MY house!" He reaches for his coat lying on a chair. "You ain't getting me outta here!"

I feel spit assault my face as he shouts, "Now get your sorry ass outta my way. I'm going to Chuck's."

I let go of the doorknob and step aside. After the door slams shut, I slide down the wall into a huddle of shattered hope. As the stun diminishes, I cry softly. Then I cry hard. Then I sob and sob until I finally cry myself out.

"God, what do I do now?"

> Journal Entry — 2/8/2003 — Been five weeks since he agreed to find an apartment. To begin with, I tried to help him by looking at the listings in one of those "Rentals" catalogs I had picked up at the grocery store. Supposedly, he checked them out and found something wrong with every one of them – too small, has roaches, too far from the boys, too far from work. I finally quit helping him. Then the last time I asked him about it, he didn't answer. But the anger in his eyes said I'd better drop the subject. I guess he's still looking because he leaves for work early quite often and other days he gets home after the boys and I are gone for the day.

***

I am putting the last load of laundry in the washer when Ronnie bellows at me from the garage. "Sara! Get your fat ass out here!"

"What do you need?" I ask from the doorway between the laundry room and garage.

"About damn time," he growls.

All I can see of him are his legs sticking out from underneath the passenger side of the car. His hand appears with a bolt in it. "Here, go to Advance Auto and get one of these," he orders.

As I step over a bag of grass seed, my eyes focus on the long, yellow car jack handle balancing the car above him like the mouth of a hideous monster. I can't pull my focus away. *If I "accidentally" bump this . . .*" I gasp and cover my mouth with my hand.

"Hurry up, bitch," he says, shaking the large rusty bolt at me.

I stare at the handle again, my vision tunneling in on it. *No one would know it wasn't an accident.* I move forward and step over the jack handle with the caution of someone facing a coiled rattlesnake. I bend down and take the bolt with my trembling hand.

"Hurry up! I want to get this done before KU's game starts."

"Okay." Safely back on the other side of the handle, I rush through the house and out the front door to my car. When I get in, I throw my purse into the passenger seat. My fingers tremble so much I can barely turn the ignition key. Brushing away the sudden tears that blur my vision, I start the car and put it in gear. The car moves along the street in a jerking gait due to my leg shaking. I pull to the side of the street.

Loud and strong tears course from my eyes. My moans are deep and full of anguish. I can't believe they're coming from me.

As I get quieter, I pray, "Dear God, help me." I rest my forehead against the steering wheel. Opening the door, I throw up in the street as the horror of what I was considering becomes all too clear. *So many times Ronnie's said that if my family knew me the way he does, they wouldn't think I'm so great and wouldn't love me. Maybe he's right. How could I even think of doing such a thing?*

"Oh God . . . oh my God . . . forgive me . . . forgive me." I feel as if hurricane forces pound me with wave after wave of shame, draining all emotions from my being. I pull myself together and go to Advance Auto.

> Journal Entry — 2/9/2003 — I've decided the only way I can live with what I almost did today is to shove it into a black hole to never be thought of again. I vow to myself

that I'll never, ever tell anyone about today. The unanswered question still spins in my mind, though, how do I get him to move out of the house?

Journal Entry — 2/15/2003 — Aunt Lola is taking the boys to Joplin and Ronnie is working overtime, giving me freedom to do some research. Today I went to a bookstore where I drank coffee and read 9/11 survivor stories, hoping to find the connection to my nightmares. A sales clerk visited with a man sitting at a table nearby who appeared to be copying notes from a book and went back to it when the clerk walked away. I decided to take a chance of doing the same thing because I don't have enough money for one of the books, much less all of them. No one bothers me for the next several hours.

My list: numb, anesthetized, unfeeling, shocked, overwhelmed, exhausted, powerless, terrified, petrified, frozen, horrified, trying to reclaim reality, fearful of next attack, fatigued, it was tragic, vulnerable, my world changed that day.

When it seemed I was writing variations of the same words over and over, I stopped with seven pages of nightmare paragraphs. That's when I realized it was almost time for Ronnie to be home. I didn't want to answer his questions or endure a long lecture. I jammed my computer in its bag and left the books lying on the table – job security for someone.

Chapter 25 – It Happened

"Hello, Sara. How -? You're pale. Are you sick?"

I sit down in my usual chair, pulling the tissue box onto my lap, and move the trash can closer. "No, Carol."

"What happened?"

"Well . . . " The words catch in my throat. I swallow hard. "Ronnie . . . threw a . . ." I feel safe here to let go of my days of pent up emotions. Tears gush from my eyes that I've been holding back from the boys and Ronnie.

Carol's face shows concern as she waits. I take deep breaths and blow my nose several times.

"Are you okay?" Carol asks, gently.

I shrug.

"Were you trying to tell me Ronnie threw something at you?"

I nod. "He threw a plastic spaghetti ladle. It hit the cabinet right next to my head." I lean forward, putting my elbows on my knees and clasping my hands together. "The worst part of it was that it bounced right into Logan's first place trophy and broke it."

"Why was that the worst part?"

I lean back heavily into the chair. "Because it broke Logan's heart, too."

"I'm sorry Logan's trophy got broken, but the worst part is that Ronnie's violence has escalated to the point of him throwing things – at you!"

Tears burn my eyes. "I'd rather talk about Logan's broken heart . . . not mine."

"Okay, we can talk about Logan's . . . first." She smiles and jots a note on the yellow legal pad. "How did all of this happen?"

"Ronnie was there with us Saturday when our pack raced against Raytown's. He spoke up when Logan's car got overlooked. That little wooden car brought out the best in Ronnie – then something, I don't know what, brought out the worst – both on the same day. We sit in silence. "How do I decide if living through the times of hell with Mr. Hyde is worth the waiting for Dr. Jekyll to return?"

"I wish I could pull a sheet of paper from my file cabinet that says when such and such happens, it's time to leave. But there isn't any such magic. Each situation has so many variables that the person in the midst of it is the only one who knows when and if that time comes."

"So it's up to me to make the decision?"

"Yes, but I'm here to help you look at all your options and make the best choice with the fullest amount of knowledge possible. You're not doing this alone."

"Thank goodness I'm not struggling alone any more. I think I would have had a nervous breakdown by now. In fact, last week I told Nancy thank you for making me come here."

"And what did she say?"

"That I'm welcome and she's glad my work has improved so much." The tightness in my neck eases. "Then she added that she knew the counseling is helping because I don't look like I'm about to burst into tears every day, just once in a while."

"Are any of your coworkers acting different towards you?"

"Oh my gosh. Yes they are!" I grin. "They're talking to me more and seem friendlier." I frown. "Ohhhh . . . wow . . . Ronnie's anger spreads far and wide like a pebble tossed into a pool."

"Exactly. People tend to think domestic violence only affects the abusers and victims. What you just said shows how it impacts all of us." Carol reads from my nightmare pages. "I see the nightmares are still happening.

"Yeah. I haven't woke Ronnie up with any of them since he moved back home. I'm not as exhausted as I used to be."

I open my purse, take out my list of 9/11 emotions I found at the bookstore, give it to Carol and walk to my window.

After looking my list over, she says, "You put a lot of work into these definitions."

"That was the most I've used a dictionary since high school."

As Carol reads more, I pick at a hangnail until it bleeds. I turn around when I hear Carol get out of her chair. At her desk, she picks up a clipboard, sheets of paper, and a pen and hands them to me. I sit back down.

"Let's see if we can fit more of the nightmare puzzle pieces together today. As I mention things from your nightmares, write them down and say out loud the first emotion you feel."

"Okay."

"Finding hand with wedding rings on it."

Tightening chest muscles limit my breathing. I say and write, "Horrified. Wonder if she was married to an abuser."

"Feeling Ronnie's presence but him not answering your call for help."

The outer corner of my right eye twitches as anger rises in me. "Infuriated. How can he not answer me with all we've been through together."

"Your homeless self," Carol says.

"Hope Ronnie pays child support so the boys and I will never have to endure being homeless."

When I look at Carol, she's skimming through my pages. I shift my weight back and forth in the chair as my heart rate increases. I wipe sweat from my upper lip with the back of my hand.

"How about we try a different approach now?" Carol says.

My muscles relax slightly at the thought of moving our conversation away from Ronnie. "All right."

"As I mention the emotions I felt on 9/11, tell me what you were thinking on that day."

"Okay."

"When the second plane hit, I couldn't believe we were being attacked in our homeland!"

I massage my arms, which are cold and prickly. "Terrorists attacks can't be happening here! Scenes from Ground Zero that night looked like they were from the other side of the world or like I was watching a movie, not real life here at home."

Because Carol knows how dry my mouth gets, she once again goes to the mini-fridge for two bottles of water, and hands one to me on the way back to her rocker. "When the plane dived into the Pentagon, I wondered if there were places in St. Louis that could be their next target," she says.

"I just wanted to get my boys and go home to hibernate until I knew the attacks were over." It's taking great effort to control my lurching emotions. I grip my jacket tight around me.

Carol continues, "Later, when anthrax killed people, I felt there was absolutely no place safe, NOT even our homes."

I stand and walk to the window. The impact of realizing that my marriage has slipped from my tenacious grip sends my emotions into a frenzy. Rain angles down the window and I jump when lightning sizzles across the sky. *I don't feel safe in my home.* As reality sinks in and understanding matures that my nightmares are triggered by Ronnie's words and actions, my feelings surface with raw force. I drop to the floor. NUMB!

I barely notice Carol sitting down beside me and placing her hand on my knee.

My whirling mind unlocks. I strive to find words huge enough to express my agony, terror, pain, and fear. A chill ripples through my body as groans explode from my mouth. My heart thumps against my chest and feels like it's twisting. *What's happening to me? Am I having a heart attack, or is this a nervous breakdown? Can't do that to the boys! Have to calm down! Lord Jesus, help me!*

The groans change to sobs; deep racking sounds fill the room. I bury my face in the palms of my hands and rock back and forth. I cry. And cry. And cry.

Carol waits, patting my knee.

A hot surge of anger curls up inside me, simmers, and grows to a boil. I suddenly look up at Carol. I jump to my feet and pace. Carol moves back to her rocker.

I stop in my tracks as I visualize a split screen. On one side, the World Trade Center towers stand tall and beautiful. On the other side, Ronnie and I face each other, saying our wedding vows. I blink. The scenes change to the towers collapsing on the left while on the right Ronnie stands over me with his fist raised. I'm sliding down the kitchen wall. Pure evil radiates from his eyes.

My tongue feels heavy, and my mouth is so dry I can barely say, "I have a damn terrorist living in my house."

She nods.

> Journal Entry — 1/29/2003 — What a day! Only time will tell if this is the last connection to my nightmares. Most important thing now is to find a way to get Ronnie out of the house. I've quit counting how many weeks it's been since he agreed to get an apartment. It's too

discouraging. He says he's looking but I find it hard to believe anything he says to me anymore. Trust is completely gone. Knowing he's a terrorist puts a whole new, ugly meaning to what I thought my relationship is with him. The only way I can make it through the days with him is to take them in small bits of time. Have to get distance from him for me and the boys, some how, some way. In Jesus' Name, I pray for wisdom to make smart choices to protect me and the boys.

Chapter 26 – Two More Women

"This is Sara. I'm here for support group," I say into the speaker box on the post.

Then, "Just a minute," a woman answers. After the gate opens, I pause, and park. At the front door of the building, I hear someone from behind me say, "Sara, so glad you're back." The door clangs open as I turn and see Kristen. "Hi. It's good to be back.

In the conference room, we all chat except two women I don't know who are sitting across the table from me. "Hi," I say. They nod. I try to not stare at the one with blackened and swollen eyes. The other one is so well dressed, she looks like she should be at a country club enjoying dinner instead of here.

"Hello, everyone," says Monica, as she walks into the room.

"Hello," we chorus.

"We have a couple of items for business . . ." Monica starts, but my attention drifts. *Wonder what she got hit with to make her eyes swell so bad that one is completely closed and the other looks like a slit of white and blood red. Hope she's not going to have permanent damage.*

Monica saying "I want to welcome Helen and Rachel tonight" draws my attention back to the meeting. "They may choose to share their situations with us later. For now, let's get started."

"Sara, we haven't seen you in quite a while," Kristen says.

"I had to lie to my husband about where I am tonight. I'm not used to doing that." I feel both hot and cold at the same time. "Uhhh . . . I like the brainstorming we did for Julie the last time I was here. Can we do that for ideas of how I can get my husband to move out? He agreed to get an apartment, but he hasn't done it."

Monica looks at Kristen as she says, "This is a tough one, but we'll give it a try. First, tell us about the agreement."

I swallow the hard lump in my throat. "Thanksgiving weekend, he was very drunk and threw a coffee cup through our front window. He felt so bad about scaring me and our sons that he agreed to move to his brother's house for a while. That's when things started changing for the better."

"Better how?" asks someone. I don't see whom because I'm looking down, picking at my cuticles.

"He started going to the boys' activities and eating with us at the dining room table instead of in front of the TV. Uhhh . . . he sent me roses at work." Blood is now oozing from where a hangnail had been. "And he bought me a hot tub for Christmas."

"Pretty desperate to weasel himself back home, isn't he?" asks Kristen. I jerk my head up and glare at her. *That's a mean thing to say.*

As I look at the women, I gradually realize they are reinforcing what Carol said about his motives for giving me the tub. *Still surprised no one has commented on what a great gift it is.*

"When did he move back?" Monica asks.

"Mmm-humm. Over New Year's weekend, while I was out of town picking up our sons."

"Figures," says Kristen disgustedly. "What's happened since then?"

I don't remember Kristen being so mean. "At Red Lobster, we talked about how things were going downhill since he moved home. He agreed to move to an apartment."

"That was smart, — talking to him in public, I mean," either Rachel or Helen says. I don't know which is which yet. Heads bob up and down.

"Much as I love that hot tub, I'd give it up so he'll have money to get an apartment. But he said it was too late to return it."

"Did you call the dealer to confirm that?" asks Kristen.

"No, why would I do that?"

"Because he may not have told you the truth," she states.

"Why would he lie to me about that?" I gasp.

"Because he really isn't planning on moving out. He's just placating you, hoping you'll give up on it – eventually," answers the well-dressed woman. "How long's it been since he agreed to move?"

"Six weeks ago," I answer in a sad voice.

"A restraining order can force an abuser to move out of a jointly owned home. But, if I remember correctly, you said he's never hurt you physically," Monica says.

"No, he hasn't. But he threatens me with violence almost every day, and he did throw a ladle at me recently. It barely missed me."

"I'm sorry to hear that, but I've seen very few restraining orders granted without evidence of bruises or broken bones," Monica says.

"Every time this subject comes up, I hope someone will have a new solution. But so far . . . it hasn't happened."

Everyone turns quiet. "Helen, would you like to tell us why you're here?" Monica asks.

The woman with the swollen eye starts to sit up straight but stops, grimacing in pain. "Okay. I've been married 32 years. Two things happened on my wedding night – the abuse started and I got pregnant. Wish there'd been a place like this when my kids were small." Kristen reaches over and pats Helen's hand. "Last night, some lady from here came to the emergency room in the middle of the night to tell me about this place." She sighs slowly and gently. "I figured if she cares enough to interrupt her good night's sleep, get dressed, and drive to the hospital to talk to me, the least I could do is to come check this place out." She shifts in her chair, wincing. "The police brought me here. Today, they took me to my house to get some things and pick up my car. I threw a few clothes into suitcases, but, mostly, I got the items my husband will destroy if I don't go back home." She gulps. "Almost all of our children's photos are gone, thanks to him."

The tissue box makes a circuit around the table. "In fact, last night I shoved him out of my face, knowing he would hit me. Just wanted to get the beating over with because I knew it was coming."

I hear myself gasp. *Oh my gosh!*

Helen looks at each woman around the table and stops at me. "Believe me, the day is coming when that bastard of yours is going to hit you!"

I suck air. My body shakes. Kristen puts her arm around me.

"Sorry to talk so much. It seemed to tumble out once I got started," Helen concludes.

"That's okay," Monica assures her. "We understand how comforting it is to talk to other women who understand what you're going through." Monica looks at the other new woman. "Rachel, do you want to share with us?"

Rachel sits tall and straight in her chair. "I grew up in Mission Hills, married a man right out of college, and I have two children." She takes her Bill Blass jacket off and hangs it on the back of the chair. "From the outside, we look like the ideal family. On the inside of that beautiful mansion, the children and I live in terror of the perfect lawyer." She breaks off talking and swallows hard. "Six months ago, after he broke my ribs and backhanded our son so hard it knocked him unconscious, I moved out. Going from a five-bedroom house to my parents' basement has been really terrible." She pauses to wipe away tears. "Every time I pull a number ticket to wait in line at the welfare office, use my food stamp card, or have to take more money from my parents, I consider moving back to that luxurious life in Mission Hills and rationalize the abuse away – again." She shakes. "Can't do that after what he did to my son." She pulls the jacket off the chair, slips her arms in and tightens it close around her. She pulls tissues from the box, blows her nose, and stares at her lap.

"Rachel, this sounds really tough," says Kristen. "Having this safe haven to talk about everything has been a life saver for me. I hope you'll keep coming."

Rachel looks up and bites her lip. "Just being with people who understand without having to explain everything is a great relief. It's already helping me stop my thoughts from going around and around"

Monica puts her hand on Rachel's shoulder. "We are here to be part of the support system you need." She removes her hand and looks at Kristen. "You don't seem quite yourself tonight. What's going on?"

"I'm surprised at how many conflicting emotions are bombarding me now that my life with Michael is officially over." She lets out a long, ragged sigh. "He finally went to trial Tuesday after seven postponements. He got three years probation and was ordered to attend anger management classes." She moves around in her chair. "Doesn't seem like a fair sentence for him almost killing me."

Anger explodes within me. "Why wasn't he charged with attempted murder?"

"That's what the police initially charged him with but it was later reduced to assault. His parents have a great deal of influence in the community and plenty of money for high priced attorneys. What I got out of it was a permanent restraining order and this raspy voice."

A little later as we filter out of the room, I maneuver close to Helen. "Thank you for being so direct with me. I needed that jolt of reality."

"I wish someone had been that blunt with me years ago. My children might not've become alcoholics and drug addicts." She takes my hand in hers. "Your children are being as devastated by his words and actions as you are."

"I-I try . . . t-to protect . . . them," I stutter.

She pats my shoulder. "I know you do, hon. See you next time – gotta go take a pain pill." She walks away.

> Journal Entry — 2/20/2003 — When I was in the hot tub tonight, my heart started pumping wildly. By the time I got out and wrapped a towel around me, I suddenly felt cold. Sitting on the couch, I wrapped myself in blankets because I couldn't stop shaking and my chest hurt. I desperately needed to have a good hard cry but couldn't do that because I didn't want to wake the boys or scare them. I started to think I was having a break down or something. I was about to call Aunt Lola for help when I noticed the pounding blood in my heart subsiding at the same rate as my waterfall of silent tears. I wrote stream-of-consciousness pages until I realized I'm grieving at the loss of my marriage. I don't know which hit me harder, knowing I'm living with my own personal terrorist or losing my marriage.

Chapter 27 – Wife-Swapping

"About time you two got here. What happened to starting this party at four?" Amy asks, making a sucking noise with her toothless gums while pointing at the kitchen clock.

"We were partying at home. Just the two of us," Ronnie says with a twinkle in his eye. "I'll take your coat, sweetheart." He winks at me as his hand brushes against my breast.

"Mike, Melissa, this is my baby brother, Ronnie, and his wife, Sara," Chuck says.

Mike stands, holding his hand out to Ronnie. "Nice to meet you, Ronnie." Mike's steel-gray eyes have been locked on me from the time we came in the door. "Hello, Sara. What a lovely name."

"Hello, Mike," I say. *Tall, dark hair, muscular – have to be careful to not look at him too often or Ronnie will accuse me of wanting to have an affair with him.* I turn and extend my hand to Melissa.

"Nice to meet you, Sara," Melissa says. "Mike's right — lovely name for a beautiful woman." She holds on to my hand so long it makes me uncomfortable.

She turns to Ronnie. "Nice to meet you," she says, hugging his hand with both of hers.

"Sara, how 'bout a beer?" Chuck laughs in a way that I know his first beer was at noon. The Farley family believes that as long as they don't drink before noon they can't be alcoholics.

"Sure, I'll have one," I answer.

As soon as we sit down, Ronnie slips his hand into mine. "Yeah, have four or five and we'll play strip poker when we get home," he jokes.

"How long are the boys gone?" Amy asks.

"A week for Spring Break," I answer. I wink at Ronnie.

His mouth curves into a seductive smile. "We're both on vacation and going to do some projects around the house while the boys aren't there to interrupt them, and our fun," he says as his hand moves down to my thigh and gives it a squeeze. "I'm sure we'll be having a lot of fun in that new hot tub, too."

"Sounds delightful," says Mike. "We've never had kids 'cause they'd put a damper on our sex life."

Melissa adds, "And we like to spend our time and money on ourselves."

"I understand that," Amy says. "With four kids in our house, Chuck and I go to the bars to get away from them." Everyone laughs. I smile half-heartedly.

"How about a game of poker to get you guys warmed up for later?" suggests Mike.

"How about it, Sara?" says Ronnie, leering. "You could use some practice. You're usually half naked by the time I take anything off." My cheeks feel warm.

"Wait a minute here. Come eat first," says Amy. "I didn't cook for fun, ya know." The six of us sit at the table, eating corned beef and cabbage.

"Where did you all meet?" I ask.

Because I happen to be looking at Amy, I see her avert her eyes to her plate with a disgusted and angry look. "At the All Nighter Bar . . . last weekend," she says quietly.

"Where's that? I don't remember hearing of it before."

"It's a new one over in the old neighborhood," Chuck answers.

Mike bumps Chuck with his shoulder. "I asked this guy if I could dance with his wife because mine doesn't like fast dancing."

"At breakfast, after closing the bar, we discovered we're neighbors," says Melissa. "That's when Chuck invited us over for this little get together."

Melissa keeps staring at me with eyes as brown as leftover coffee. "I can tell we're going to be best friends." Her blond hair is pulled up on top of her head the way Ronnie likes it.

I excuse myself to go to the bathroom so I don't have to watch Ronnie ogling Melissa's butt in her skinny, skin-tight jeans every time she stands up. *These two characters don't seem like Chuck and Amy's type.*

As I return to the kitchen, I hear Ronnie saying, "Sara only drinks with me when the boys aren't with us. Something about it's not good for them to see both of their parents drinking." I wonder why he's telling them that. As I pass by Mike, he grabs my hand and pulls me down into the chair between him and Chuck. "Times a wasting. Let's get this poker game under way,"

Why has everyone shifted chairs? Ronnie is sitting between Melissa and Amy now. The poker game is friendly to me for a change with two high pairs and a full house. When I glance at Ronnie, he gives me smiles conveying encyclopedias of sensual promises. *I'm not sure I want any sex with the way he's flirting with Melissa. And Mike doesn't seem to care.* He has a way about him that makes me smile even when I'm aggravated at him. The after-effects of his seductive smile make me lose count of how many beers I've had so far. I return his smile, conveying lots of fake, sensual promises to him.

I look at Amy, who is uncharacteristically quiet tonight. She hasn't been joking around – just getting drunker and concentrating on her poker hand. *There's a weird vibe in this bunch tonight – nah, probably just too many beers in me.*

Each time Mike reaches in front of me to take another beer from Chuck, his arm inches closer to my chest. *Wish Ronnie hadn't insisted I wear this blouse – it's the lowest cut neckline I have.* I scoot back in my chair, and Mike's arm follows still closer and finally brushes against me. I frown at him and he scoots his chair away from me an inch. I keep playing risky poker hands, hoping to be out of the game so I can move a chair and be in between Ronnie and Melissa. That would slow them down.

Chuck and Mike put new beers in front of me when they see a low beer line in my bottle. Almost every time I look at Ronnie Melissa is staring at me and has winked at me twice. I drink too many beers too fast. *The way I feel right now is pretty great – but what's the hangover going to be like tomorrow?* "I've gotta pee again." The clock on the wall seems to sway as I stand. I'm hoping someone gets up while I'm out of the room so I can move to a different position at the table.

As I return from the bathroom, I feel Mike's eyes strip me of my blouse and skirt, leaving me standing in my underwear. I return to my seat between the two jerks and focus on peeling beer bottle labels off, hoping to slow the rate of the beers lining up in front of me.

Melissa inches closer and closer to Ronnie until she's almost in his lap. I frown at him. He mouths the words "I love you," to me. I can't help smiling at him. A bare foot caresses my leg. I don't remember if Ronnie is wearing slip-ons or not. It's out of character for him to do something like that. I pull my feet under my chair.

Around ten o'clock, with exaggerated stretching, yawning, and a smile from ear to ear, Ronnie says, "Sara, let's go home." He winks.

Did he just wink at me or Mike?

"Okay. I've drank too many cards anyway." Hiccup. "And won way too many beers." It takes a bit for my foggy mind to comprehend why they're laughing. "Oops," I say as I stand up and sway. Mike seizes the opportunity to grab me with both arms and squeeze me too tight. I give Ronnie a look of desperation but he takes his time getting around the table to me.

As Chuck gives me a tight hug, I wonder why he doesn't get those rotten teeth fixed with all the money he makes. *Spends too much on beer.* I can't quit staring at him for some reason. My head feels foggy, and everyone's words are mixing together, making no sense to me at all.

***

I hear our house phone ringing as Ronnie unlocks the front door. He rushes in to answer it. "Hello . . . Oh, really?. . . Uh-huh."

I put a hand on each side of the hall, hoping to make it to the bathroom. *Almost there. No, not in the sink.*

"Sara, where are you?"

"I'm . . . here . . ."

"Melissa and Mike are at the motel down the street. They want us to join them for a drink," I hear Ronnie say with excitement as he approaches the bathroom.

"What? " I say as the first hurl hits the side of the stool. "Oh, shit."

"What the hell's wrong with you?" he asks from the doorway

I point to the side of the stool.

When I glance up, he stands framed in the doorway. "Guess we won't be going any place now," he says in a loud bellow like an angry bull. I feel the oddness of his anger. A few moments ago, he was telling me how much he loves me. He stomps away.

Between heaving and waves of nausea, I hear TV noise. I attempt to clean the vomit from the side of the stool but my movements stir up the nausea and cause more heaving. Finally, my stomach empties enough that I make it up the stairs and into bed. *Why are they in the motel close to our house if they are neighbors of Chuck and Amy's?* Sleep finally comes.

***

"Well, it's about time you get up, sleepyhead," Ronnie says as I walk into the kitchen.

I shuffle around the breakfast bar, shielding my eyes from the bright sunlight pouring in through the window. "Uggg . . . so this is what your hangovers feel like." I sit. "I'm in desperate need of coffee to chase the cobwebs out of my head."

Ronnie cackles as he pours a cup and scoots it over in front of me. I put my hands to my head.

"You really tied one on. I've never seen you so looped before."

"Shhh . . . not so loud." I glance at him.

"Okay, okay." He moves a bottle of aspirin in front of me. It's the same bottle that has permanent residence on the counter for his hangovers.

I swallow the aspirin with coffee. "I'm never doing this again," I say, grimacing at the stale beer taste in my mouth.

"Melissa called while you were sleeping. I invited them to join us in the hot tub tonight."

"Chuck and Amy, too?"

"No, just Mike, Melissa, and us. They want to get better acquainted," he says, smiling and wriggling his eyebrows at me.

"I don't want to get to know them any better!"

"Why not? You sure seemed to enjoy them last night."

"That was the beer. I hated dodging Mike's hand and the fake apologies every time he bumped into me. And I sure as hell didn't enjoy Melissa gluing herself to you like a fly stuck on flypaper."

He laughs strangely. "Oh, that was just harmless fun and flirting. That kind of stuff livens up a marriage."

"I liked you caressing my leg under the table — not what they were doing."

"I didn't touch you under the table." He looks puzzled at first. Then both corners of his mouth curl up into the Cheshire Cat grin.

I manage a swallow of coffee from my shaking cup. My brain connections catch hold.

I jump to my feet, crashing the stool to the floor. "Those two aren't friends of Chuck and Amy's, are they?" I yell.

He shakes his head no, smiling so large his face stretches out of proportion.

"Did Chuck and Amy know what was going on?"

"Sort of." He pours himself more coffee with a steady hand.

"All of it . . . every bit of it . . . was a damn setup for wife-swapping!"

"I wouldn't exactly put it that way. It was just fun."

"FUN? YOU thought if I got drunk enough! But the answer is still NO!" I feel like I am going to explode. He sits there, calmly drinking coffee, as if we are discussing what to have for dinner.

Through clinched teeth, I say, "Bye." As I go past him, he grabs my hand. I yank it away. "Don't *you* dare touch *me*!" Running for the front door, I snatch only my purse and go out into the cold March wind.

* * *

I watch waves crash onto the rocks of Longview Lake waiting for my shaking to subside. My heart races. Questions fly at my brain, demanding answers. I start talking out loud. "How could I have been so stupid?" I gently bang my head against the steering wheel. "Sometimes I think I'm as stupid as Ronnie says I am." I throw myself upright. "Stop it, Sara! Carol and you know you're not stupid. You didn't notice it was a setup because you were so focused on trying to keep Ronnie in a good mood while the boys are in Joplin." Frantically, I dig through pages in my notebook, looking for blank pages. Slow, helpless groans jerk out of me as I yank some pages out and write on the back of last month's journal in a stream of consciousness. Several pages later, my shaky handwriting stabilizes. I start over, writing a legible journal entry on new pages.

> Journal Entry — 3/8/2003 — Looking back, I see I've spent way too much time and energy trying to be the woman Ronnie wants me to be. I've gradually given pieces of myself away to him in small increments at a time. First, it was more and more makeup, then whatever hairstyle he likes, whether I liked it or not. And clothes – two different wardrobes – my normal clothes and the "date" clothes, as he calls them. The higher the hemline and lower the neckline, the better he likes them. I'm always worried someone I know will see me dressed like a whore when we're out in public. I feel like I have to be two different women. I really dislike the one Ronnie likes! Then the porno!

I get out of the car and amble down to the water's edge. The March wind blows the brilliant, shiny water into the bank, making small waves. I close my eyes and remember the rhythm and sounds at the beach when I was there a lifetime ago. It soothes my turmoil. I pull my coat and blanket tighter around me as I walk out onto the marina. Watching the movement of the water reminds me of how the boys love feeding the carp in the summer time. The fish battle each other for food, pushing one another up on top of the water.

My mind goes back to the night before. *I'm almost as mad at Chuck and Amy as I am at Ronnie. I wonder what his . . .* "Eureka!" I exclaim to the empty lake. I race to my Chevy and turn it toward home to evict Mr. Hyde out of my house – forever!

***

"Oh good, you're here," Ronnie says as I walk in the front door. "Come here, sweetheart, let's kiss and make up," he croons. He grabs my hand and tries to pull me in for a hug. I shove him away, rushing to the kitchen. I cough so he can't hear the click of the back door unlocking as I pass it. I sit on the stool closest to the door for a quick exit. With a steady hand, I pour myself a cup of coffee.

Without taking his eyes off me, he walks around to the other side of the counter and sits down. "What's going on?" he asks, looking worried.

In a calm, assured voice, I answer, "To begin with, I'm absolutely shocked Amy joined you and Chuck in that charade last night."

"But– " he starts. I hold up my hand to cut him off.

"What do you think your mother would say if she knew what the three of you did?"

His eyes darken. "She would be shocked. Why?"

"Because I'm going to tell her."

Panic jumps onto his face and grows in intensity. "You wouldn't dare!"

"Oh yes, I would . . . and I will!" It takes determination to keep the sound of my voice normal and to not reveal my overwhelming fear to him.

"That would break her heart!" He glowers at me.

"There is only one thing that will stop me from telling her."

"What's that?" he asks. A cold, hard look grips his features.

"You finding an apartment and getting your ass moved out of here by Friday at five p.m."

"Hell . . . that's not enough time!"

"You've been 'looking' for nine weeks. Move back to Chuck's or whatever, but get yourself out of this house!"

He smiles the kind of smile that suggests he knows something I don't. He turns his stool away from the counter and stands up. "You're bluffing, you damn wuss. Don't make me knock the piss out of you, you defiant bitch."

I am on my feet with my left hand on the doorknob by the time he moves in front of me. *Oh God!*

His blue eyes are so cold my trembling becomes a terrible shudder. My legs shake, and, for a moment, my knees almost fail me. He grabs my wrist and makes his right hand into a fist. It seems my world is crashing in as I close my eyes. I hear heavy breathing. I tremble with anticipation.

My wrist goes free. No fist is pounding me. I wait. I open my eyes slightly. He's stepping back and seems suddenly aware, like someone coming out of a blackout and confused about what he was about to do. His eyes are like two holes in his face. In a flat voice, as though there is no emotion left in him, he says, "I almost hit you like Jason does Maria."

I tighten my grip on the doorknob as I turn around to open it. "I'm not taking vacation this week and when I come home from work on Friday, if you're not outta here, I'm driving straight to your Mom's house."

He steps closer, saying, "Come on, Sara, we can work this out."

I open the back door and stumble on trembling legs to my car. The cold air feels refreshing on my sweaty body. Yanking the unlocked car door open and jumping inside, I hit the lock button. By the time the engine starts, Ronnie is pounding on the driver's window. "I'm not done with you yet!"

I put the car in reverse, and he jumps back when it starts moving.

"The boys and I will make it without you!" I scream back.

> Journal Entry — 3/9/2003 — I'm spending the week at Aunt Lola and Uncle Steve's house. Oh my God, what have I done? I'm terrified of living with Ronnie, and now sitting here in Aunt Lola and Uncle Steve's house, I'm terrified of living without him! I feel like the depression abyss is pulling me down. SARA! GET A GRIP ON YOURELF! It's way past time to quit playing this game of pretending his bullet words and threats weren't abuse because he never hit me physically. His words strike so hard, it's like being whacked full force with a belt. Remember all the things you've learned in the last few months. Be proud of yourself for not being sucked into the wife-swapping, for standing up to that monster, and for no longer making excuses for him because it's too hard to face the reality of what he really is. You've come a long way, baby! I'm so thankful I can stay here all week so I won't have to deal with him trying to talk

me out of my demand every day. Thank God for the family I have. With him moving out, I have to make some decisions. In order to keep him giving me money every week, I'll have to perform sex on demand the way he likes it, not forgetting anything. Can't think about anything more tonight. My brain and emotions are mush. I can't wait to talk to Carol on Wednesday.

Chapter 28 – Deadline

The receptionist says Carol is waiting for me in her office. Rushing in, I blurt out, "Hi. There's so much I've got to tell you. An hour's probably not long enough. I'm so glad you introduced me to the support group. Ronnie's finally moving out because I threatened to tell his mother on him." I stop because I feel breathless.

"Hi, Sara," says Carol, with a big smile. "Ronnie's moving out? Tell me how this happened."

I take my jacket off and toss it on a chair. "I think the support group and coming here is giving me courage. I finally stood up for myself." I'm so wound up and excited, I pace as I talk.

"That's good to hear. Did you say you're going to tell Ronnie's mom on him?" Carol closes the office door. "Seems a strange thing to say about a grown man."

"Guess so. But it worked! He's seriously looking for an apartment."

I take several deep breaths. I tell her about the travesty at Chuck and Amy's and the fallout from the evening. I put three breath mints in my mouth. Carol gets each of us bottles of water from the mini-fridge. I take a long swig.

"The whole thing was a . . ." I shiver. ". . . setup for the . . . wife-swapping Ronnie's wanted to do for a long time." I feel heat stealing up my neck. Despite the mints and sips of water, my mouth still feels like cotton.

Carol writes notes.

"When I calmed down and my thinking became clear, I knew Ronnie had given me the means to get him out of the house." I smile weakly.

"Really? Do you think he believes you?"

"I think so." I feel like I can stay sitting in a chair now, so I sit. "He told me last night he thinks he found an apartment."

"Sounds like he does. But are you ready to follow through with your threat if he doesn't move by the deadline?"

"I didn't think that part through very well before saying it. But I think this ultimatum is the only means I have to get him out of the house again. I dearly love his mom, but I'm fighting for me and my sons' survival." I clench my fists so tight my fingernails imprint my hands. "If Ronnie forces me to tell her, that's on him."

"How have things been since Saturday?"

"Okay. I'm staying at Aunt Lola and Uncle Steve's house while they're in Joplin with the boys for the week."

"Has Ronnie been trying to get you to change your mind?"

Will he actually hit me if I have to tell his mom? "Yeah, when I get to the house after work each day, there are eight to ten messages on Aunt Lola's answering machine. In some of them, Ronnie is begging and pleading. Others, he's ranting threats at me."

"Has he come by the house?"

"Every evening on his way to work. He can't tell if I'm there or not because I'm parking in the garage. He pounds on the door, rings the doorbell over and over, and tries seeing in through the blinds." Sadness wells up inside me. "I just stay quiet until he leaves. He's so pathetic. I feel sorry for him some times, but then I remember last Friday night and that stops me from taking back my ultimatum."

"What do you think would happen if you did take it back?"

I stand and move to the red chair. "He wouldn't move out. I'd lose all the ground I've gained,"

Carol nods. "Sara, I've watched your strengths appear and grow by leaps and bounds in the time you've been coming here. You're a strong woman. I have confidence you'll follow through with whatever actions are necessary."

"Thanks. Every time you tell me I'm strong, I feel more empowered. I've only got two days to keep my resolve steady. When he's gone on Friday, I can fall apart then." My heart starts beating faster. "Hopefully, I'll be able to pull myself back together before the boys get home on Sunday."

"What are you going to do Friday when you get home from work and he's moved out?"

"Umm . . . be relieved he's finally gone . . . watch some TV – anything but sports." I smile. "Then soak in the hot tub until I can go to sleep."

"Do you have caller ID on your phones?"

I nod.

"Are you going to answer his calls?"

"Uhhh . . . don't think so. I'm glad you're making me think this through ahead of time."

"That's my job." She smiles.

"What are you going to do if he's not moved out?" asks Carol.

My heart feels like it skips a beat. I wipe my hands on my skirt. "Umm . . . go tell Mom Farley." I stand and walk past Carol to the window. *Where are the damn birds when I need them?*

"Sara, I really hope you don't have to talk to her, but it's extremely important to be emotionally prepared for whatever happens."

As I turn to look at Carol, I notice I'm gritting my teeth. Back in my chair, I close my eyes momentarily.

"Something else happened Saturday. Don't really wanna talk about it, but guess I'd better." I scoot the trashcan closer to me and grab tissues. "After I gave Ronnie his ultimatum, he almost hit me." My voice cracks and tears fall.

"What happened?" she ask, her voice almost too loud.

"It's still so terrifying and unreal at the same time."

"Take as much time as you need."

I give her the details. Feeling my chest tighten, I lean my head back against the wall and close my eyes.

"Sara, are you okay?"

"Yes, just need to unwind myself a little." I breathe slow and easy several times. I open my eyes. "When he realized I was serious about telling Mom Farley, I really believed he was going to hit me for the first time. As I waited, waited, and waited – nothing happened. He turned loose of me. When I opened my eyes, he had taken a few steps back. His hands were curled into fists down at his sides. His face . . . looked utterly frozen and shocked. I reiterated the ultimatum and ran out the back door to my unlocked car. He came out the front door yelling at me to stop. I just started driving and kept on driving." I feel like a bottomless sadness is trying to swallow me. I look out the window at a sea of floating white clouds that soothes my turmoil.

Carol goes a shade paler as she quietly says, "Oh my God, Sara." I see her swallow hard as she looks down, flipping pages in my folder. "Let's take another look at your safety plan."

"Okay."

Carol has regained her professional composure. "Is your emergency bag still at Lola's?"

"Yes, and I also hid an extra set of car and house keys in Pepper's dog house."

"That's a good idea. Sara, I think you are ready for Friday. Will you tell the boys when they get home Sunday?"

"Probably. I don't want Ronnie to be there. The boys will ask questions and say what they're feeling if I talk to them alone." Wearily I pull my hands through my hair. "I'm making the choice for the three of us to start our lives without him on Sunday."

I start to put my coat on.

"Sara, wait a minute. I have an observation about Logan and Derek that I want to share with you."

I take my arm out of my coat and sit back down. "Okay, what is it?"

"On Monday I had a client cancel at the last minute, giving me an hour to review some files. As I read through your journal entries, I noticed Derek was sleeping with Logan in his room when Ronnie moved out in December."

"Yes, he was."

"Then Derek started sleeping in his own room right after Ronnie moved out?"

I start to see where she's going with this. "And by his birthday in January, he was sleeping with Logan again."

"Yes. I think Derek or maybe both of them need the comfort of being together when Ronnie is in the house," Carol says.

A long sigh comes from me unexpectedly. "How much damage have I allowed to happen to them because I wouldn't face the reality of what their dad is?" Tears rain silently down my cheeks.

Carol scoots forward in her chair and reaches over, patting my hand. "Sara, Logan and Derek are going to be okay. With Ronnie out of the house, they can go with you to the children's group at Rose Brooks."

"That's true. I am looking forward to that."

Chapter 29 – Friday, 5:00 PM

Journal Entry — 3/13/2003 — Less than 24 hours until Ronnie has to be moved out. I pray he does so I don't have to hurt his mom. I read some place that when a couple is separating, it's a good idea to let someone close by know what is going on in case you need their help. If only Uncle Steve were here. A neighbor? Crosswhites are too old. Mrs. King is the neighborhood gossip. Guess it has to be Karen. She and Norman have been separated several times, so she should understand. I'll get up early in the morning and drive over to talk with her before I go to work.

As I walk to the car Friday morning, I notice how clean the spring air smells and hear birds singing making this a beautiful day. I hope it stays beautiful. Slowly, I drive down a street close to my house, looking to see if Ronnie's truck is in our driveway. I let out a deep breath as I round the corner. It's not there. I drive around the block and park six houses away. Ronnie won't be able to see my car if he gets home from work while I'm talking to her.

I knock on Karen's door. *She already knows Norman and Ronnie have the same temperament because of their ongoing feud about the exact location of the property line between our yards. Ronnie has found ways to alienate every neighbor we have,*

"Hi, Sara," interrupts my thoughts.

"Good morning, Karen. Do you have a minute?"

Glancing at her watch, she says, "A few minutes."

I bolster my courage to say, "Ronnie and I are separating today." I notice a dent in her door that looks like a foot has tried to open it. "Don't know if you ever hear our arguments."

"I've heard yelling from your house a few times but didn't want to embarrass anyone by asking questions," Karen says. "Would you like to come inside?"

"Yes, thanks. Privacy would be better."

Standing in her living room, I smile feebly. "I may need your help with something around five this afternoon?"

"Not sure if I can, but I'll try," she says, appearing nervous.

I let out a big sigh. "Ronnie and I are separating today," I repeat. "He's reluctantly agreed to move out." With my heart pounding, I say, "He's been threatening to hit me more and more lately. If he gets out of control this afternoon, I'd like to know I can come over here to get away from him."

She stares at me, her eyes widening. She turns and goes into the kitchen without saying a word.

Should I follow her? My emotions swirl back and forth between fear and determination. Think I'll just leave.

As I put my hand on the door handle, I hear her say, "Sorry I left you like that, but I had to check Norman's work schedule. She pulls her sleeve up to her elbow revealing deep purple fingerprints on her forearm.

I put my hand to my mouth and gasp.

"I quit babysitting your boys three years ago because I didn't want them to see Norman doing things like this to me." She gently pulls her sleeve back down.

My mind races, trying to process what she's just revealed to me. My mouth gapes.

"Norman isn't supposed to be home until seven. I'll be working out in my front yard ready to help if you need me."

Tears blur my vision as I look at my watch. "Thanks so much. I have to get to work. Now that we know we're in similar situations, maybe we can be of help to each other."

"Perhaps . . . but for me, it's impossible to make ends meet on my own." She opens the front door. "Seems I'm between a rock and a hard place with five kids to feed," she adds as I step onto the front porch.

"Thank you again so much, Karen. Hopefully, Ronnie will be gone when I get home."

***

Fear and dread of five o'clock blocks my concentration. It walls me off from doing my job efficiently as the second hand creeps ever so slowly all day long.

Thank goodness I've only had four new minor injury claims today. Hope double-checking each task kept me from making too many mistakes. Can't afford to lose my job now. God, if I have to talk to Mom Farley, help me to say the right words and ease any pain I cause her. My thoughts race back and forth between wanting this day to be over so I can know if he's moved or not and fighting the powerful urge, out of fear, to call him and take back my ultimatum.

"Goodnight, Sara," Nancy says. "Have a great weekend."

"Thanks, you too," I answer. *Mine will be if Ronnie's gone.*

***

"Wreck on 435 has traffic at a standstill," comes from my car radio. After exiting the interstate, I reduce my speed to as slow as possible without being a road hazard. "God, give me strength to follow through with this," I beg as I make the last turn toward my house.

My heart rate jumps with excitement when I see NO TRUCK in the driveway. After getting out of the car, I walk to the edge of the street to be sure he hasn't parked down the block like I did this morning. I don't see him anywhere. I quit holding my breath.

Standing at the front door, I wipe sweat from my face with the back of my hand as I turn the key in the lock. Hesitantly, I turn the handle and go in.

Silence thunders ominously from every room in the house. My muscles start to unwind. *Definitely not here.*

I go to the kitchen for a drink of water. Looking out the window, I smile at the sight of Pepper sprawled on her back, sleeping in the sunshine. *Wonder how many times I've washed dishes in this sink with my tears raising the waterline.* I take several cleansing breaths. *Hard to believe our whole future hinges on whether his clothes and shoes are out of our closet.*

I walk up the stairs and purposely step on the creaky step. Then I stand in front of the closet, looking at my image in the mirror. My sweaty palm slips as I turn the doorknob. The clothes rod on Ronnie's side is empty.

"It worked! He's gone! He's gone!" I shout, twirl, and dance. "Thank you, God, I don't have to go see his Mom." It is the most excitement our bedroom has seen out of me in a long time. I turn to collapse on the bed, exhausted. I hadn't realized how much the fear and dread of this moment was taking out of me. I close my eyes and rest.

The phone rings. Out of habit, I reach for it. "Hello."

"Hi, Sara," Ronnie answers. "Did you see I've moved out?"

"Yes."

"Just wanted to be sure you know you don't need to go see Mom tonight."

"Okay."

"Talk to you later. Gotta go to the grocery store."

"Bye."

Have to remember to look at the caller ID. Must go tell Karen before Norman gets home. I run out the front door.

As I step over the indefinable property line, Karen says, "I can tell by that big smile on your face, he's gone."

"Sure is. What a relief!"

"That's great news," she says, smiling slightly. She turns and walks toward the house, saying, "Better get dinner started. Norman will be home soon."

"Okay. Thank you again. If you ever need my help, please, please, don't hesitate to ask."

She nods. We each go back to our respective houses. They look so normal from the outside but contain so much anger and violence on the insides.

> Journal Entry — 3/14/2003 — So much relief! Such pain, dread and fear! Pain that my marriage is over, dread of the overwhelming responsibility of being a single mother, fear of how I'm going to make ends meet. Wish I had the courage to take the chance Ronnie will continue to give me child support payments if I refuse to have sex with him. Just can't take that chance right now – maybe some day soon. Too much to think about. Going to just let it be okay to ignore my emotions for tonight.

Chapter 30 – In My Cave

Soon as I get home from church, I settle down on the sofa to watch for the boys' arrival. I read my Bible, trying to find peace about divorce. When I hear a car horn, I go outside. Derek runs at me, talking and smiling. "Granny and Poppa have new kittens. Can we have one when they're big enough to leave their momma?"

"Hello to you, too, question box," I answer, hugging him. "We'll have to wait and see about kittens." He walks with me back to Aunt Lola's car.

"Hi, Mom," Logan says, pulling things from the back seat into his backpack.

"Hi, Logan. Did you have fun?"

"Sure did. Have lots to tell ya." He smiles real big. "Can we go to Kyle or Zach's, whichever one of them is home?"

"I knew that question was coming when you got here. Kyle's expecting you. Put your stuff in your rooms before you go."

"Thanks, Mommy. We will," he yells over his shoulder as he runs to the front door with Derek in his wake.

"How are you doing?" Aunt Lola asks.

"Good. I slept a lot, did some journaling, and cleaned the boys' rooms."

Uncle Steve moves over beside me and puts his arm around my waist. "I can't tell you how excited we all were to get your phone call that Ronnie's moved out. And I want you to know we will be here to help you whenever you need us."

I swallow a lump in my throat. "Thanks. That's one of the things that's helped me make the choices I'm finally making." I pick up a couple of sacks belonging to the boys. "When do you leave for Australia?"

"April 25th and get back May 12th," Aunt Lola says. "Wish you could go with us."

"Sounds wonderful. Maybe I can go to Switzerland or Italy with you after the boys are grown."

"We'll start planning for that," Uncle Steve says. He reaches for Aunt Lola's hand.

"We've got to get going," Aunt Lola tells me. "Have laundry to do before Steve leaves for Dallas tomorrow."

As I watch them back out of the drive, the phone rings.

"Hi, Ronnie."

"Did the boys get home yet?"

"Yes. They've gone to Kyle's."

Awkward silence. Then he says, "Since I'm off on Tuesday, how about I come take the boys to Kanagy Park after school, if the weather's nice? I'll bring your money, too."

Better not ask how much. "I'm sure they'd love that! What gave you that idea?"

"I was at a close-by park watching some kids play. I was thinking about how Logan loves swinging higher and higher until the chains jerk." I can hear a smile in Ronnie's voice.

Silence. *He's never gone to a park by himself before. Strange.*

***

Logan comes out of his bedroom, rubbing his eyes. "What time is it?"

"Seven." I stretch and pat the sofa on each side of me. "Sit down, boys. There's something I need to talk to you about."

"What's wrong?" Logan asks.

"Nothing. In fact, what's happened seems quite right." I put a hand on each of the boy's knees. "Remember how everything felt better when Daddy was staying at Uncle Chuck's?" I feel muscles tighten under both of my hands.

"Yeah, but he brought mean daddy back home with him," Derek says, disgustedly.

"He's more scary now," says Logan.

I feel my muscles tense. "More scary? How?" I ask.

Logan stands, shoves his hands into his pockets, and sways sideways. "Last week, when you were gone to the grocery store, Daddy took a nap. We made too much noise playing with our cars in the dining room, and he yelled at us to go to our rooms."

Derek starts tapping his foot.

"It isn't unusual for him to send you to your rooms," I say.

"I know. But I had to go pee terribly bad. I tiptoed to the bathroom in my sock feet and the door squeaked when I opened it." I see Logan's Adam's apple bob as he swallows. "He told me . . . I'd better never, ever F-blank-blank-ing wake him up again. It's so wrong for him to say that word to me. So wrong!"

Derek's incessant foot tapping is getting to me. I press down on his knee to get him to stop. "You're right. He shouldn't be saying any bad words to any of us. Sounds to me like you'll be happy to know Daddy moved to an apartment Friday."

The boys' eyes open wide, looking at each other.

"I won't m-miss him," Derek says in a small voice.

"Good," says Logan. "I don't ever want to see him again in my whole life!"

I motion at Logan to come back to the sofa. He sits down on the other side of Derek. "We're not going to have him yelling at us, and we're going to be okay," I assure them.

I scoot forward on the sofa and half turn toward them so I can see both of their faces. "Derek, when I was cleaning your room, I found your blanket and pillow in the closet again with almost all of your stuffed animals in there. How come?"

He drops his head. Logan reaches over and hooks his finger in Derek's belt loop. "Time to tell her, little Bro."

Derek's chin quivers as he looks at me. "When Daddy's yelling really, really loud at you, and Logan isn't here, I pretend my animals and me are climbing down into a blanket cave and then I pull a pillow in on top of us. Then I ca–ca–can't hear Daddy anymore." His knees squeeze his hands between them.

"Do you mean every time he yells at me?" I ask in surprise.

"No, Mommy," Logan answers. "It's when Daddy gets the loudest and when . . ." He swallows and goes on. " . . . when he's saying you'll be picking yourself up off the floor." He slouches back into the couch as if all his energy has drained from him.

"Oh, dear God," I say, feeling like Logan looks. I hear sniffles from each of them as I struggle with my swirling emotions. Words finally come. "What do you do when Logan's here?"

Logan answers. "We get in my bed, pull the covers over our heads so we can't hear him, and make each other sing happy songs."

"Is Daddy's yelling why you want to sleep with Logan sometimes?"

"Yeah. It's not as scary in Logan's bed."

I move off the couch and squat in front of them. "Now that you've told me this, I'm really glad Daddy is moved out." They both come off the couch at me.

"Uh, Mommy . . . I can't breathe," says Derek.

"Let go, Mommy, you're hugging too tight," adds Logan.

"Oh, sorry," I say, relaxing my grip on them." We all laugh. "I have an idea. How about we ask Zach and Kyle to come spend next Friday night with us?"

"Really?" Derek asks, jumping to his feet.

"Oh, yeah," says Logan. "Daddy won't be here to spoil our fun."

Chapter 31 – Wreck

With Aunt Lola and Uncle Steve in Australia, calling Ronnie is my only option when I'm running late. "I'm on my way home from Kansas City from a business meeting and can't make it to daycare before they close at six. Will you go pick the boys up and stay at the house till I get there?"

"Where are you?" he asks, impatiently. "How long before you'll be home?"

"I'm on I-70 and will be there in about an hour."

"Okay, but hurry up. I've got plans."

"Thanks. See ya."

Wipers aren't designed to move fast enough for the downpour pounding my windshield. Emergency lights and slowing traffic appear between the swipes of the windshield wipers. "Great. Ronnie's gonna really be pissed," I say to the empty space keeping me company in the car.

Twenty-seven minutes later, the creeping traffic is finally moving again. *Eighty-nine m.p.h. — way too fast. Cruise on 74 should get me there a little faster but not enough to get me a ticket.*

Five miles down the road, I feel a strange vibration through the steering wheel. *Car problems are the last thing I need.* The vibration intensifies as I hit a puddle, causing the car to glide sideways to the right onto the bumpy ridge at the edge of the pavement. That's when I remember Ronnie's warnings to not use the cruise control in the rain, something about hydroplaning. When I tap the brake to turn it off, my car slides over into the passing lane. A semi's air horn blares at me from behind. I jump! All I can see in my rearview mirror is truck grill. I yank the steering wheel to the right. The car floats across the lane and shoulder, flying me into pitch-black darkness. I hear the crunch and shriek of metal tearing apart. I scream like a banshee at the noise of the airbag exploding, sounding like a hundred parachutes opening all at once.

***

The hardness of the steering wheel presses into my face from beneath the deflated airbag as I regain consciousness. I put my hands on the wheel to push myself back in the seat – PAIN – in so many places! I hold my breath as long as I can. I gingerly lean back down against the steering wheel, then I breathe slow and shallow. I wait for the dizziness to subside. In my mind's eye, I see Ronnie's face giant and menacing, spraying spittle on my face. The vision motivates me to inch myself upright in the seat. *Have to get my cell – call 911 – need light.* With dread, I raise my hand toward the dome light. Just as it illuminates, a knife-pain pierces my right side.

Continuing to breathe shallow, I survey my surroundings. The front of the car is leaning down and to the left with glass pebbles glistening everywhere. A chill ripples through me, as I notice my purse containing my cell phone is against the passenger side door. When I try to reach for it, excruciating pain shoots through my left ankle. I scream! My vision goes out of focus and then clears as I think I'm going to pass out. Something wet and sticky trails down the left side of my face. I press napkins against a wound and they stick. "Lord, help me stretch far enough to get that phone," I say while steeling myself for the oncoming pain. I reach. *Just a little more.*

***

A faint light above me gradually focuses as I stare at it. *COLD — I'm so cold.* I pull my spring coat from the passenger seat. It's damp, but better than no cover. Then I notice my purse strap in my hand. "Hallelujah, I got it. I got it!" I fumble for my phone and dial 911. SILENCE. "Oh my God. . . no . . ." The unbearable pain in my side instantly stops my sobs. "I'm so tired . . . " Darkness everywhere. I hear an empty soft-drink can trundle across the floor. No flickering lights. *Boys – if Ronnie left them with Chuck and Amy's hooligans — I'll file for divorce tomorrow.* Shivers rack my body. *Rest . . . need rest.* Merciful unconsciousness comes back . . .

***

Sirens . . . voices . . . someone's hands touching me. "We're putting a cervical collar on you. The firemen are getting you out."

I raise my eyebrows, trying to pull my eyes open. *Too tired.* "What time is it?" I ask, relaxing my face.

"Six a.m. Your car's in a ravine – we couldn't find you until daylight," answers a different voice.

OH . . . warm blanket.

I drift into sleep. "I'm putting in an IV" rouses me. "You're going to feel a stick."

I smile slightly at the voice warning me about a needle stick compared to my night of agony.

"What is your name?" someone asks.

"Sara Sutherland." I moan deep in my throat like a trapped animal. "Uh . . . Sara Farley."

"Sara. Talk to me. What day is it?" the voice asks.

"Monday."

"Do you have children?"

"Two boys . . ."

"How old are they?"

"Derek's one. Uh . . . Logan's eight . . . no, can't be right. Uh, they're in grade school." It's too uncomfortable to lay still and it hurts so much, I dread movement. I concentrate on the whooping of the siren, hoping to ignore the pain. "That pain med isn't helping any! I'll tell you my boys' ages if you give me more of it."

"No. I can't give you pain medications, but tell me Logan and Derek's ages."

"How do you know their names?" I ask, feeling panicky that a stranger knows my kids' names.

"You told me their names when we were getting in the ambulance."

"Oh, yeah. Come on, just let me have some ibuprofen," I bargain.

"Sorry, can't do that. St. Mary's Hospital is the next exit."

* * *

"Sara, you're in the ER. My name is Jenny. Are you allergic to any medications?"

"No, just shrimp. Don't feed me shrimp. No throwing up."

Jenny laughs. "Okay, no shrimp."

"I have to have something for this shittin' pain!"

"All we can do right now is put ice packs on your ankle and head until we find out what the nature and extent of your injuries are."

"No wonder I'm so cold." I try to kick the one off my ankle, but the pain stops me. "Get these damn things off of me!"

"Okay, for a minute."

I feel something warm being put on top of me. I go to sleep or pass out again, don't care which.

I see Ronnie's face appear above me, with a tear trailing down his cheek. *NO, no, no, not you!* "Don't want you here!"

Through the thickness in my head, I hear a voice saying, "Ma'am, I'm here to take you over for tests."

"Oh, sorry. Thought you were someone else." My bed starts moving with the ceiling tiles and lights above me starting a parade.

***

Another warm blanket soothes me as I rouse again. "Dr. Vaughn says I can give you some medication to take the edge off of your pain," Jenny says. She injects yellow liquid into my IV.

"Thanks."

Jenny raises the head of my bed higher, making me wince. "We're going to get this collar off of you, too." I hear the Velcro fasteners pulling loose, then she checks tape on the bandage above my left eye. "I'll bring your family in to stay with you while we wait for the test results."

I see a familiar small hand pulling on the curtain. With eyes wide and full of fear, Logan comes into sight with Derek behind him. Derek's eyes are red, and watery. I brace myself at the sight of Ronnie.

"How are you doing?" Ronnie asks from the foot of my bed.

"Okay, I guess." Logan is on the left side of the bed, rubbing my hand, and Derek is on the other side, squeezing my hand tight. "Hello, boys. I'm okay," I say, looking at one and then the other, squelching the need to moan and groan.

"Daddy, will you lift me up so I can give her a kiss?" As Derek gets close to my face, he asks, "Will it hurt if I kiss you?"

"You can kiss my cheek." His sweet, teary kiss feels great. When Ronnie puts him down, Derek's hand slides back into mine.

"I'm big enough I can stand on my tiptoes to give you a kiss," Logan announces. His kiss is quick and light.

"Mommy, how many boo-boos do you have?" Derek wants to know.

"Lots. You can count them later if you want to."

Ronnie smiles at me. "How ya doing?" he asks me again.

"Hurting a lot," I answer impatiently.

"It'll get better. I called your job and left a message telling them you've had a car accident and won't be in today." He speaks matter-of-factly as if he is in charge of my life.

I look around at the sound of the curtain trailing back in its track. A blond, curly-haired young man comes to my bedside. "Mrs. Farley?"

"Yes. Please call me Sara."

"Sara, I'm Dr. James Vaughn. I understand you tangled with an air bag when your car went off I-70 last night."

"Sure did. This is Ronnie and these are my sons, Logan and Derek." Dr. Vaughn shakes Ronnie's hand. He then extends his hand to Logan, who straightens up a little taller for his handshake. Derek follows suit with a big smile.

Dr. Vaughn opens my chart. "You've got a serious concussion but no hemorrhaging." He moves from the foot of the bed to my side. "You'll have bad headaches for a few weeks, but they should fade as time goes by. Pain medication for your other injuries should keep them at a tolerable level."

"What about this knife in my side?"

"Your ribs are deeply bruised, but nothing's broken. Time is the best medicine for both of those injuries."

"What about her ankle?" Ronnie asks, nosing into our conversation.

Dr. Vaughn continues looking at me. "Looks like your ankle got smashed pretty hard in the accident."

"The metal wadded up around it when the floorboard buckled in the crash," Ronnie informs him.

"The x-rays show several fractures." The boys squeeze my hands. "I spoke with an orthopedic surgeon who looked at your x-rays. He says you're going to need surgery."

"Can Mommy come home now?" interrupts Logan.

"Not for a while. She needs to stay with us a few days until we get her fixed up," Dr. Vaughn answers. Turning back to me, he adds, "The nurse is arranging a room for you right now."

Derek starts crying.

"Oh," says Logan, reaching over and pulling Derek close to him. Logan and I squint back tears.

"But I have to go home today," I insist.

"I'll stay with the boys until you're able to get outta here," volunteers Ronnie. "Just stay here and do what the doctors say."

"But . . ."

Ronnie puts his finger to my lips. "Stay here and get better," he says, in his nicest voice. "I'll take good care of the boys."

"Guess I don't have any choice," I say dejectedly, as I wipe his touch from my lips.

My pain is easing. The heated blankets distill my shivers. Sleep is suddenly very inviting. I relax into the warmth and close my eyes.

"Sara, Dr. Perry will be by tomorrow to discuss your surgery." Dr. Vaughn smiles at the boys and says, "Your mom will be home in a few days and I'm sure you'll take good care of her." He disappears behind the curtain.

"Come on, boys, time to go to school," Ronnie says.

"But I want to stay with Mommy," whines Derek.

I open my eyes. "It won't be any fun watching me sleep all day. Go have a good day at school." I try to rouse myself long enough for them to leave. "Then Daddy can bring you back for a visit this evening." I look at Ronnie for confirmation.

He nods. "Yes, boys. I'll be there to pick you up when you get out of school."

They give me forced smiles and put their jackets on.

"I'll let school and daycare know what's going on."

After kisses from the boys and an unwanted peck from Ronnie, they leave. I pull my blankets closer, trying to ignore the physical and emotional pain. *Timing of this wreck sure sucks! Aunt Lola and Uncle Steve won't be back home for another 14 days. No one else to help me but Mr. Hyde. Damn it! Hope I've learned enough at group and counseling to keep Ronnie at a distance and not let my feelings rebuild.*

***

I think I am dreaming when I hear Derek saying, "Mommy, Mommy, look at the pictures I colored for your room!"

"Hello, guys," I mumble through grogginess. Pain stabs my side as I struggle to sit up. "Here, let me help you," Ronnie says, pushing the button to raise my head.

Then Logan pushes a button, raising my knees. "Don't do that!" Ronnie says gruffly.

I frown at him, and his voice softens as he explains to Logan how those buttons can fold me into a pretzel.

"Sorry, Mommy," Logan apologizes.

"It's okay," I answer, forcing a smile through my pain for him. "How was school today?"

Derek has pushed a chair to the wall and is up on it with his colored pictures and scotch tape in hand.

"Mrs. Jennings let us learn about hydroplaning today," Logan answers. "It's amazing how water can lift a big heavy car up off the road."

"Sure is. I don't ever want to do that again!" I answer.

"Hey boys, I need to talk to your Mom. That window ledge looks like a good place for car races." They grab their backpacks and scramble to the window.

Ronnie moves the tray table out of the way and pulls a chair against my bed on the opposite side from the boys. I look past him at some far-off thing on the wall.

"Did you have the cruise control on when your car went off the road?" he asks quietly in icy tones.

I glance in the boys' direction, buying time. I am unsure how to answer him when the door to my room opens at the perfect time. "Sorry to interrupt the visit with your family," the nurse says. "I have medications for you so you'll be ready for surgery tomorrow."

"We'll finish this later," Ronnie hisses under his breath. The corner of his mouth twitches. "How's my lovely wife doing?" Mr. Hyde asks, flashing his best smile.

"Mommy, I brought Rafael to sleep with you," Derek says. He pulls his floppy-eared rabbit out of his backpack and runs over to my bed. He arranges his sleeping buddy on my left arm, tucked in so tight, he's almost under me.

"Don't you need him to sleep with?"

"No." He hooks a finger in one of Logan's belt loops. "Logan's letting me sleep with him in his big bed till you get home." He attempts a smile.

"Yeah, he won't be afraid sleeping with me," Logan assures me.

"Sounds like a good plan to me," I say. "Come, give me easy hugs and kisses."

I lean left slightly to get their affection. As Logan kisses my cheek, he whispers in my ear, "Don't worry, Mommy. I'll take care of the little guy until you get home." He gives me a hug that's too tight, but it's worth the pain.

Ronnie picks Derek up high enough to hug me.

"Thank you so much for sharing Rafael with me. We'll sleep well tonight."

"Love you, Mommy."

"Come on boys, let's go," Ronnie says. "I'll see you in the morning before surgery." He winks at me as he closes the door behind them.

***

> Journal Entry — 5/2/2003 — Really nervous about going home. Ronnie is being so great about all this that I'm having difficulty keeping my emotions restrained. Have to keep my guard up though and remind myself Mr. Hyde will return first chance he gets.

"Good morning, Sara," says my nurse, waking me for vitals. "I understand you may get to go home today."

"Yes, finally. Seems like I've been here for a month instead of a few days. Do you know when Dr. Perry will be here?"

"Shouldn't be long. I saw him in the hall just before I came in here."

"Great. I'll call Ronnie to tell the boys the good news."

Moving around on crutches is slow and frustrating as I gather things to go home. *With Ronnie in the house, it's either going to be a long two weeks until I can walk on this ankle, or . . . nice if he continues acting the same as he has been so far.*

Chapter 32 – Going Home

About mid-afternoon I hear, "Mommy, Mommy."

"You get to go home today," says Derek.

"Looks like it." Both boys hug me softly.

"I'll tell the nurse we're ready to go," Ronnie says, starting out the door.

'Wait a minute, Ronnie. Wait! Dr. Perry still has to come by and release me before we can go." *Hope he doesn't blow his stack about having to wait.*

He frowns. "Why'd you call me if you're not ready to leave yet?"

"I said, 'If Dr. Perry gives the okay, I'll be released this afternoon' and that you could come on over or wait for me to call you after I see him." I glance down at my notepad. "Then I said it was your choice."

His face looks stormy. I shudder and tighten my arms about me. He smiles. "Come on, boys, let's watch cartoons with Mommy until Dr. Perry gets here."

I relax, gradually.

Scooby Doo and Power Rangers fill the next hour as we wait. Occasionally Ronnie stands, walks to the door, looks both ways in the hall, and returns to his chair. Each time he gets up, my body tightens, as I fear his rage will erupt.

As Transformers starts, Dr. Perry comes in the door. "Hello, everyone." He smiles at me. "Looks like you're ready to go."

"Sure am," I answer, happily.

Ronnie's eyes sparkle as he looks at me, picks up my hand and kisses it. *His charm is on a flip-switch just like his anger.* I pull my hand away.

Dr. Perry turns the pages in my chart, pauses, and then goes on. My stomach clenches a little more with each pause. "Everything looks good. Remember, no weight on that ankle for two weeks. Call my office on Monday, schedule an appointment. Do you have any questions?"

"Don't think so. Thanks for everything, Dr. Perry."

"You're welcome. I'll tell the nurse you're ready to go, and she'll be in with a wheelchair shortly. Take good care of her, boys," he says as he walks out the door. Logan and Derek wiggle with joy, giving each other high-fives. Ronnie gives me his best disarming smile.

* * *

On the way home, I rest with my eyes shut, enjoying the feel of the sunshine on my face. From the back seat, I hear the boys chattering excitedly about how they are going to take care of me like that nice Dr. Perry told them to.

"Sara, do you feel like stopping at the park for a few minutes?" It gets quiet in the back seat. "If not, we'll go after we get you settled in at home."

"This warm sunshine feels so good, that sounds nice if we don't stay too long." I hear "Yeah!" and "All right!" from behind me.

As Logan and Derek hit the slides, I feel Ronnie take my hand. He is shaking. When I look at him, I see perspiration trickling down the side of his face.

He clears his throat. "When you were late getting home the other night, I got mad. Then you not answering your cell for hours got me worried. When the highway patrol couldn't find you all night, I was just plain scared." He swallows hard. "Then I started thinking about what I might have to say to the boys if you weren't okay."

I can't stand to see him in such pain, so I turn away to watch the boys chasing each other. Ronnie strokes his thumb on the back of my hand, his hand trembling less. When I look back at him, tears are streaming down his face. The only other time I've ever seen him cry like this was when my Grandpa died.

"I promised God that if He'd just bring you home safe, I would treat you the way I should have been doing all along." Now he is holding my hand with both of his. "On my way home from the hospital Monday night, it dawned on me that it didn't matter if you had the cruise control on or not. I'm sorry I asked you about it." Tears stream down his face. "From now on, I'm going to focus on showing you how much I love you." His magic touch shoves against my resistance. "I love you. Please, please, give me another chance."

Unable to force my eyes from his, I whisper, "Ronnie . . . I don't know what to say. You've sure taken me by surprise." I take my hand from his, lean back in my seat, trying to stop the flood of emotions hitting me with earthquake force.

"Mommy, are you tired yet?" asks Logan, through my rolled down window. "You have your eyes closed."

At the sound of Logan's voice, I hear Ronnie sniffling. I assume he is wiping away tears.

"Yes, I am. I think it's time to go home."

* * *

"Derek, how about unlocking the front door?" Ronnie asks as his truck stops in our driveway. "Logan, will you carry some of Mommy's stuff into the house?"

"Yeah, Daddy" echoes from both of them as they go to do their tasks.

The pain pills are wearing off as I loosen my seatbelt. I am dreading the long trip hopping to the house on crutches. Ronnie comes around the truck and opens my door. "Here, Sara, put your arm around my neck. I'll carry you into the house." When I look at him, his eyes are still red from crying. He eases me out of the seat. His muscles feel oh so familiar and good. Another increment of resolve melts.

He sits me down on the sofa. Logan goes to the kitchen for a glass of water while Derek and Ronnie prop my foot up, rearrange pillows to just the right spots, and cover me with a blanket.

"This is wonderful, guys. I'm impressed and pleasantly surprised." Each of them wears smug, pleased-with-themselves smiles. "There's just one thing wrong." Their faces go solemn. "I've got to go to the bathroom." I give them an obnoxious smile.

Their frowns change to grins. Derek giggles, and the rest of us join him.

"Come on boys," Ronnie says, "Let's get her up to go to the bathroom. That was a good practice run."

* * *

At bedtime, I sit in the recliner with a son on each side of me, reading a chapter from Derek's Power Rangers book. When Ronnie comes into the living room after cleaning the kitchen, he sits down on the sofa. He watches us instead of turning on the TV.

Derek lightly touches the bruises up and down my left arm. As I close the book, he says, "Mommy, you have thirteen boo-boos on this arm. Do they all hurt?"

"Not any more. They're getting better."

"I'm soooo glad you're going to be okay," Logan says. "And that you're home."

"Me, too." I pull them both in close for hugs.

"Time for bed, boys," Ronnie tells them.

"But I want to stay up with Mommy," moans Derek.

"Hey guys," Ronnie intercepts the bargaining I know is coming. "Mommy needs lots of rest so she can get better. You'll have the whole weekend with her starting after school tomorrow."

"Okay," Derek says with resignation and starts toward Logan's room.

* * *

After getting the boys settled into bed, Ronnie sits in a chair next to me. Feelings I thought long gone bubble. My resistance wanes.

"Sara, I think what I said to you at the park must have been quite a shock. Just let me stay here to help you like I did when you were in bed before Derek was born. If things get difficult for either of us, I'll go back to the apartment." He reaches over and strokes my cheek.

"I really do need help right now. Living in this split-level with so many stairs doesn't work for crutches." I am bone weary. "Okay, we'll give it a try — but no going to the bars!"

"I don't need the bars when I'm here with you and the boys." He raises my hand to his lips and starts a trail of kisses at my fingertips. I pull my hand away because a dozen unexpected emotions are hitting me with a warning light flashing in my heart to proceed with caution.

His melodious laughter still makes a ripple of goose bumps race across my flesh. He stands in front of me and holds out his arms toward me. "If you're ready for bed, I'll carry you upstairs."

"I am exhausted." As I scoot forward in the chair, I stop and look up at him. "Wait a minute. Just what do you have in mind upstairs?"

His eyes crinkle at the corners. "To just let you sleep and get better. Nothing else. I promise."

I study his face.

He takes a step back and holds up his hands. "Honest, no sex. I can see how tired you are, and I'd guess you're ready for another pain pill."

"Sure am." He takes my hand to help me stand.

> Journal Entry — 4/24/2003 — I want to get today's happenings on paper while Ronnie's watching TV. Wish I could switch my emotions to "none" or "newlywed" intensity for responding to Dr. Jekyll or Mr. Hyde, whichever Ronnie is at any particular moment. Since it isn't humanly possible, I'm stuck with the status quo of being on this roller coaster of emotions with him.
>
> Reality Check — must have his help for two weeks until I see Dr. Perry. By then, Aunt Lola and Uncle Steve will be home — will re-evaluate options then.
>
> Sex — hardest area to deal with due to his insatiable sex drive — like when I had pneumonia last August and Dr. Motley ordered me to complete bed rest for one week. Ronnie said we didn't have the $500 deductible for me to go to the hospital (I bet he had it in his savings account). Actually, he didn't want me away from him where I was inaccessible for sex. He figured two to three times a day wasn't too often since I was already in bed and had plenty of time to get rested for the next time the urge hit him. If his sex drive becomes a problem this time, I'll reissue the threat to tell his Mom about the wife-swapping charade. I AM A STRONG WOMAN — I CAN DO THIS!

* * *

"The boys are on the bus. How about breakfast in bed?" Ronnie asks, coming through the door with a tray of scrambled eggs, toast, and coffee.

"A girl could get used to this," I say, pulling myself up to a sitting position. He arranges pillows between me and the headboard.

He smiles wide. "Feels good to be spoiling you. Go ahead. Eat."

He sits down at the foot of the bed, drinking coffee and watching me. I feel self-conscious.

"Tell me what needs to be done, laundry, vacuuming, what?"

"Let's see . . . both bathrooms need cleaned, the grass could use a mowing . . . I'll think of more by the time you get those done."

"Cute, real cute." He comes to me and kisses the top of my head like he used to a long time ago, then goes downstairs.

Ronnie being, doing, and saying things that I'm starved for causes a maelstrom of emotions to whip around and blend together within me, igniting an ember of happiness like I haven't felt in years. Once again, my psyche wants to filter out the terrible things that have happened, and automatically revert back to the dream marriage every cell in my body still craves, like an addiction.

With breakfast finished, another pain pill working on me, and pillows everywhere, Ronnie lays down beside me. He kisses my cheek and lips with passion and gentleness that reduces my emotional starvation. "Just what do you have in mind?" I ask.

"Sweetums, I know you're way too sore and in too much pain for sex." That was his favorite name for me when our marriage was good. "I just want to lie here with you for a while, maybe take a nap, and then I'll get busy on your 'honey-do' list." I curl into the cradle of his body, enjoying the memories of days and nights gone by.

* * *

"Mommy, I don't want to wear pink," gripes Logan. When I look up from my book, I see him holding a pair of pink-splotched underwear in each hand. I try to not laugh, but can't help myself.

"Ain't that funny?" Derek says in an angry stance. "Mine's pink, too!" He holds a pair out in front of him with the waistband stretched tight.

Having heard the boys' comments, Ronnie comes through the dining room door, looking sheepish. "Boys, we'll go to Wal-Mart for new underwear after dinner." He glances at me and tries to keep a straight face.

The boys glance at each other. Smiles gradually spread across their faces and laughter echoes through the house.

* * *

Lying in bed at night, Ronnie and I rediscover things we like about each other. I am feeling so comfortable with him in the house again that I decide to ask a question that I know will truly test our relationship.

"Remember me telling you I'm going to counseling?"

It takes so long for him to answer, I don't think he heard me. "Yes, I remember. Are you still going?"

"Yes, I am. I'm wondering if you'll drive me there Wednesday."

He is quiet again. My body tenses as I wait.

"I'll ask for a day of vacation so I can take you."

> Journal Entry — 5/19/2003 — I shudder at the horrendous thought that if I had completely quit on my marriage, we would have missed out on the dream life we've had since the wreck. The memories of his bullet words hitting me full blast causing my body to recoil are becoming hazier and hazier as his words of love flow over me like warm satin. And, oh, his touch – closes my eyes in pleasure, is as soft as butterfly wings, melts the residual resistance left in me, and feels like he's touching my heart in a very special way. The question of whether I dare trust him with my heart is becoming a moot point as time goes by.

> Last week Ronnie couldn't find a hammer to hang a picture for me. His voice started rising with accusations of the boys losing it. I don't know what kind of looks the boys and I had on our faces, but Ronnie suddenly stopped, looked at me, and, back at his normal voice level, asked if any of us knew where he had last used it. Deep, ragged sighs from Logan and Derek drew our attention. Ronnie dropped to his knees and gathered them into his arms while looking at me. His face softened as he apologized for scaring us. Derek retrieved the hammer from where Ronnie had left it, and the three of them hung the picture, then went outside to play catch. A difference of night and day from what would have occurred before our last separation.

Chapter 33 – Intimate Terrorist

When Carol opens the door to the waiting room, a deep look of concern crosses her face. "What in the world happened to you?"

"Car wreck. I had a concussion and fractured my left ankle."

She lets out a big sigh. "What a relief."

As she sits in her rocker, she says, "I was afraid Ronnie had done this to you. Tell me what happened."

"I don't remember much about it. I was coming home from meetings in Kansas City and the state troopers say I hydroplaned off of I-70. It took until daylight for them to find me."

"Who was with the boys?

"Ronnie. When I was running late, I called him and asked him to pick them up. He did and stayed at the house. He called the highway patrol when I didn't get home by ten."

"I'm pretty sure the pain pills aren't what's put that big smile on your face. What else is going on?" she wants to know.

I swallow hard, then say, "Ronnie's been staying at the house helping with the boys, cooking, cleaning, doing laundry, and he brought me here today." I wait uncomfortably.

"Sara, from the beginning of you coming here, I've said my job is to help you think things through. But I need to remind you abusers almost never change for the long-term."

"Maybe he's the exception. After all, he has controlled his sexual appetite since I came home from the hospital. I think he can stop being an abuser." I move my foot to a different position, hoping the zings of pain will stop.

Carol scoots her footstool over to me. "Is he staying at the house or the apartment?"

"Both. He's stopped at the apartment a few times to pick up clothes." Wish I could tell what Carol is thinking.

"As I said, very few abusers change for the long term. Which phase of the Cycle of Abuse are you in right now?"

I need to walk to the window. "Honeymoon." I gather some calmness from my limited view of the pink and white blossoms outside. I move my foot over about a half-inch.

"Is there no one besides Ronnie to help you?"

"No. Aunt Lola and Uncle Steve don't get home from Australia until a week from Tuesday. I'm hoping Aunt Lola can come stay with us a few days when they get back. Uncle Steve will be out of town a lot due to being gone from the office for so long."

"In the meantime, maybe neighbors and people at your church can help you."

"I don't want to be a burden to anyone," I answer quietly.

"Have you ever helped someone who needs help?"

I nod.

"How did that make you feel?"

"Great. It always feels good to see thankful smiles on peoples' faces."

Carol leans forward in her chair. "Sara, when you don't ask others for help, you are robbing them of opportunities and the pleasure of them seeing that thankful smile on your face."

"Hmm . . . " I smile. "Never thought of it that way before."

"Why do you think Lola and Steve help you with the boys?"

"Because they're so much fun and they've never had kids of their own."

"And why do they give you things they know you can't afford to buy?"

"Because we're family."

"Not because they like you and you're fun?"

"Maybe . . . "

"Have any of your neighbors ever helped you with anything?"

"Yes, Karen next door. She took care of Logan when I was on bed rest with Derek. Then she took care of both of them when I went back to work."

"Perhaps the way Ronnie is helping you now feels reminiscent of when you were on bed rest."

"I don't want to admit it, but, yes, it does. That's one of the reasons it's so difficult to keep my hope of permanent changes from overtaking me – again."

"Let me remind you of two very good reasons to not give those hopes room to grow." She holds up one finger. "Shattered window." Adding a second finger, she says, "Ladle thrown at you. Men who are cruel, indifferent, abusive, addictive, and unable to be loving and caring don't change for the long term."

I sob. In an effort to control my lurching emotions, I swallow and grip my jacket tightly around me.

"Sara, if you can't keep from being drawn in by Ronnie's charm and game-playing for your own benefit, do it for Logan and Derek."

Carol waits.

"I don't see how . . . how I can make it without him."

"Can't make it in what way specifically?"

"Mainly financial."

"He has consistently given you child support every week that you've been separated, hasn't he? That isn't why he's staying at the house, is it?"

"No, but I have to give him most of what he wants and right now him being at the house is what he wants."

Carol puts bullet points on a sheet of paper. "Does your church know about your accident?"

"No, haven't been there since the wreck."

"Call the church office to see what kind of assistance they can give you."

"That will be hard for me to do . . . "

"Next, I think the boys are old enough to warm up food and put dishes in the dishwasher with your supervision. I bet they can even do laundry with some instructions."

"I guess. But I can't maneuver the stairs with crutches. There's just so many of them in our split-level. He's been carrying me up and down them."

"Really?" she says. "I think Ronnie is counting on you feeling exactly how you're feeling. He knows how badly you want things to work out between the two of you, and he's taking advantage of the situation."

My blood rises in my cheeks. "If that were the case, he would be demanding sex from me, wouldn't he?" I wiggle around in my chair as much as the cast will allow.

"I don't know why he isn't. Have you considered he might be getting his needs met someplace else? Has there been anything out of the ordinary to suggest that's a possibility?"

I struggle to get up on my crutches so I can walk out on this bitch. Before I can accomplish it, Carol squats down in front of me and puts her hand on my knee.

I sling her hand away. "Leave me alone!"

Gently and in a kind voice, she says, "Sara, when someone is in the middle of something, they have a skewed perspective and little ability to step back and see what is really going on. Do you think there's a possibility this is happening in your situation?"

My powerful feelings frighten me. I seem to go into a white arctic zone of acceptance and my anger drains away, leaving me exhausted.

> Journal Entry — 5/20/2003 — I'm out of the cast and wearing one of those ugly black boots that is so clunky. Scooting up and down the stairs on my butt works pretty well. As I've been able to do more for myself and am able to get the boys up and off to school, Ronnie's been sleeping at his apartment when he gets off at 4:00 am and then comes over here about noon. He is still being a great husband and father. I'm still scared to trust that it will last though because Carol's words of "skewed perspective" keep popping into my head. I'm just biding my time waiting for him to prove everyone wrong. He's even been giving me extra money to make up the difference between my workers compensation and regular pay. Thank goodness I go back to work next week.

Chapter 34 – "Mean" Daddy Room

> Journal Entry — 5/27/2003 — I love spring with nature's beauty bursting to life after a long winter's rest. Having Ronnie here since my accident, it seems my marriage is renewing in the same way. The feeling of crunching eggshells beneath my feet is lessening as time passes. I've had moments when I've noticed I'm holding my breath, waiting to see who he is, Dr. Jekyll or Mr. Hyde. Seeing frozen looks on the boys' faces as they wait to see which father is talking to them has decreased. Dare I hope Ronnie is one of the few abusers who have chosen to change? Only time will tell.

As I switch the car off in my driveway, I hear yelling. *Sounds like it's coming from next door. Hope Norman isn't beating Karen again.* The yelling continues as I limp toward the house, carrying a gallon of milk.

"Bend over, Logan. You're getting an ass whipping like you've never had before!"

"Oh my God!" I shout. "That's Ronnie!"

I drop the milk jug. It bursts when it hits the corner of the step, splashing milk on my legs and skirt.

"But I didn't mean– " I hear Logan start to say.

"Shut the fuck up! I'm getting this done before your damn mother gets home."

My mothering instincts ignite. I shove the screen door open so hard, it snaps the retainer chain and slams against the side of the house. As I rush down the hall to Logan's room, I scream in a voice louder and stronger than any I'd ever heard come out of myself before, "His damn mother's here!"

I see Ronnie's belt in his hand stop in mid-air above Logan, who is bent over his desk chair. Derek is backed into a corner, sobbing and trembling.

Ronnie takes his hand off Logan as if his son were suddenly electric. With his eyebrows knitted together, the lurking danger is strong and thick. As Ronnie turns, he trips on Logan's baseball bat and falls onto the bed. As I watch him trying to get up, I see my opportunity. I grab Logan and Derek's hands, pulling them into the hall out of Ronnie's view.

I bend down to their level. "Go to Karen's house and stay there. If she's not home, go to Kyle's or Zach's. I'll come find you soon as I deal with your dad."

They both stare at me with frantic terror in their eyes.

"Damn you, Sara! Bring that boy back in here right now!" Ronnie bellows.

Logan's head jerks around to see how close his dad is. "I have to get my baseball bat," he says, trying to get past me.

"Not now! Logan, take your brother and get outta here!" I move them down the hall pressing on their backs with my hands. They resist, looking over their shoulders, then take off running when Ronnie appears in the bedroom doorway.

I turn to stand my ground against the drunk. My body urges me to back away, but I force myself to not give an inch to the bastard swaying back and forth in front of me.

"Where the hell they going?" he slurs.

"Some place safe from you." Barely hearing a siren in the distance gives me an idea. "Someone must have called the police. My guess is you have one, maybe two minutes before the police get here."

"Why they coming?"

"To see what's going on here. I'm sure all the neighbors heard you screaming at Logan through the open windows."

"Damn!" he says, shoving past me. He slams the front door shut as if that was where his yelling had escaped from the house. I move closer to the back door, grabbing his truck keys off the counter. He follows me.

"Two minutes, huh? That gives me one to pound the shit out of you and be gone before they get here." The corners of his mouth foam as he moves toward me.

I am ready to fight back for my life. "Stop!" I shout. He stops, looking dumb-founded.

I heave myself past him, yank open the front door, and step out onto the porch. I hold out the keys as if I'm tempting a dog with a bone.

"Give me those damn keys," he says, swaying toward me.

He trips on the threshold and grabs my hand to catch his balance.

I yank my hand free from his. The keys stay in his hand.

"They're almost here," I say, hearing a siren coming closer.

He clutches the keys in his fist and raises them to my face. I don't flinch. "I *guarantee* you will spend the night in jail if you touch me," I say with force and confidence.

His fist loosens in slow motion, dropping to his side. The sirens grow louder as he backs down the steps. As he gets closer to his truck, he pauses and starts back toward me with his eyes glaring evil. "You dumb-ass bitch!" he yells.

I step inside, close the door, and turn the lock with my shaky hand. He glances down the street for the siren, maybe a block away. "I'll be back soon as those damn cops are gone."

He gets into his truck and backs out of the drive. As his truck turns the corner, a police car with blazing lights and siren zips right on past my house.

Trembling, I hobble out into the yard, shaking my fist in the air. "Go run yourself into a tree some place!" I collapse to the ground, exhausted and in tears. Hugging myself, I rock back and forth.

Suddenly I stop. *He said he'd be back. Gotta change the door locks.* I run next door to Karen's. When she opens the front door, both of my boys jostle past her and into my arms.

"Are you okay?" asks Logan, his face white with fear.

Derek's eyes are teary and wide. "Did he hurt you?"

"I'm okay, guys. I'm okay." When I look up at Karen, she looks panicked. "Did you call the police?" I ask.

She drops her eyes to the porch. "No . . . I couldn't do it. I thought you were okay because he quit yelling." Blinking back tears, she looks up. Just then her husband's car pulls into the driveway.

"Or, he could have been killing me was why he stopped yelling."

She gasps, putting her hand to her mouth as the three of us walk away.

* * *

"We did it all by ourselves," I brag to the boys while tightening the last screw on the new door lock.

"Can Daddy still come in some times?" asks Derek.

"Yes . . . but only when we want him to."

"Come on, Derek, let's go play Zelda," says Logan.

"Will you help me get to the next level?" Derek wants to know.

I go upstairs. I stare at my wedding ring, turn it slowly around and around, take it off and drop it in a drawer. *What do you do with wedding rings when the marriage is gone?* Despair over my lost marriage clings to me like a wet garment after a rain.

With a blank journal page lying on the counter in front of me, I take deep breaths. I listen to the boys playing their video games as though this day hasn't been a life-altering day for our family. My muscles release. My emotions stabilize. The cobwebs clear from my brain, and I start writing.

An angry, loud voice from the living room interrupts my thoughts. "Do what I tell you to or you'll be picking yourself up off the floor!"

I stub my big toe running for the living room, trailing drops of blood. I don't feel a thing. "LOGAN!" He looks like a mini-sized, threatening Ronnie.

Derek turns around, runs and grabs hard onto my legs, sobbing heavily. I put my arm around him.

Logan stands about five feet away, looking angry, cords straining hard in his neck. He pounds his tight fists against his thighs.

In a calmer but firm voice, I instruct Logan to go sit in the rocking chair while I talk to Derek. I peel Derek loose from me, move us to the sofa, and sit us down. "Derek, breath slow . . . slower . . . slow." I take both of his hands in mine. "Now, tell me what happened."

"He . . . he said I have to sleep in the "mean daddy" room by myself if I don't give him my Blue Eyes White Dragon card." He sobs.

"Why does he want your card?"

"'cause it's the best Yu-Gi-Oh! card there is."

I look at Logan. His face is covered with both hands, tears leaking from between his fingers. I look back at Derek.

Tears fill my eyes as I pull him into a hug. "It's okay."

He tries a smile and wipes his teary, slimy face on his shirtsleeve.

"Why don't you go take a bath while I talk to Logan?"

"'kay," he says. As he goes toward the bathroom, he keeps looking back at me.

"Logan?" Tears no longer drip. "Logan, come here please." He shakes his head. "Yes. Come here," I say strongly.

He reluctantly stands and moves to the other end of the sofa from me. "Threatening to hurt Derek is absolutely unacceptable. Why did you say that?"

"'cause he wouldn't give me that card!" He looks straight ahead with his body rigid.

"Did you think threatening him would make him give it to you?"

He turns his head, glaring at me. "You do what Daddy wants when he says it!" He turns away.

My breath catches. My hand flies to my mouth. I start shaking. "Oh, dear God!" I take a deep breath and move down the sofa closer to him. I reach for his hand. "Logan, I was afraid of Daddy." I hold tight as he tries to pull away. "I believed he would hurt me really bad if I didn't do whatever he said to do. That's one of the reasons he doesn't live here anymore."

His hand tightens around mine.

"Do you want Derek to be afraid of you like that?"

He suddenly looks at me. "No, Mommy, no! He's my little bro."

I see tears building. "I know how much you love him. I'm sure you also know how scared he is of sleeping in your room, especially by himself."

He bobs his head up and down. "I don't want to sleep in the mean daddy room, either."

"I know you don't, and we're going to remake your room tomorrow so it won't remind you of daddy anymore. And, I'm going to tell you something you can do instead of making threats."

"Like what?" He seems curious now.

"Like . . . running ten circles in the front yard. Do you wish you had known that before you got upset with Derek?"

"Yeah. Can I go tell Derek I'm sorry?"

"Yes, you may."

He squeezes my hand before he slips free.

I slowly walk to the kitchen, listening to Logan's apology. Derek asks him to play in the tub with him. My shaking hand makes it difficult to write, but their laughter slowly calms me.

Snuggled between my precious little ones, I pray for strength to climb the mountains in front of me. And I go to sleep making plans of how to change the "mean daddy" room.

***

"Logan, which one of these blues do you want your room to be?"

His eyes widen and he starts a smile, then stops. "But Daddy won't let us paint it anything but that silly baby-blue. And I'm no baby!"

"I know. But since Daddy isn't living at our house any more, we're going to paint our rooms with colors we like . . . your room first."

"Can we paint mine yellow like the canary bird at Zach's?" Derek wants to know.

"Yes, we'll do yours next Saturday."

"Yippee!" Then he stops jumping up and down. "What? I want mine done today tooooo."

I squat in front of him. "We're going to paint Logan's today so it won't be a 'mean daddy' room any more."

His pout fades as he points to a paint chip in my hand. "That one, Logan. That one."

"Yeah, Mom, I like that one." We watch the paint shaker mix the paint, pick out brushes and rollers. Walking out of the store, all three of us have smiles as bright as the sun in the sky.

Medium blue paint splatters the plastic covers that protect the floor and furniture. The boys paint up as high as they can reach while I paint from there up to the ceiling. We take turns starting songs and finish them together. As I close the hallway door so I can paint behind it, Logan's baseball bat hits the floor. We all jump. I hand it to Logan. "Put this in the closet with your glove and balls."

Slowly he walks over to me and takes the bat. "It has to go back behind the door after the paint dries."

"Why?"

Derek's lower lip quivers. Logan hangs his head. "'cause, just 'cause," says Logan, staring at the floor.

I sit down on the floor for a much needed rest. "Come… sit with me," I say, patting the plastic covered floor. They look at each other and slowly sit. "You have to tell me why the bat can't be in the closet."

"Zach's dad hits his mom," Derek blurts out.

"How do you know that?" I ask, shocked by his revelation.

"Zach told us and we've seen her black eyes," Logan adds.

"But we go to church with them every week," I mutter, trying to process what they are telling me. "Christian men don't hit their wives," I say, wondering if that's really true. (Appendix I)

"Zach's dad started his own church and is the preacher, so he can say it's okay for dads to hit moms," says Logan.

"But what does that have to do with the baseball bat?" I ask.

"'cause Daddy's always tells you that you'll be picking yourself up off the floor," says Logan.

"We know he means he's going to hit you," Derek says and scoots closer to me.

With vengeful anger on his face, Logan jumps up into a batter's stance with his bat. "If we ever hear him say that again, we're coming after him with this!" Logan drops the bat to the floor.

I jump!

Logan collapses to the floor and stares at new paint on the wall. "That's why it stays behind the door, not in the closet!"

I am stunned.

I hear "Mommy?" like it's coming from afar. I feel a paint-crusted little hand slip into mine bringing me back to the moment. I gulp air. "Boys, you have to tell me what happened yesterday!"

They stare at each other. Logan swallows hard.

"Logan was being a good, big brother," Derek finally says.

"What happened?" I ask again.

He blinks tears. "I woke Daddy while h-he… was taking his nap."

Logan's voice is brought back by his anger. "Yeah, Daddy said Derek was too noisy when he walked through the living room and that Derek woke him up!"

"Yeah. He… he… started yelling at me to go to my… room," Derek says hesitantly. "After he went back to sleep, I wanted to play with Logan. So I tiptoed to his door. When I opened Logan's door, it made noise. Daddy ordered me back to my room." Derek rubs a paint splotch on the plastic, making the splotch bigger.

Logan lets out a sigh much too big for an eight-year-old. "After Daddy had more beer he went in Derek's room and was going to whip him. Because Derek was so scared, I told Daddy I was the one that opened the door. He came into my room and yelled for Derek to get in here, too."

Derek's tears flow like a river. "He was ta-taking off his belt."

Logan stands up and paces in the paint splatters with his bare feet. "Daddy said, 'cause I nosed into his business with Derek that I was the one getting a whippin' and Derek had to watch." He plops on the floor.

"That's when you got . . . home," says Derek, wiping snot on his tee-shirt sleeve.

I stand and pace in the paint. Then I sit back down. "Come closer, boys." I take their hands. "It's extremely, extremely important you tell me the truth." I take a deep breath, steeling myself for their answers. "Has Daddy ever hit either of you with his belt before?"

They look at each other as if they are trying to be sure the other one is going to give the same answer. "No," says Derek quietly.

"No, he hasn't," says Logan, reinforcing Derek's answer.

"Guys, remember what they teach you in Sunday School about lying. Are you telling me the truth?

They both nod. Logan holds up his right hand. "I promise, Mommy. We're telling you the truth," he says. Derek puts his right hand up and crosses his heart with his left hand.

"Okay guys." I pull a new gallon of paint close to us.

Logan glances around his room. "I like my new room." His tear-stained face smiles at me.

"The best is yet to come." I tell them to strip to their underwear. I open another can.

Puzzled, they strip while I pour dark blue paint into the tray. I touch my hand to the paint and then handprint the wall. Their eyes light up as they scramble to join me. An hour later, the three of us lay on the floor with our feet on the wall, admiring our handiwork of hand, foot, elbow, fingers, and nose prints all around the room. I vetoed the butt-print Logan wanted to do.

"Thank you, Mommy, for giving me my new room," said Logan, putting his crusted blue hand in mine.

"We do this to my room tomorrow?" asked Derek.

"No, next Saturday."

"Maybe we can paint all the rooms in the house to get rid of the mean daddy," ponders Logan.

"Maybe so," I answer him, wishing it were only that easy.

"Time to get you two in the tub before you stay blue, permanently."

After I scrape and wash paint off them, they go to Kyle's for the afternoon. I paint trim, clean up the mess, and plan our futures.

Chapter 35 – Final Journal Entry

Journal Entry — 9/11/2004 — It's been fourteen months since Ronnie left for the absolute last time. My courage hit its peak that day. I'm amazed how I went into action. It felt like I was watching someone else stand up to our intimate terrorist. Our lives changed forever in those few moments. But it was *me*! Girl, I'm finally proud of you!

I now know why Ronnie didn't resist either of the separations more than he did. One day in the middle of July, he called me at work pleading that I come to his apartment immediately. I heard fear in his voice unlike anything I'd ever heard before. Inside his apartment, I stood at the patio door looking at the St. Louis skyline. He told his "life and death emergency" to me as he sat on the couch across the room behind me. He chain-smoked as he relieved his guilty conscience by confessing to an on and off affair that started one week before he moved to Chuck's in December. I wanted to bludgeon that SOB into unconsciousness! But . . . I'm not an abuser . . . so I wouldn't let myself do that.

My ears became radar antennae, seeking out his exact location so he wouldn't have time to stand up before I responded to him. I felt as though a bomb had exploded in my stomach. When I turned on him, my legs didn't want to move; all my muscles, even the bones, seemed twice their usual weight. MY rage forced my legs to move. Instantly I was standing over him like he has done to me hundreds, maybe thousands, of times.

I felt tendons stand out on my neck. My voice rose to a scream, saying, "You have ripped and shredded my emotions into nothing for years. If we didn't have two sons the law demands I have to let you see, you would never, ever see any of us again. You have abused me for the last time!" I walked out the door and out of his life for the final time.

Ronnie's confession included the fact he had actually rented his apartment in February so he could be with his mistress. Learning about the girlfriend explains so many things — leaving early and getting home late from work, she is the woman Amy was trying to warn me about Christmas Eve, the phone call on the day he threw the spaghetti ladle was her telling him her husband had found out she was cheating and that she was ending the affair — that was the real reason he threw the spaghetti ladle — it had nothing to do with me.

How did I feel? — angry, hurt, betrayed, humiliated, pained, abandoned, horrified, disgusted, resentful, depressed, rejected, abandoned, injured, embarrassed, bewildered, vengeful, indignant, and torn. Thanks to Carol, there is no doubt about how I feel about him. It has been difficult to not beat myself up at not recognizing the obvious signs he had a girlfriend, but Carol has helped me to not do that. I am finally convinced he is an abuser who will never change. Very seldom does he remind me of the charismatic, charming man I married and remembering the day in his apartment is my permanent reality check.

Without the monumental support of Carol, the group, Aunt Lola and Uncle Steve, I would have stayed with Ronnie for the rest of my life. Kristen recommended her attorney to me, and the divorce became final in February. I keep a cautious relationship with Ronnie like two enemies forced into a truce.

When I told the boys about the divorce, they only wanted to know how often they have to see him, which is every other weekend. When he picks them up, they go to McDonald's or Fun House for a couple of hours, and then he brings them home. They've stayed overnight at his apartment once. They're more interested in spending time with their friends. I now know the abuse will not impact our lives forever, and that we will know happiness some day. As the boys become young men, they'll have to figure out what kind of relationships they want to have with their father.

Logan and Derek started going to Rose Brooks for the children's sessions the week after Ronnie left for the last time. Derek's stuttering lasted a couple of weeks, and then went away. I was surprised to find it on the list of problems children have when they live in homes where there's domestic violence. He's learning to express his emotions through drawing. The first few pictures were in shades of gray and black with small bits of color. Recently, they've become lighter with more color and some smiles.

Logan's stomachaches stopped within one week of Ronnie moving out (that's on the list, too). Logan uses physical activity to assuage his anger. He's becoming a good basketball player. He moved his baseball bat from behind the door within a month of Ronnie's departure, and it's still in the closet.

The three of us have settled into a good routine. Homework is done at the kitchen counter while I cook dinner. Instead of sitting in front of the TV like zombies, we play board games and read books in the evenings. They now come home from Zach's when his dad gets there. Recently Zach's mother commented about how Logan and Derek seem calmer and happier these days. I've told her about Rose Brook. No response from her. I don't know how Maria is because I'm never at Chuck and Amy's any more.

I've spent a lot of time talking to God about my disastrous marriage and divorce. I know in my head He forgives me, but the feelings don't match up yet. Forgiving myself for failing still seems impossible. I now thank God for my 9/11 nightmares. They were the catalyst that forced me to stop my intimate terrorist in his tracks.

To get reacquainted with myself, Carol suggested I make a list of things I like and dislike. At first, I couldn't name any of mine, but I knew all of Ronnie's. She says this is normal. I had lost myself during the years I was married.

It astounds me how the terrorists' attack on 9/11/2001 parallels women and children being terrorized in their own homes. That now infamous day has given every American a hint of what it feels like to be a domestic violence victim. What would America's recovery level have been like if more terrorist attacks had occurred on 9/12/2001, if thousands more had died on 9/13/2001, and more attacks and deaths followed on 9/14/2001? This is the world of domestic victims. They are being terrorized in anger-blasted homes day after day, month after month, year after year. I wonder how many domestic violence victims would leave abusive situations if given a small semblance of support, such as what was shared across America on 9/11 and in the following days.

Maybe I'll find a way to help people connect their 9/11 experiences with domestic violence victims trapped by personal terrorists. Empowered with this knowledge, thousands of women and children imprisoned behind closed doors can be rescued. Maybe I can be the one by talking to small groups about it — no, not *me* who got a D- in speech class. But I might write a book and be on Oprah some day. These ideas make me laugh out loud.

Laughter and freedom feel so good!

APPENDICES

Appendix A – Am I a Victim of Domestic Violence?

RATE YOUR RISK :

Are You At Risk To Become A Victim of Family Violence?

TAKE THIS SELF-TEST TO SEE IF YOU ARE AT RISK TO BECOME A VICTIM OF FAMILY/DOMESTIC VIOLENCE.

Rate yourself for risk by answering each question with Yes or No:

DOES THE PERSON YOU LOVE . . .

_____	"Track" all of your time?	_____	Control all finances and force you to account in detail for what you spend?
_____	Constantly accuse you of being unfaithful?	_____	Humiliate you in front of others?
_____	Discourage your relationships with family & friends?	_____	Destroy personal property or sentimental items?
_____	Prevent you from working or attending school?	_____	Hit, punch, slap, kick or bite you or the children?
_____	Criticize you for little things?	_____	Use or threaten to use a weapon against you?
_____	Anger easily when drinking or using other drugs?	_____	Threaten to hurt you or the children?
		_____	Force you to have sex against your will?

If you find yourself saying "yes, this has happened to me" to any of these, then you are at risk to become a victim of domestic violence and IT IS TIME TO GET HELP.

San Antonio Police Department web site

http://www.ci.sat.tx.us/sapd/SAF_Risk.htm

The following is a list of warning signs for potentially abusive relationships. They are presented as guidelines and cues to pay attention to, not as judgments on the worth of the other person.

Question relationships with partners who:

- Abuse alcohol or other drugs.
- Have a history of trouble with the law, get into fights, or break and destroy property.
- Don't work or go to school.
- Blame you for how they treat you, or for anything bad that happens.

- Abuse siblings, other family members, children or pets.
- Put down people, including your family and friends, or call them names; accuse them of being "trouble makers".
- Manipulate you with phrases like, "You're hurting me by not doing what I want," and "If you love me, you will/will not do that."
- Is hypersensitive – easily insulted, perceives the slightest setbacks as personal attacks.
- Is cruel to animals or children,
- May expect children to perform beyond their capability (i.e., spanking a two-year-old for wetting a diaper).
- Always angry at someone or something.
- Make you feel guilty for wanting to slow the pace or end the relationship.
- Expects you to meet all of his needs; take care of everything emotionally and domestically.
- Try to isolate you and control whom you see or where you go; expect you to spend all of your time with them or "check in" to let him know where you are and who you are with.
- Nag you or force you to be sexual when you don't want to be; restraining you against you will; acting out fantasies in which you are helpless, initiating sex when you are asleep, demanding sex when you are ill or tired, "playful" use of force during sex.
- Shows little concern for your wishes.
- Explosive behavior and moodiness that can shift quickly.
- Threatens, breaks or strikes objects to terrorize you.
- Extremely jealous and/or possessive of you – equates jealousy with love; can't stand to be apart from you.
- Cheat on you or have lots of partners.
- Are physically rough with you (push, shove, pull, yank, squeeze, restrain).
- Take your money – controls finances – makes you account for every penny spent.
- Accuse you of flirting or "coming on" to others or accuse you of cheating on them.
- Don't listen to you or show interest in your opinions or feelings.
- Things always have to be done their way.
- Disrespectful and puts you down.
- Put down your family, friends, dreams, ideas and goals.

- Lose temper frequently over little things.
- Makes you feel as if walking on eggshells to keep the peace.
- Make threats to hurt you or your children, leave you, injure your pets, and destroy your property.
- Ignore you, give you the silent treatment, or hang up on you.
- Plays mind games.
- Refuse to take responsibility for his actions. Blames you for his behavior.
- Lie to you, doesn't show up for dates, and maybe even disappear for days.
- Make vulgar comments about you and others.
- Blame all arguments and problems on you.
- Tell you how to dress or act.
- Threaten to kill them if you break up with them, or tell you that they cannot live without you.
- Experience extreme mood swings; tell you you're the greatest one-minute and rip you apart the next minute.
- Tell you to shut up or tell you you're dumb, stupid, fat, or call you some other name (directly or indirectly).
- Compare you to former partners.

Some other cues that might indicate an abusive relationship might include:

- You feel afraid to break up with them.
- You feel tied down, feel like you have to check-in.
- You feel afraid to make decisions or bring up certain subjects so that the other person won't get mad.
- You tell yourself that if you just try harder and love your partner enough that everything will be just fine.
- You find yourself crying a lot, being depressed or unhappy.
- You find yourself worrying and obsessing about how to please your partner and keep them happy.
- You find the physical or emotional abuse getting worse over time.

Your relationship is healthy if:

- You trust your partner.
- You treat each other the way you want to be treated, and accept each other's opinions and interests.
- You each feel physically safe in the relationship.

- Your partner likes your family and friends; encourages you to spend time with them; wants to include them in his/her life as well as yours.
- You make important decisions together.
- Your partner understands when you spend time away from him or her.
- You don't feel responsible for protecting your partner's reputation or for covering for his/her mistakes.
- Your partner encourages you to enjoy different activities (like joining the volleyball team or football team, running for student government, or being in a play) and helps you reach your goals.
- Your partner likes you for who you are " not just for what you look like.
- You are not afraid to say what you think and why you think that way. You like to hear how your partner thinks, and don't always have to agree.
- You have both a friendship and a physical attraction.
- You don't have to be with your partner 24/7.
- Your partner doesn't force sexual activity or insist that you do something that makes you uncomfortable.

What are your rights in a relationship?

- To express your opinions and have them be respected
- To have your needs be as important as your partner's needs
- To grow as an individual in your own way
- To change your mind
- To not take responsibility for your partner's behavior
- To not be physically, emotionally, verbally or sexually abused
- To break up with or fall out of love with someone and not be threatened

Source: Domestic Abuse Project (http://www.domesticabuseproject.org)

Appendix B – Verbal Abuse

Verbal Abuse and its Devastating Impact
by Patricia Evans - **http://www.verbalabuse.com/**

Although many people have heard sticks and stones may break our bones but words will never hurt us, those who have suffered from verbal abuse know that words do hurt and can be as damaging as physical blows are to the body. The scars from verbal assaults can last for years. These psychological scars leave people unsure of themselves, unable to recognize their true value, their talents and sometimes unable to adapt to life's many challenges.

The circumstances under which verbal abuse takes place make a real difference in how to respond to it. In the workplace, for instance, an appropriate response to a very abusive boss might be to prepare a resume or to read the want ads. On the other hand, a child can't very well escape from an abusive parent and so we, the observers and relatives of the child must be alert and ready to speak up for him or her. Keeping a record and letting others know what is going on are often good first steps.

Frequently Asked Questions - Reprinted with permission from iVillage.com

Is name-calling verbal abuse?

Yes! Name-calling is abusive because it says that you are BLANK, but actually you are a person. Batterers define their mates as objects. It isn't healthy to be in the same room with a person who defines you, and it is harmful to children who witness it. They either see their survival threatened or they think it's normal, or both.

Why does it seem that after he abuses me verbally he is happy, like he feels relieved? Also, he will act like it never happened. It's like he has no memory of it. I try hard to not fight with him because it's not worth it -- it only makes him say more things. I end up asking myself if I am blowing things out of proportion or overreacting.

This is what verbal abusers do. Verbal abusers almost universally act like nothing happened, like they feel fine and the relationship is fine. This is because they feel they have more control. Maybe they got you to back down, believe them or doubt yourself. Being more compliant and more slave-like makes them happy.

My husband's counselor doesn't think my husband's abusive nature is all that bad, and doesn't consider it domestic violence. Since when is breaking picture glass, slamming doors and breaking doorjambs not violent? I have the feeling they think it's just a "communication problem," and they are encouraging couples therapy. I said no way. What do you think?

The problem of finding a counselor who understands that verbal and physical abuse come from the same underlying control issues, and neither is justified, is difficult. Often counselors are trained to look for a 'cause (you) and effect (abuse)' relationship. But you and your mate are not mechanical -- therefore what you do doesn't make him be abusive. If your relationship were mechanical, then when you push up like on a seesaw, he would be affected: he'd go down. But that's not how it is. I refer therapists and counselors whom my readers have discovered and whom they refer on to me as "someone who understands abuse." The easiest way to find one is to call my office -- the number is 925-934-5972. Information is at my Website, **www.PatriciaEvans.com.**

My husband's abuse is the very quiet, insidious kind. He always finds a way to make me the problem. When he gets angry, he is enraged. There does not seem to be any degree between not being angry and rage. He has agreed to go a licensed therapist, but I have already reached a point of depression myself. The question is, what to do now? He has his first appointment this week with the counselor. Do I wait to see what she says? How long will it take before things are right? Will they ever be right?

The abuse you describe usually happens behind closed doors, so some people may not see the problem. I do. Most abusers present a "perfect" image to their therapist, admitting to a mistake or two, which they swear wouldn't happen if only their wives would "whatever." Also, most women don't take to an abuser, sexually, once he shows his controlling side. Most who are abused are too traumatized to regain the level of trust necessary for physical intimacy. Please trust your intuition and take care.

After years of verbal abuse, the abuse turned physical when my partner tried to rape me. He has been in counseling, but now that he knows more about abuse, he accuses me of abusing him. His counselor told me he can change with time, therapy and will, but I don't believe he wants to change. If he's acting this way while he's still on probation, I shudder to think how he'll be when he no longer is. Am I just being paranoid? Can an abuser really change?

Most abusers take years to change and most women aren't turned on to anyone they've been afraid of, and that's just the way it is. It's a natural protective instinct. Women aren't likely to want to have a child with a controller. It's a commitment to a life either of pain and suffering, or divorce and possible difficulty with custody. I think that the instinct to stay away from an abuser is built into the survival of the human race and well worth attending to. Women ignore this instinct at their own risk -- and sometimes put themselves at risk just to placate the person who has abused them.

I know I'm being verbally abused, but I just can't bring myself to leave. What's wrong with me?

There are many reasons why it's hard to go. People who suffer from frequent verbal abuse need plenty of support. If you have family or friends to go to, just get away and see what it's like. Know that while you stay, you're with the same mentality as a batterer. Physical abuse is always a possibility, but the emotional abuse is worse in the long run. See if you can find a support group at a local shelter. Abusers get worse over time and always blame the victim.

Appendix C – Cycles of Abuse

Domestic abuse falls into a common pattern, or cycle of violence:

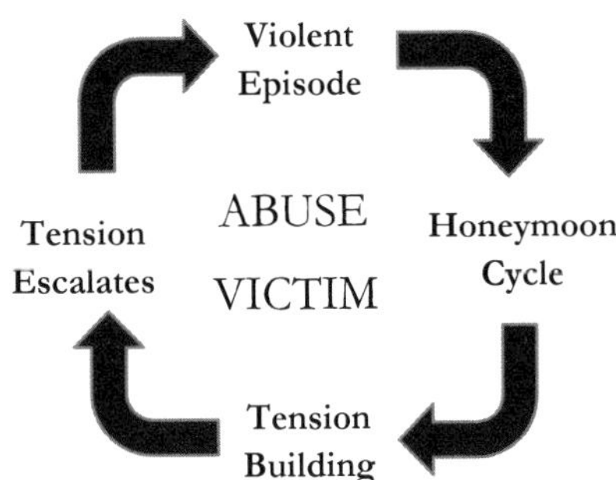

- Abuse – Your abusive partner lashes out with aggressive, belittling, or violent behavior. The abuse is a power play designed to show you "who is boss."
- **Guilt** – After abusing you, your partner feels guilt, but not over what he's done. He's more worried about the possibility of being caught and facing consequences for his abusive behavior.
- **Excuses** – Your abuser rationalizes what he or she has done. The person may come up with a string of excuses or blame you for the abusive behavior—anything to avoid taking responsibility.
- **"Normal" behavior** — The abuser does everything he can to regain control and keep the victim in the relationship. He may act as if nothing has happened, or he may turn on the charm. This peaceful honeymoon phase may give the victim hope that the abuser has really changed this time.
- **Fantasy and planning** – Your abuser begins to fantasize about abusing you again. He spends a lot of time thinking about what you've done wrong and how he'll make you pay. Then he makes a plan for turning the fantasy of abuse into reality.
- **Set-up** – Your abuser sets you up and puts his plan in motion, creating a situation where he can justify abusing you.

Your abuser's apologies and loving gestures in between the episodes of abuse can make it difficult to leave. He may make you believe that you are the only person who can help him, that things will be different this time, and that he truly loves you. However, the dangers of staying are very real.

The Full Cycle of Domestic Violence: An Example

A man **abuses** his partner. After he hits her, he experiences self-directed **guilt**. He says, "I'm sorry for hurting you." What he does not say is, "Because I might get caught." He then **rationalizes** his behavior by saying that his partner is having an affair with someone. He tells her "If you weren't such a worthless whore I wouldn't have to hit you." He then **acts contrite**, reassuring her that he will not hurt her again. He then **fantasizes** and reflects on past abuse and how he will hurt her again. He **plans** on telling her to go to the store to get some groceries. What he withholds from her is that she has a certain amount of time to do the shopping. When she is held up in traffic and is a few minutes late, he feels completely justified in assaulting her because "you're having an affair with the store clerk." He has just **set her up**.

Text from: *Mid-Valley Women's Crisis Service*
Graphic designed by Susan Grace Napier

Appendix D – Making a Safety Plan

Your safety is the most important thing. Listed below are tips to help keep you safe. The resources in this book can help you to make a safety plan that works best for you.
Domestic violence shelters may be able to provide you with a cell phone that is programmed to only call 911. These phones are for when you need to call the police and cannot get to any other phone.

If you are in an abusive relationship, think about...

1. Having important phone numbers nearby for you and your children. Numbers to have are the police, hotlines, friends and the local shelter.
2. Friends or neighbors you could tell about the abuse. Ask them to call the police if they hear angry or violent noises. If you have children, teach them how to dial 911. Make up a code word that you can use when you need help.
3. How to get out of your home safely. Practice ways to get out.
4. Safer places in your home where there are exits and no weapons. If you feel abuse is going to happen try to get your abuser to one of these safer places. Avoid kitchen and bathrooms.
5. Any weapons in the house. Think about ways that you could get them out of the house.
6. Even if you do not plan to leave, think of where you could go. Think of how you might leave. Try doing things that get you out of the house - taking out the trash, walking the pet or going to the store. Put together a bag of things you use everyday (see the checklist below). Hide it where it is easy for you to get.
7. Going over your safety plan often.

If you consider leaving your abuser, think about...

1. Four places you could go if you leave your home; someone the abuser does not know is a good choice.
2. People who might help you if you left. Think about people who will keep a bag for you. Think about people who might lend you money. Make plans for your pets.
3. Keeping change for phone calls or getting a cell phone.

4. Opening a bank account or getting a credit card in your name.
5. How you might leave. Try doing things that get you out of the house - taking out the trash, walking the family pet, or going to the store. Practice how you would leave.
6. How you could take your children with you safely. There are times when taking your children with you may put all of your lives in danger. You need to protect yourself to be able to protect your children.
7. Put together a bag of things you use everyday. Make copies of as many of the following documents as possible. Leave it with someone where you can get to it easily in case of an emergency – again, with someone the abuser does not know is a good choice.

ITEMS TO TAKE, IF POSSIBLE

☐ Children (if it is safe)

☐ Money

☐ Keys to car, house, work

☐ Extra clothes for you and your children

☐ Medicine

☐ Birth certificates

☐ Social security cards

☐ School and medical records

☐ Bankbooks, credit cards

☐ Driver's license

☐ Car registration

☐ Welfare identification

☐ Passports, green cards, work permits

☐ Lease/rental agreement

☐ Mortgage payment book, unpaid bills

☐ Insurance papers

☐ Protection or Restraining orders, divorce papers, custody orders

☐ Address book

☐ Pictures, jewelry, things that mean a lot to you that abuse may destroy

☐ Items for your children (toys, blankets, etc.)

8. Think about reviewing your safety plan often.

If you have left your abuser, in addition to the list above, think about...

1. Your safety - you still need to.
2. Changing the locks. Consider putting in stronger doors, smoke and carbon monoxide detectors, a security system and outside lights.
3. Telling friends and neighbors that your abuser no longer lives with you. Ask them to call the police if they see your abuser near your home or children.
4. Telling people who take care of your children the names of people who are allowed to pick them up. If you have a protection order protecting your children, give their teachers and babysitters a copy of it.
5. Telling someone at work about what has happened. Ask that person to screen your calls. If you have a protection order that includes where you work, consider giving your boss a copy of it and a picture of the abuser. Think about and practice a safety plan for your workplace. This should include going to and from work.
6. Not using the same stores or businesses that you did when you were with your abuser.
7. Someone that you can call if you feel down. Call that person if you are thinking about going to a support group or workshop.
8. Safe way to speak with your abuser if you must.

WARNING: Abusers try to control their victim's lives. When abusers feel a loss of control - like when victims try to leave them - the abuse often gets worse. Take special care when you leave. Keep being careful even after you have left.

This section on personalized safety planning is adapted from the Metro Nashville Police Department's personalized safety plan.

Appendix E – Helping Children Handle Anger

Children need to know there is nothing wrong with being angry and that everyone gets angry sometimes. But they need to know ways to express their anger in a safe and socially acceptable way. When children feel helpless, tired, jealous, or hungry are some feelings that can manifest into anger. Make certain they do not get what they want by throwing tantrums. Don't just tell your child what **not** to do; tell them what they **should** do.

- Comment on your child's behavior when it is **good.**
- Talk with them about why and what makes them angry.
- Count to 10 slowly; for older children, have them count from 10 backwards.
- Be still for a full minute and be quiet – works better when parent does it along with children.
- Blow or breathe out very forcefully.
- Breathe in for a count of their age – breathe out for a count of their age.
- Take "time-out" or "alone-time" to calm down.
- Make angry faces in the mirror.
- Draw or color pictures about what makes them angry, how they felt before they got angry, and how they feel as they get over the anger.
- Hit or scream into a pillow.
- Run in circles until get dizzy and they may laugh when they fall down.
- Use modeling clay to squeeze, knead, make into object of anger and tear it apart.
- Give them a stress ball or toy to carry in their pocket.
- Put a feather on an empty table and have them blow it across the table – make it into a game.

http://www.kidsource.com/kidsource/
http://www.livestrong.com

Appendix F – Restraining and Protection Orders

Restraining and protection orders are two options for people being threatened or physically abused. They are similar in whom they protect, but are different in how long they are good for and the penalties for violation. In the United States, each state has specific laws for abuse, stalking and sexual assault. No filing fees are usually charged for restraining and protection orders. Check with your state and local authorities for definitive information.

Restraining Orders

Restraining order laws establish who can file for an order, what protection or relief a person can get from such an order, and how the order will be enforced. It's literally a piece of paper a judge signs stating the terms someone must follow or risk legal consequences. They are often used to give legal protection to victims of domestic abuse, harassment, stalking and neighborhood disputes. Parents and guardians can seek restraining orders on behalf of children. The scope of them can be wide. The purpose is to give victims protection until a hearing can be scheduled.

Protection Orders

A protection order requires individuals to refrain from directly or indirectly contacting the victim and from threatening, abusing or harassing any member of the victim's household. It can give you some time to find a safe place to live away from abusers.

Experience suggests that protection orders might be most effective with men who ordinarily obey the law and have something to protect, such as their standing in the community or their employment. For the batterer who has contempt for all authority, has a history of other criminal behavior or is determined to control his partner at all costs might not obey protection as well. On the other hand, having protection orders can enhance local law enforcement's efforts to assist the victim, and repeated violations of a protection order eventually are likely to result in legal consequences for a perpetrator.

For most women, becoming a victim of a violent crime is their first introduction to the legal system. Statistically, a woman's danger increases 75% when she tries to escape her abuser. It is vitally important to have a well-thought-out safety plan (see Appendix C). Protection orders are NOT ironclad shields against any abuser's assaults. Even law enforcement agencies that have strong resolve to respond to victims' needs cannot provide officers to be with her 24 hours a day.

If an order is granted, you should make numerous copies and keep one with you at all times. Also leave a copy of the order at work and your children's school or daycare. An abuser or harasser breaks the law when they don't follow the restraining order's terms, and the police should be called immediately.

Typical Information Needed to Apply for Orders

In the Kansas City metropolitan area Emergency Rooms, domestic violence shelter advocates can assist in getting emergency orders issued (even in the middle of the night). The process for obtaining these orders starts with filling out the needed paperwork. You can get the forms at your local courthouse, shelters and domestic abuse prevention organizations, and online. It will save you time and can be more complete if your statement is prepared in advance of going to apply for the order. If not, it will need to be written at the time of your interview at the courthouse. Generally the forms will ask:

1) What your relationship is to the abuser?
2) Write a detailed statement of incidents involving abuse (be very specific about the abuser's actions, threats, etc.) with dates or approximate dates, and descriptions. Start with the most recent incident and work your way back in time that the abuser did any of the following to you or your children (indicate which child):
    a. Physically abused any of you (hitting, punching, choking, sexual abuse, etc.).
    b. Did something to make any of you afraid of physical harm (restraining, raising a fist, etc.).
    c. Interfered with any of you making an emergency call.
    d. Indicate if the police were involved. Was the abuser arrested? Charged? Were you injured? Did you receive medical attention? Where?
3) Addresses for locations you would like protected by your order (usually restricted to you and your children's residences, workplace, school, daycare).
4) Take your forms, your ID, and identifying information about the person you seek protection from (including name, addresses,

social security number or driver's license number and photo, if available) with you to your local courthouse.

5) The court clerk takes your forms and information to a judge, who decides if a temporary restraining order is needed until a hearing can be scheduled.
6) If the order is granted, the court arranges for service of process to the alleged abuser, giving them legal notice and the date for the court hearing.
7) At the hearing, you must show the abuse or harassment, and your need for protection. The judge decides whether to issue the permanent restraining order. Domestic violence shelters may have advocates available to assist with preparing for and going to court.

<u>You have the right:</u>

- To physical and emotional safety and security. No one has the right to hurt another person.
- To keep your own income and determine how it will be used.
- To be treated with respect and consideration.
- To say no to sex and to sexual advances. It is rape when a man has sexual intercourse with a woman against her wishes.
- A man can be convicted of raping his own wife. A wife who is forced to have sexual intercourse with her husband against her will can take action against him for sexual assault.
- To be protected by the police. The police have a duty to keep the peace. The police have a duty to stop, and arrest anyone who has committed a criminal offense. If you have been hit, this is an assault and the police have a duty to protect you.
- To be treated with fairness, respect, and dignity. To be free of intimidation, harassment, or abuse.

Appendix G – Summary of Dr. Jekyl and Mr. Hyde

by Robert Louis Stevenson – first published in England in 1886

Every Sunday, Mr. Utterson and Richard Enfield take a stroll through the city of London. Mr. Enfield tells of an incident of an extremely unpleasant man trampling a small girl while running from something, or to somewhere. A large crowd gathered and held the stranger, Mr. Edward Hyde. The crowd forced the man to make retribution in the form of money. They held him until the banks opened.

About a year later, an upstairs maid witnesses the vicious murder of a kindly, distinguished old gentleman and the maid positively identified the murderer as Edward Hyde. On another walk, Utterson and Enfield step into Dr. Jekyll's courtyard and see him in an upstairs window. As they greet Dr. Jekyll, his face is covered with abject terror and, after a grimace of horrible pain, he suddenly closes the window and disappears. Utterson and Enfield are appalled by what they have seen.

Some time later, Utterson receives a visit from Poole, Dr. Jekyll's man servant who suspects that foul play is associated with his employer. Dr. Jekyll has confined himself to his laboratory for over a week. Dr. Jekyll has ordered all of his meals to be sent in, and has sent Poole on frantic searches to various chemists for a mysterious drug. Poole believes his employer has been murdered and that the murderer is still hiding in Jekyll's laboratory. Mr. Utterson and Poole return to Jekyll's house, where they break into the laboratory. There, they discover the body of Edward Hyde. They search the entire building for signs of Jekyll and can find nothing, except a note addressed to Utterson, which is the "confession" of Dr. Henry Jekyll.

Jekyll had been born wealthy and grown up handsome, honorable, and distinguished, and yet, he committed secret acts of which he was thoroughly ashamed. Intellectually, he evaluated the differences between his private and public lives and, ultimately, he became obsessed with the idea that at least two different entities, or perhaps even more, occupy a person's body. His reflections and his scientific knowledge led him to contemplate the possibility of scientifically isolating these two separate components. With this in mind, he began to experiment with various chemical combinations. Having ultimately compounded a certain mixture, he then drank it, and his body, under great pain, was transformed into an ugly, repugnant, repulsive "being," representing the "pure evil" that existed within him. Afterward, by drinking the same potion, he could then be transformed back into his original self.

His evil self became Edward Hyde, and in this disguise, he was able to practice whatever shameful depravities he wished, without feeling the shame that Dr. Jekyll would feel. Recognizing his two "selves," Jekyll felt the need to provide for, and protecting, Edward Hyde. He drew up a will leaving all of his inheritance to Edward Hyde. Thus, this double life continued until the murder of the elderly gentleman by Edward Hyde.

This horrible murder caused Dr. Jekyll to make a serious attempt to cast off his evil side, Edward Hyde, but that side of his nature kept struggling to be recognized. One sunny day while sitting in Regent's Park, he was suddenly transformed into Edward Hyde. After awhile, Edward Hyde almost totally occupied Dr. Jekyll's nature, and the original drug was no longer effective to return Mr. Hyde to Dr. Jekyll. After having Poole search throughout London for the necessary "powder," Dr. Jekyll realized that his original compound must have possessed some impurity that cannot be duplicated. In despair at being forced to live the rest of his life as Mr. Hyde, he commits suicide at the moment that Utterson and Poole are breaking down the laboratory door.

Appendix H – Why She Stays

Women stay in abusive relationships for many reasons. They do not stay because they "want to be abused".

A battered woman may believe:

- His violence is temporary.
- Her abuser when he tells her that his abuse is "her fault".
- With loyalty and love, she can make him change.
- His promises that it will "never happen again".
- It's her responsibility to keep the family together.
- There will be more good times.

She may tell herself:

- He's had a hard life.
- He needs me.
- All men are violent; it is to be expected.

Fear is a major factor. Many women believe their abusers' will kill her if she leaves him. She may fear:

- More severe abuse.
- Retaliation if he finds her.
- Destruction of her belongings or home.
- Harm to her job or reputation.
- Stalking.
- Charging her with a crime.
- Harming children, pets, family or friends.
- His committing suicide.
- Court or police involvement.

Economics:

- Few job skills.
- Limited education or work experience.
- No access to bank account, Limited cash.
- Fear of poverty, homelessness.

Pressure from community of faith/family:

- Family expectations to stay in marriage "at any cost", deny the violence, blame her for the violence.

- Religion may disapprove of divorce, leader may tell her to "stay and pray".

Guilt/Self Doubt:

- Guilt about failure of the relationship, guilt about choosing an abuser.
- Feelings of personal incompetence.
- Concern about independence.
- Loneliness.

Concern for Children:

- Abuser may charge her with "kidnapping," sue for custody, and fears losing custody of her children.
- Abuser may abduct or abuse the children.
- Questions whether she can care for and support children on her own.
- Believes children need a father.

Lack of community support:

- Unaware of or isolated from services available to battered women.
- Lack of adequate childcare, affordable housing.
- Negative experiences with service providers.
- No support from family and friends (takes **average of 7 attempts** for victims to successfully leave).

Will it get better? Studies show that over time, without intervention, abuse in the home gets more frequent and more violent.

www.estesvalleyvictimadvocates.org/

Appendix I – Statistics of Domestic Violence

Department of Justice 2010

NOTE from author: research on the internet for statistics of domestic violence in churches is almost non-existent. Based on reading a large number of web sites, my very unscientific estimate is between 34-50%, equal to the general population.

- Every 9 seconds in the United States a woman is assaulted and beaten.
- 4,000,000 women a year are assaulted by their partners.
- In the United States, a woman is more likely to be assaulted, injured, raped, or killed by a male partner than by any other type of assailant
- Every day, 4 women are murdered by boyfriends or husbands.
- Prison terms for killing husbands are twice as long as for killing wives.
- 93% of women who killed their mates had been battered by them.
- 70% of men who batter their partners either sexually or physically abuse their children.
- Women are most likely to be killed when attempting to leave the abuser (75% higher risk).
- 60% of all battered women are beaten when pregnant.
- 2/3 of all marriages will experience domestic violence at least once.
- Weapons are used in 30% of domestic violence incidents.
- It is estimated that between 20% to 52% of high school and college-age dating couples have engaged in physical abuse. Liz Claiborne survey says 50%.
- In homes where domestic violence occurs, children are abused at a rate 1,500% higher than the national average.
- 50% of the homeless women and children in the U.S. are fleeing abuse.
- The amount spent to shelter animals is three times the amount spent to provide emergency shelter to women from domestic abuse situations.

Appendix J – Shelter Information

National Hot Line – 1-888-799-SAFE (7233)

KANSAS CITY SHELTERS

816-HOT-LINE (816-468-5463) - Metropolitan Family Violence Coalition is an umbrella organization for the six Kansas City metro area domestic violence shelters.

Rose Brooks☐ is located in south Kansas City, MO. Twenty-five beds are being added in 2011 due to the overwhelming need of victims. A pet area is also being added because the ". . . therapeutic benefits that pets can have on a family greatly outweigh the cost and inconvenience of housing them," was stated by Susan Miller, the center's chief executive, in a recent interview. Hotline 816-861-6100. Office 816-523-5550. **(www.rosebrooks.org)**
Hope House is located in Independence, MO and Lee's Summit, MO, Hotline 816-461-HOPE. **(www.hopehouse-ejc.org)**
Friends of Yates (formerly Joyce H. Williams Battered Women's Shelter) is located in Wyandotte County, KS. Office 913-321-0951.
Newhouse is located in Kansas City, MO. Office 816-474-6446.
www.newhouseshelter.org
Safehome is located in Johnson County, KS. Hotline 913-262-2868. Office 913-432-9300. **www.safehome-ks.org**
Synergy Services/Safe Haven servicing Parkville and other areas of Ray County, MO. Office 816-587-4100 **www.synergyservices.org**
Mattie Rhodes Center is for Spanish Speaking Victims. Located in Kansas City, MO. Office 816-471-2536. **www.mattierhodes.org**

ST. LOUIS SHELTERS

800-941-9144 or 636-583-5700 - Franklin County Hot Line.
877-462-1758 - Lincoln County Hot Line
877-946-6854 - St. Louis County Hot Line.

Appendix K – Faith Community References

Christian Coalition Against Domestic Violence (CCADV) - Abuse in any form is NEVER God's design for relationships. That is why we believe that all abuse - child abuse, dating abuse, spousal abuse and elder abuse must STOP! Reminder: Abuse does not take a holiday! There is never a day off! What is your place of worship doing to bring awareness to the issues? We invite you to encourage them to speak out about domestic abuse through a sermon, maybe an announcement, maybe a special speaker, maybe a special offering. **http://ccada.org/default.aspx**

The Christian Network Against Domestic Violence was founded in November 2004 as an online organization. Tamika Johnson-Hall, Executive Director, is a survivor and conqueror that understands the devastating effects of domestic violence. **http://www.freewebs.com/cnadv/**

Focus on Christ for Ultimate Satisfaction - not-for-profit 501(c)(3) organization offering hope, encouragement, support, education, spiritual direction, and assistance to teens, women, and families who experience domestic violence, destructive relationships, separation, or divorce. Through counseling, education, training, support groups, and tangible resources, we are dedicated to helping others.
http://www.focusministries1.org

The Faith Committee - Mission is to educate and empower McHenry County faith communities to identify, understand and respond to issues of family violence. Faith communities play a significant role in healing the individual, community and society that are damaged by family violence. One of their main goals is to encourage faith communities to develop a proactive response to family violence in their community and in the whole community.
http://www.co.mchenry.il.us/familyviolencecouncil/Pages/index.aspx

The Faith Trust Institute is a national, multi-faith, multi-cultural training and education organization with a global reach working to end sexual and domestic violence. Faith Trust provides communities and advocates with the tools and knowledge they need to address the religious and cultural issues related to abuse. **http://www.cpsdv.org/**

Note from Ms. Napier: I am including this section because I am sure I would not have survived my 25-year marriage without having had God to hold on to. Depression has oppressed me the majority of my life and I believe it would have indirectly ended my life during the worst 10 years of verbal abuse, if God, Jesus, and His angels had not been there with me during those darkest of times. I often stood at the kitchen sink washing dishes while asking God to give me strength and courage, and that He would use what I was living through to help someone else, some day. As of the publishing date of this book, God has answered my prayers because I have assisted two women and six children escape domestic violence. I believe there will be many more victims who become survivors because God is opening doors in many unexpected places and ways. I pray God's peace for you.
Romans 1:20-21: "For ever since the world was created, people have seen the earth and sky. Through everything God made, they can clearly see his invisible qualities – his eternal power and divine nature. So they have no excuse for not knowing God. Yes, they knew God, but wouldn't worship him as God or give him thanks. And they began to think up foolish ideas of what God was like. As a result, their minds became dark and confused." God's divine nature and personal qualities are revealed in His beautiful creations.

Romans 3:23: "For everyone has sinned; we all fall short of God's glorious standard." We must recognize that we are sinners and that we do not meet God's perfect standards. Sin is serious in God's sight and includes thoughts, words and actions. All sin (i.e. hatred, lying, lust) makes us sinners not just the obvious ones like murder and adultery. The greatest sin of all is to not accept Jesus as our savior. Romans 5:12: "When Adam sinned, sin entered the world. Adam's sin brought death, so death spread to everyone, for everyone sinned."

Romans 3:10: "As the Scriptures say, no one is righteous – not even one." No one can earn right standing with God. Our sins cannot be canceled out by good deeds, religion or works. Each of us accepting Jesus Christ's payment on the cross for each of us is the only available payment method of our sin debts.

Romans 6:23: "For the wages of sin is death, but the free gift of God is eternal life through Christ Jesus our Lord." God's holiness demands a payment for our sin, which is death. Eternal death is separation from God forever in Hell. God is a just God.

Romans 5:8: "But God showed his great love for us by sending Christ to die for us while we were still sinners." God sent His Son Jesus Christ to pay the penalty for our sin by dying on the cross. God is a God of mercy and He sent Jesus to take our sin upon Himself and the punishment we deserve. Mercy is not getting what we deserve. We all deserve death. Jesus willingly took our place on the cross to pay our sin debt for us.

Romans 6:23: "For the wages of sin is death, but the free gift of God is eternal life through Christ Jesus our Lord." Eternal life is a free gift from God. Grace is getting what we don't deserve and God's grace is amazing. He has given us eternal life through Jesus Christ!

Romans 10:9-10: "If you confess with your mouth that Jesus is Lord and believe in your heart that God raised him from the dead, you will be saved. For it is by believing in your heart that you are made right with God, and it is by confessing with your mouth that you are saved." Each of us must believe that Jesus Christ is the Son of God and that He died for us on the cross, rose from the dead, and is Lord. We must put our trust in Jesus alone to make us right with God.

Romans 10:13: "For everyone who calls on the name of the Lord will be saved." Becoming saved is no complicated formula. Jesus paid the price of our sin for us. Our responsibility is to accept Jesus as our Lord and Savior. If we do, we will be saved from eternal death in Hell to eternal life in Heaven.

Romans 8:1: "So now there is no condemnation for those who belong to Christ Jesus." By accepting Jesus' death as a payment for our sins, our sin debt is gone as far as the east is from the west. Knowing Jesus died on a cross is not enough. Each of us must believe that He died for each of us individually.

Romans 5:1: "Therefore, since we have been made right in God's sight by faith, we have peace with God because of what Jesus Christ our Lord has done for us." Because of what Jesus willingly did for us on the cross, we can now have peace and a relationship with the living God because our sin no longer separates us from our Heavenly Father.

If you were to die today, do you know where you will spend eternity – heaven or hell? You can know for sure that your destination is in heaven if you accept Jesus Christ as your Lord and Savior today. You can claim God's salvation right now by saying a simple and sincere prayer similar to this: **"Heavenly Father, I admit that I am a sinner and need Your forgiveness. I believe Jesus Christ is Your Son and that He died for the sins of the world, including mine. I believe by Him dying on the cross and rising to life again that He paid my debt sin for me. I now ask You to forgive me and to cleanse me completely. I take Jesus Christ as my Lord and Savior. I ask the Holy Spirit to come help me to live according to Your teachings in the Bible. I ask these things in Jesus' name. Amen."**

If you have accepted Jesus as your Lord and Savior today, God, Jesus and the angels in heaven rejoice! I praise God for your decision! Salvation involves inward belief (praying the above prayer) and an outward confession that Jesus is Lord (find a church that is a Bible believing, teaching church where you can tell them about your salvation and get acquainted with your new family, the family of God).

If you would like to let me know you I am now your sister in Jesus Christ, please contact me at www.SusanGraceNapier.com, or, SusanGraceNapier@gmail.com

Appendix L - References

Books

Beller, Thomas, edited by Thomas Beller. Before & After Stories from New York. Winnipeg, Canada, Mr. Beller's Neighborhood Books, 2002. These stories were originally published on the web site, **www.mrbellersneighborhood.com**.

Berry, Dawn Bradley. The Domestic Violence Sourcebook. Lincolnwood, IL: NTC/Contemporary Publishing Group, 2000.

Braiker, Harriet B. The September 11 Syndrome: Anxious Days and Sleepless Nights, Seven Steps to Getting a Grip in Uncertain Times. New York: McGraw-Hill Companies, 2002.

Brown, Lou, Francois Dubau, and Merritt McKeon. STOP Domestic Violence: An Action Plan for Saving Lies. New York: St. Martin's Press, 1997. Nicole Brown Simpson's father, Lou Brown, is the founder and president of the Nicole Brown Simpson Charitable Foundation that provides urgently needed funding to battered women's shelters across the country. He co-authored this book with Francois Dubau, a pastor in Laguna Beach, CA and Merritt McKeon, a domestic violence survivor.

Hampton, Wilborn. September 11, 2001: Attack on New York City. Cambridge, MA: Candlewick Press, 2003.

Evans, Patricia. Controlling People: How to Recognize, Understand, and Deal with People Who Try to Control You. Avon, MA: Adams Media, 2002.

Hawker, Lynn and Terrt Bicehouse. End the Pain: Solutions for Stopping Domestic Violence. New York: Barclay House, 1995.

Hunt, June. How to Rise Above Abuse: Victory for Victims of Five Types of Abuse. Eugene, OR: Harvest House Publishers, 2010.

Jones, Ann. Next Time, She'll be Dead: Battering & How to Stop It. Boston, MA: Beacon Press, 1994. Written by a formerly battered woman who is now an educator on domestic violence. Included are suggestions for working with battered women and facilitating support groups, and provides necessary supplemental material.

Kilgore, Nancy. Every Eighteen Seconds: A Journey Through Domestic Violence. Volcano, CA: Volcano Press, 1992. A series of letters the author wrote to her son explaining her relationship with her abusive husband. At the end of each letter are exercises to educate and help the reader's understanding of their own situation.

Kindig, Eileen Silva. Goodbye Price Charming: The Journey Back from Disenchantment, Creating the Marriage You've Always Wanted from the Ashes of Storybook Romance. Colorado Springs, CO: Pinion Press, 1993.

Luchsinger, Jason and Susie. A Tender Road Home: he Story of How God Healed a Marriage Crippled by Anger and Abuse. Nashville, TN: Broadman & Holman Publishers. Susie Luchsinger is a sister of Reba McIntire and has sung with Reba at various times,

Martin, Del. Battered Wives. Volcano, CA: Volcano Press, Inc., 1976, revised and updated 1981. One of the first books written about domestic violence.

McNulty, Francine. The Burning Bed. Harcourt Brace Jovanovich, 1980. True story of Francine Hughes who burned her husband to death while he slept. Her court case was the first in the country to use the "battered woman syndrome" as a defense.

Murphy-Milano, Susan. Getting Away from Domestic Violence & Staying Safe: Defending Our Lives. New York: Doubleday Dell Publishing Group, 1996.

Nyala, Hannah. Point Last Seen: A Woman Tracker's Story of Domestic Violence and Personal Triumph. New York: Penguin Books, 1997.

Norwood, Robin. Women Who Love Too Much: When You Keep Wishing and Hoping He'll Change. New York: Pocket Books.

Peck, Maria J. Silent Cries: A Woman's Journey to Freedom. Austin, TX: Bridgeway Books.

Price, Nancy. Sleeping With the Enemy. New York: The Berkley Publishing Group, 1987. This has been made into a move starring, Julie Roberts.

Quindlen, Anna. Black and Blue. New York: Dell Publishing, 1998. On the New York Times bestseller list.

Rivers, Victor Rivas. A Private Family Matter: A Memoir. New York: Atria Books. This actor shares the chronicle of his escape from the war zone of living under the rule and wrath of his father. Victor managed to seek help for his family and criminal punishment for his father. He has been a spokesperson for the National Network to End Domestic Violence.

Roy, Maria. Children in the Crossfire: Violence in the home – How does it affect our children? Deerfield Beach, FL: Health Communications, 1988.

Stevenson, Robert L. Dr. Jekyll & Mr. Hyde and Other Stories of the Supernatural. New York: Scholastic Magazines, 1963.

Schwartz, Dianne, Whose Face Is in the Mirror?. Carlsbad, CA: Hays House, 2000.

Turner, Tina with Kurt Loder. I, Tina. New York: Avon Books. This story about Tina's life with Ike Turner has been made into a movie.

Wakefield, Maria. Dodging Her Chariot. Independence, MO: Cartiful Publishing, 2009

Weiss, Elaine. Family and Friends' Guide to Domestic Violence: How to Listen, Talk and Take Action When Someone You Care About is Being Abused. Volcano, CA: Volcano Press Inc., 2003.

Weitzman, Susan. "Not to People Like Us" Hidden Abuse in Upscale Marriages. New York, NY: Basic Books, 2000.

Weldon, Michele. I Closed My Eyes: Revelations of a Battered Woman. Center City, MN: Hazleden, 1999.

Web Sites

20 Reasons Why She Stays, A Guide for Those Who Want to Help Battered Women - Susan G. S. McGee - **SusanGSMcGee@aol.com**

Choose Respect is designed to encourage positive action on the part of adolescents to form healthy, respectful relationships. Supported by the Centers for Disease Control, it offers fact sheets and scripts for parents who need clear-cut advice on supporting safe and respectful relationships.

Jane's Due Process - a nonprofit organization ensuring legal representation for pregnant minors in Texas. Our goal is to have every pregnant teen know that she has the right to seek legal help, to be treated with respect and sensitivity by those who work in the legal system, and to participate in legal proceedings where everyone is interested in following the law. Web site is geared toward teenagers. **http://www.janesdueprocess.org/**

Futures Without Violence (formerly Family Violence Prevention Fund). The FWV works to prevent violence within the home, and in the community. They work to help those whose lives are devastated by violence. - http://www.futureswithoutviolence.org/

Leaving Abuse is an individual's website and this is a quote from there: "I am a woman who escaped SAFELY from an abusive relationship without the abuser knowing I was leaving, or having any idea where I had gone. Before I left, I planned for my future practically, emotionally and financially. I did it and so can you." **http://www.leavingabuse.com/**

Love is Respect is a national campaign to end teen dating abuse. Love is Respect offers a number of ways for young people, and their parents, to get involved in the national movement to educate young people on safe dating and relationships. **http://blog.loveisrespect.org/**

Missouri Coalition Against Domestic and Sexual Violence- MCADSV works to organize and provide support to the various agencies who offer services to those in need in the State of Missouri.
http://www.mocadsv.org/

National Coalition Against Domestic Violence - The NCADV works to organize and support the efforts of communities as they work to eradicate domestic violence. **http://www.ncadv.org/**

National Network to End Domestic Violence - The NNEDV is dedicated to creating a social, political, and economic environment where violence against women no longer exists. - **http://www.nnedv.org/**

Violence Against Women National Online Resource Center (VAWNET) - Resource library is home to thousands of materials on violence against women and related issues, with particular attention to its intersections with various forms of oppression. **http://www.vawnet.org/**

Women's Law Organization - A project of *NNEDV*, providing legal information and support to victims of domestic violence and sexual assault. **http://www.womenslaw.org/**

ABOUT THE AUTHOR

As the first anniversary of 9/11 came and went, Susan Napier experienced a deep depression. Searching for the source of her rising anxiety and loss of functionality, she came to the realization her emotions paralleled the trauma experienced in a 25-year abusive marriage. As a volunteer at Rose Brooks domestic violence shelter in Kansas City, she educated victims being treated in emergency rooms and assisted them in finding immediate assistance. The author envisions family, friends, communities, and the nation coming together in similar ways that Americans did for each other on 9/11.

Through SGN Seminars, Ms. Napier does presentations of "Listen – Learn – Save Lives." Topics of Domestic Violence and Elder Abuse are tailored to audiences of businesses, churches, community organizations, educational institutions, and health care professionals. She inspires audiences to make a difference by teaching them recognition of abuse symptoms, ways to initiate conversations about possible abuse, how to assist victims in escaping violent situations, and, as importantly, things to avoid in order to NOT escalate the danger for victims or to put themselves in harm's way.

Ms. Napier can be contacted at: **www.SusanGraceNapier.com**